D1575887

TORCHWOOD

SLOW DECAY

TORCHWOOD

SLOW DECAY

Andy Lane

BBC
BOOKS

4 6 8 10 9 7 5

Published in 2007 by BBC Books, an imprint of Ebury Publishing.
Ebury Publishing is a division of the Random House Group Ltd.

The Random House Group Ltd Reg. No. 954009.
Addresses for companies within the Random House Group can be found
at www.randomhouse.co.uk.

A CIP catalogue record for this book is available from the British Library.

ISBN 978 0 563 48655 8

The Random House Group Ltd makes every effort to ensure that the papers
used in our books are made from trees that have been legally sourced from
well-managed credibly certified forests. Our paper procurement policy can be found at
www.randomhouse.co.uk.

Torchwood is a BBC Wales production for BBC Three
Executive Producers: Russell T Davies and Julie Gardner
Producer: Richard Stokes

Project Editor: Steve Tribe
Production Controller: Peter Hunt

Cover design by Lee Binding @ Tea Lady © BBC 2007
Typeset in Albertina and Century Gothic
Printed and bound in Germany by GGP Media GmbH, Poessneck

To Dave, Alison and Jamie Trace,

for providing me with a Hub of my own in Plymouth

And dedicated to the memory of Craig Hinton

— best friend and best man

ONE

The sky was taking on the appearance of an old bruise as the sun slipped inevitably toward the Cardiff skyline. Yellows and purples were layered across it, each sliding into the other in a cascade of disturbed colour, like an Edvard Munch painting. Lights were beginning to come on across the city, in buildings and on streets, gradually replacing the actual city with a pointillist copy of itself.

The top of the tower block where Gwen stood was covered in weeds, moss and grass. The vegetation had drifted up, in seed or spore form, from the countryside beyond Cardiff's suburbs. From where she stood, by the top of the stairway that led down towards street level and the rational world below, the far edge of the building was an impossibly straight cliff edge and the man standing there was poised on the edge of the void, coat eddying around him in the breeze like wings. Ready to fall or to fly.

'Where can I get a coat like that?' she asked.

'You have to earn it,' Captain Jack Harkness said without turning around. 'It's a badge of office. Like bowler hats in the Civil Service.'

'They don't still wear bowler hats in the Civil Service,' she replied scornfully. 'That went out back in the 1950s, along with tea trolleys and waistcoats. And I speak as someone who worked alongside loads of Civil Servants when I was in the police force.' She caught herself. 'I mean, when I was *really* in the police force, not just *telling* people that I'm in the police force to avoid having to tell them that I hunt down alien technology for a living.'

'I bet they still wear them,' Jack said. The wind ruffled his hair like a playful hand. 'I bet when all the Civil Servants arrive in their offices in the morning they lock the doors, unlock their desks and take out their ceremonial bowler hats to wear where nobody else can see them. Like a kind of administrative version of the Klu Klux Klan.'

'Have you got some kind of downer on the Civil Service?'

He still didn't turn around. 'In an infinite universe,' he said, 'there are undoubtedly planets out there where the entire population has grey skin, wears grey clothes and thinks grey thoughts. I guess the universe needs planets like that, but I sure as hell don't want to have to visit them. I prefer the thought that if there's a planet of Civil Servants then there's also a planet where everyone has an organic TV set built into their back, and you can just follow people down the street, watching daytime TV to your heart's content.'

The colour was slowly bleeding from the sky in front of Jack Harkness: yellows dissolving into oranges, oranges melting into reds, and everything dripping from the sky, sliding off the back of the night and leaving velvet darkness behind.

Gwen gazed at Jack's back, trying once again to try and separate out the complex mess of feelings she felt for this man. When he talked about Civil Servants wearing bowler hats, it was almost as if he had only recently seen them. When he talked about alien planets, she could almost believe that he'd been to them. Almost. But that would have been mad. Wouldn't it?

She wondered, not for the first time, how her life had managed to take such a right-angled turn without any warning. One day she was taking statements and guarding crime scenes whilst technicians in overalls scraped evidence up into plastic bags, and the next she was part of Great Britain's first and last line of defence against... what? Invasion. Incursion. Infiltration. A whole bag full of words beginning with 'In', because that's where things were coming. In – to her reality. In – to Cardiff.

And it was all because of this man standing on the edge of a roof twelve storeys above the ground. This man who had arrived in her life like a flash flood, drowning her in strangeness and adventure.

Impulsive. Impressive. Impossible. A whole dictionary of words beginning with 'Im'.

'Most people spend their time looking up,' she said eventually, 'looking at the stars. You seem to spend far too much time looking down. What are you looking for, exactly?'

'Perhaps I'm looking for fallen stars,' he said after a moment.

'It's the people, isn't it? You just can't help watching them.' She caught herself. 'No, that's not it. You're not watching them; you're watching *over* them.'

'Ever seen a two-year-old tottering around a garden?' he said softly, without turning around. 'There might be poison ivy, or rose bushes, or hawthorn around the edges. There might be spades or secateurs lying on the lawn. The kid doesn't care. He just wants to play with all those brightly coloured things he sees. To him, the world is a safe place. And you might want to rush out and cut back all those sharp, spiky plants so they can't hurt him, and you might want to clear away all those dangerous tools just in case he picks them up and cuts himself on them, but you know you shouldn't, because if you keep doing that then he will either grow up thinking the world can never hurt him, or he might go the other way and think that everything is dangerous and he should never go far from your side. So you just watch. And wait. And, if he does get a rash from the poison ivy, or if he does cut his finger off with the secateurs, then you get him to hospital as quickly as you can, in the reasonably sure knowledge that he'll never make that mistake again.'

Small points of light were appearing in the darkness beyond Jack. Within the space of a few minutes, it seemed to Gwen that he had gone from being a solid figure silhouetted against a slowly shifting backdrop of colour to a black shape against blackness, defined only by where the stars weren't.

'Is that what we are to you?' Gwen asked. 'Children?'

'That's all *we* are,' he replied. 'To *them*.'

'And who are *They*?'

'Who are *They*? They are the ones who live over the walls of the garden, in the wilderness outside. Me – I'm just a child as well, playing in the garden with the rest of you. The difference is, I'm just a little older. And I've already had my share of poison ivy rashes.'

Gwen gazed around at the top of the building, at the grasses and the weeds that occupied the spaces between the ventilation ducts and antennae, swaying gently in the evening breeze. 'Life survives, doesn't it?' she said, apropos of nothing. 'Finding little nooks and crannies to grow in. Putting down roots where it can, eking out some kind of existence in the cracks.'

'And that's what we do.' The wind caught his coat, billowing it out behind him, but he seemed oblivious to the possibility of being blown off the building. 'In Torchwood. We look for the things that have been blown in on the breeze between the worlds, and if necessary we eradicate them.'

Caught by a sudden premonition, Gwen looked at her watch. 'Jesus! I've got a dinner appointment.' She'd arranged to meet Rhys in a restaurant nearby – an apology of sorts for the amount of time she seemed to be spending away from him at the moment. Time she was spending with Jack. She turned to leave, then turned back, curiously unwilling to leave. 'Are you coming down at all tonight, or are you going to stay here until dawn?' she asked.

'I'll see how the mood takes me. How about you? Want to give dinner a miss and come join me on the edge?'

'Thanks, but no. Gotta go.'

'Just out of interest, why did you come up here in the first place?'

'Oh…' She racked her brain. It all seemed so long ago – the echoing space of the Hub, the conversation with Toshiko, the ride to the top of the building where she knew that Jack tended to hang out when he wasn't with them – and now the memory was strangely obscured by the image of a muscular body and a huge coat wrapping itself around the wind and billowing like a leather sail. 'Yeah… Tosh asked me to let you know something. She's picked up little bursts of electromagnetic energy somewhere in the centre of Cardiff. It's not one of the standard frequencies. She's keeping an eye on it.'

'OK.' He paused. 'Keep your mobile handy. Just in case.'

A sudden flush of anger at Jack's casual assumption that she would come running when he called brought a bloom of heat to her cheeks and forehead. 'What – just in case I actually manage to get a few hours to myself? Just in case I actually get a life?'

'You can walk away any time you want, Gwen,' Jack chided, a dark voice speaking to her out of darkness. 'I don't own you. Go back to the police, if that's what you want. But you know what will happen. You'll be on the outside again. You'll see us walking past you, pushing through the barriers, taking control of your crime scenes and stripping them of whatever we want, and you won't be part of it any more. Can you stand that? Having taken that peek over the garden wall into the wilderness, can you really pretend that it doesn't exist and that the garden – the nicely ordered garden – is all there is?'

'Go to hell,' she said bleakly. 'You know I can't.'

'Go to your restaurant. Make small talk with your friends. Fashion, politics, house prices, sport… It really doesn't mean anything. Not when it's compared with the stuff that's drifting in through the Rift. *This* is real life. Down there – it's just fantasy.'

She turned away and pushed open the door that led down through the interior of the building. Twenty minutes to get to the restaurant, and she still had to get back to the Hub and retrieve her handbag and her high heels. Just for once, couldn't they each get the chance to take one thing from the shelves and the storerooms in the Hub – one thing that would make their lives easier? A teleporter. That was all she wanted. Something to get her from A to B without having to go to all the tedious trouble of crossing the intervening ground.

The wind suddenly gusted around her, pushing her roughly against the doorframe. She thought she heard a flutter behind her, like cloth being blown away. She turned back, but the sky was completely black now, and if Jack was there then she couldn't see him.

Owen was daydreaming, sitting at his bench in the darkened underground space of the Hub and letting his mind drift away into the higher levels of the empty atrium, up where the brickwork wasn't quite so damp and the blanked-off ends of Victorian sewer pipes projected from the wall.

Sometimes, in the quieter moments – the moments between frantic chases around Cardiff in search of some piece of alien technology and long periods spent at his bench or in his lab dissecting out the form and function of the biological things they found – Owen daydreamed about writing up some of his stranger investigations in a magazine of some sort. The magazine didn't exist, of course. There was no *Journal of Comparative*

Alien Anatomy, nor even an *Extra-Terrestrial Biology Quarterly*. There was no convention he could go to where he could present his results. There was nowhere for him to get any recognition for the things he had discovered. Or even to record them for posterity before he started forgetting, went mad, or died, unremarked.

It made him feel angry and frustrated, sometimes, the amount of stuff that he knew but could never tell anyone. And who else was there to tell? Torchwood Cardiff: five people, rushing around trying to solve all the problems they could, with barely enough time left over to get on with their own personal lives, let alone sit down over a cup of coffee and chat about chlorine-based enzyme chemistry and anomalies in osmotic transfer rates.

And only one of them had any medical training.

It was a waste. A real waste. Owen had discovered so much during his time working in the Hub. Things nobody else on Earth knew. The bizarre secrets of Weevil sex, for instance, which had almost made him throw up the first time he learned about them but went a long way towards explaining the expressions on the faces of the creatures. The various senses that creatures could have in place of sight and hearing, including things like biological radar that Owen would have thought impossible unless he'd actually experienced them. The way that vast diaphanous creatures could slip through rock with the same ease that whales slipped through water. The existence of single beings that took the form of flocks of bird-like creatures, with each little part being an irreplaceable part of the whole.

There were times he felt he knew so much about alien biology that he would burst, and yet he was just scratching the surface.

And that was just with the equipment he had: cutting edge, of course, but cutting edge for Earth. There were alien things on the shelf in Torchwood that would allow him to watch biochemical reactions on the cellular level like he was watching a movie, or to guide minute robotic scalpels along arteries by the power of thought alone. And they would stay on the shelves. Nobody was allowed to touch them. The risk was too great.

After all, they all remembered Suzie, and what had happened to her when she discovered that she could temporarily raise the recently deceased.

Thoughts of Suzie led Owen on to thinking about the other members of the team. Owen probably spent more time in their company than anyone else in his life, but he still felt as if he knew virtually nothing about them. What about Captain Jack Harkness, for instance: the enigmatic leader of the team? From things he said, and more things he left unsaid, Owen sometimes suspected that Jack was as alien as some of the things that drifted through the Rift, and yet there were other times when he seemed more grounded, more part of the moment than anyone else he knew. And Toshiko, the technical expert who could strip a device she'd never seen before down to wires and bits of metal, then put it back together again just the way it had been, but who didn't know the first thing about how people worked. And Gwen. Beautiful Gwen...

The sound of the main door bursting open broke his concentration. Gwen rushed in, unbuttoning her blouse. For a moment, Owen was stunned. It was as if his dreams were coming to life.

'Gwen... er... this is... Look, I thought...'

She glared over at him. 'Down, Rover. I'm running late, and I need to get changed to go out. I left my glad rags here earlier.' She dashed across towards one of the side rooms. 'I completely lost track of time.' She vanished out of the Hub, but he could still hear her voice. 'Bloody Jack. I just went up to deliver a message from Tosh, but he kept me talking. Where is Tosh, by the way?'

'She's out trying to triangulate some signal she discovered.'

'Great.' She appeared again in the Hub, buttoning up a jacket over a silk blouse. She looked taller, and there was a *tock-tock* as she walked that suggested she'd exchanged her trainers for a pair of heels.

'So what are you all dressed up for then?' smirked Owen.

She glanced over at him. 'You know the Indian Summer?'

'Up on Dolphin Quay?'

'That's the one.'

"Contemporary Indian cuisine with a special touch, derived from the intimate geographical knowledge of our chefs". That one?'

'That one. I'm meeting... some people there tonight. I'll take the scenic route, I think. It'll save me a twenty-minute walk. In high heels.'

Without any hesitation, Owen said, 'Hold on, I'll come with you.'

13

'To the Indian Summer? Dream on!'

'No – out the scenic route.' He looked at his watch . 'It's time for me to go, anyway.' Getting up from his bench, he crossed to an area of flagstones in the centre of the underground space, picking up the remote control from a nearby bench as he went.

After a few moments, Gwen joined him. They had to stand close together to fit onto the flagstone, and Owen couldn't help noticing that Gwen was holding her body tense, ensuring that nothing touched him, no folds of cloth and no bare skin. Fair enough – if that's the way she wanted to play it. He pressed a button on the remote and suddenly the Hub was falling away from them as the flagstone rose noiselessly into the air. Within seconds they were high enough above the ground that a fall would have seriously injured them, but a faint pressure pushed them towards each other. A faint pressure that Gwen was obviously resisting.

A faint breeze stirred Owen's hair. He glanced up, to where a square of darkness was approaching them, set in between the lights of the ceiling. The dark square grew larger, and then they were plunging into it: a slab-sided tunnel which took them upwards, the stone passing fast enough to rasp the skin from their fingers if they touched it.

And then they were somewhere else. They were standing together in the Basin, shadowed by the massive sheet-metal waterfall that stood in the centre, sprayed by the wind-borne water that curved away from it. The sky was dark and starred, with wisps of cloud floating on the breeze. Owen could smell baking bread, roasting food and, strangely, candy floss. Crowds parted around them like a shoal of fish moving to avoid an unfamiliar presence in their ocean, not looking at them, not even aware that they had appeared from the depths of the earth.

'Jack told me that something had happened here, once,' Gwen said softly. 'Something was here that had the power to make people ignore it. The thing left, but some echo of the power stayed. That's why nobody can see us until we step away.'

'Whatever it was,' Owen said, 'he's obsessed by it. It's scarred him.'

'Thanks for the lift,' Gwen said. 'You can find your own way back, can't you?' For a second he could smell her skin, her perfume, her soap, and then she was gone, running off across the square.

'Actually,' he said, 'I think I need a drink.'

The Indian Summer was half-full, and Gwen spent a few moments standing in the doorway and scanning the interior before she spotted Rhys.

The restaurant walls were painted white, the artwork hanging on the walls was big and abstract, the furniture stark black, and the entire effect about as far away from the standard 'flock wallpaper and sitar music' stereotype of Indian restaurants as it was possible to get. And that was before one even saw the menu. The Indian Summer had opened less than a year before, and it had soon established itself at the forefront of Cardiff restaurants. Gwen and Rhys had been there enough times for the waiters to start to recognise them. Or, at least, they were polite enough to pretend to recognise them, which was a start.

Rhys was sitting at a table near the bar, and Gwen had to look twice before she was sure it was him. For a start he was with another woman, which she hadn't been expecting, but there was more than that. Rhys just didn't look like Rhys.

Once or twice, when she had first joined the police, Gwen had been patrolling through one of the shopping arcades in Cardiff when she had caught sight of her own reflection in a shop front. For a few moments she had found herself wondering who that rather severe person in uniform was before she realised with a sudden shock that it was her, hair drawn back in a bun and striding along the line of shops in her clunky shoes. She had the same reaction now, watching Rhys without him being aware that she was there. When was the last time he had shaved? When had his face got that chubby? And when had he started wearing his shirt untucked from his jeans in an attempt to disguise his growing beer belly?

It was bizarre that Gwen could find herself standing there, surprised at the appearance of a man she spent every night sleeping with, but how often did one look – really *look* – at one's friends or partners? She and Rhys had been together so long that they had slipped into a comfortable routine. Part of that routine, she now realised, was that they were taking each other for granted. Not even looking any more. And that was horrible – really horrible.

Waving away the waiters, she weaved through the tables, and by the time she had got to where they were sitting Rhys was Rhys again and Gwen was wondering where that sudden disconnection had come from.

And yet, part of her was asking herself what Rhys saw when he looked at her, and whether she had changed as much as, for that long moment, she had realised he had.

Rhys stood up as she arrived, grabbed her round the waist and kissed her. 'Hi, kid. I was beginning to wonder if you were going to make it tonight.'

'I promised I'd be here,' Gwen said, and turned to where Rhys's companion was determinedly avoiding watching them as they hugged. 'Hello,' she said, extending a hand, 'I'm Gwen.'

The girl was younger than Gwen by a few years: black-haired and slim. Very slim. She smiled at Gwen. 'Hi,' she said, taking Gwen's hand. 'Nice to meet you.'

'This is Lucy,' Rhys said. 'We work together. I hope you don't mind, but we bumped into each other outside. She's going through a bit of a rough time, and I thought she needed cheering up. Is that OK?' His voice contained a hint of a plea, and there was something in his eyes that made her wonder what he thought her reaction was going to be.

'That's fine,' Gwen said, aware that this wasn't the time to point out that she had been hoping for a quiet evening out, just the two of them. Time to talk, and share experiences, and shore up their rather fragile relationship. 'Have you ordered?' she added, seeing a plate of poppadoms on the table and a set of dishes containing lime pickle, raita and chopped onions.

'We thought we'd wait for you,' Rhys said as they both sat down. 'We just ordered some stuff to keep us going.'

Gwen picked up the menu and quickly scanned the familiar dishes. 'I'll have the Karachi chicken, lemon pilau rice and a sag paneer,' she told Rhys. 'And a bottle of Cobra.'

As Rhys turned to pass the order on to the hovering waiter – including, she noticed, ordering food for Lucy without having to ask what the girl wanted – she turned and said, 'So how long have you and Rhys worked together?'

'About six months. I moved here from Bristol. Rhys looked after me when I arrived: showed me how the job worked and where everything was kept. He was very patient.' She smiled. 'Rhys tells me you're something special in the police.'

'Rhys talks too much.' She smiled to take the sting out of the retort. 'I'm on plain-clothes duties now, but I used to be in uniform. That was when we met.'

'How's your day been?' Rhys asked as the waiter walked away.

'Not too bad. Pretty quiet, in fact.'

'You see,' he said, turning to Lucy: 'I can spend hours telling her about the intricacies of logistics and routing, and all I get back for my trouble is "Not too bad. Pretty quiet".'

While they waited for the food to arrive, the conversation flickered back and forth around subjects they could all contribute to: work, holidays, nightlife in Cardiff... nothing that would have excluded one of them, which meant that Gwen never got a chance to talk to Rhys about their own lives, how they felt about each other, where they were going and what was happening to them. All very superficial.

At one point, Lucy said, rather shyly, 'You probably don't remember, Gwen, but we have met before.'

'We have?'

'At a party.'

Gwen thought back. She and Rhys had always socialised with his workmates quite a bit, but that had all died away recently without her really noticing. She remembered all the parties, but she didn't remember Lucy.

'Sorry,' she said. 'I was probably drunk at the time.'

'It was over in Ely. There was a barbecue, and some of the guys were busking in the garden.' She looked over at Rhys, and Gwen was disturbed to see something in her eyes, something warm and melting. 'Rhys borrowed someone's bass guitar, and they all played some Kaiser Chiefs stuff. He was very good.'

And then Gwen remembered. It had been a hot Saturday afternoon, and she had been wearing a long cotton dress and a straw hat, just to keep cool. Rhys had been wearing black jeans and a green T-shirt. She hadn't even realised he played bass until he picked up one belonging to the man who was throwing the party, plugged it into an amp and just started playing along with the other guys. The next-door neighbours had banged on the door to complain, but had ended up staying and getting drunk in the kitchen. It had been a magical evening.

And yes, she did remember Lucy, but not the way she was now. The hair had been the same, but she had been about three dress sizes larger. A size sixteen, at least.

'But you were—' she blurted, and caught herself.

'I was a bit bigger then,' Lucy said, blushing and looking down at the tablecloth. 'I've lost quite a lot of weight recently.'

Two waiters turned up with a trolley of food, and there was silence for a moment as they deftly crammed the metal plates of food into every spare inch of space on the table. Gwen looked across and noticed, with a little twinge of some unidentifiable emotion, that Rhys had ordered a lamb dish that was heavy with cream. And he'd replaced his empty bottle of Cobra with a full one while she hadn't been looking.

'I'm sorry,' Gwen said when the waiters had retreated, 'I didn't mean to—'

'That's all right,' Lucy said. 'I'm a lot happier now. Rhys remembers what I was like before. Don't you, Rhys?'

His gaze flickered from Lucy to Gwen and back, reflecting his dim awareness that he'd blundered into a conversational minefield. 'Um… any more drinks?' he asked.

'So,' Gwen continued, 'how did you, er…'

'I went to a clinic,' Lucy explained. 'I was desperate, and I saw an advert. Actually, I think it was a flyer at a club, or something. So I went along, and they gave me a consultation, and some herbal pills. And they worked – they really worked! The weight just melted away from me!'

Gwen winced, not liking the sudden image conjured up by Lucy's words. She glanced sideways, looking to meet Rhys' eyes and share a silent moment with him, but he was looking directly at Lucy's face. And he was smiling.

And that was, of course, the perfect moment for Gwen's mobile to bleep, alerting her to an incoming text message.

She knew what it was before she even opened up the mobile to look at the screen.

Torchwood, it said. *Alien presence at nightclub. Deaths occurred.*

Gwen looked up from the screen, with its bitter message, an apology on her lips, but neither Rhys nor Lucy had even noticed the disturbance. She could probably have left the restaurant there and then without them even knowing.

So she did.

TWO

'Turn right here!' Toshiko called out, trying to make herself heard above the roar of the engine.

The Torchwood SUV swung round a corner, almost spilling her from her seat. She grabbed hold of a strut with one hand whilst the other used a trackball to keep crosshairs centred on a map on the computer screen in front of her.

Jack was driving. That was always a bad thing as far as Toshiko was concerned. Especially when she was navigating. He seemed to assume that when she said 'right' or 'left' then that abrogated any responsibility he had to check for other traffic, pedestrians, buildings or, in one instance a few minutes ago, the existence of a roundabout which he then went the wrong way around.

'Any sign of that alien tech?' Jack yelled from the driver's seat.

'Nothing,' she called back. 'I've not seen any signals since the one half an hour ago.' She glanced sideways, towards the front of the SUV, but the sight of tall buildings whipping past against a black sky made her feel sick, so she concentrated on her display.

'That's the one you triangulated to the nightclub?'

'To the block in which the nightclub is located,' she corrected. Toshiko glanced back at the map display. 'Left!'

The SUV veered again, and somewhere behind them Toshiko heard a squeal of brakes, a blaring horn and a sudden *crump* as two heavy metal objects came into an unexpectedly close proximity.

'Have you ever thought about getting hold of a Torchwood helicopter?' Owen called out. 'We could probably get there faster, and cause fewer accidents on the way. Two benefits for the price of one.'

'If I had a helicopter,' Jack yelled back, 'then I couldn't do *this*!' He threw the SUV into a screeching two-wheel skid around a corner. Falling sideways, Toshiko caught a glimpse of a red traffic light turning the windscreen the colour of blood, then they were past and straightening up again.

'Where's Gwen?' she asked, more to distract Jack from his stunt driving than anything else.

'She's gone out to dinner,' Owen and Jack answered in harmony.

'I texted her,' Jack added. 'She's meeting us there.'

'She went to the Indian Summer,' said Owen, just to prove that he knew something Jack didn't. 'I think she was meeting Rhys.'

'And even if we did have a Torchwood helicopter,' Jack continued, 'where would we land it? SUVs are easier to park.'

'Last time we went out in this vehicle,' Toshiko said quietly, 'you parked it in the foyer of an office block. The time before that, you parked it in the middle of the Taff Bridge. I can't help feeling that finding suitable parking spaces is not high on your list of priorities.' Catching a glimpse of a flashing red set of arrows on the map display, she called out: 'Stop anywhere along here.'

The vehicle slowed and then slewed sideways into what Toshiko fervently hoped was a parking space, as opposed to someone's front garden. Owen broke the sudden silence by saying, 'Wait for a moment while my stomach catches up with us. And wait… and wait… and *yes*! We're back together again. Thanks for holding on.'

Jack jumped out, while Owen pulled open the SUV's side door and gestured for Toshiko to go first.

The SUV was parked across the mouth of an alleyway off St Mary Street. They were obviously in the middle of a crime scene: the nearby shop fronts reflected the flashing lights of police cars between each other in a crazy neon chiaroscuro. Uniformed officers were standing around, staring at the Torchwood team with barely disguised hostility. It was something Toshiko was used to. Nobody liked to be outranked, especially when they didn't understand what was going on.

The street ahead of them was closed off with red and yellow striped incident tape. Turning, Toshiko could see that the street behind them was closed off as well; at least, it had been until the Torchwood vehicle had driven straight through. Now the tape just lay limply on the ground. None of the police officers standing around made any attempt to pick it up again.

Owen slid the door shut behind him, and Jack led the way down the alley to what appeared to be the entrance to a nightclub, to judge by the sign suspended from the brickwork above the door. Policemen around the doorway moved away as they approached.

'Bloody Torchwood,' one muttered as they passed. 'Who do they think they are?'

Jack sighed. 'They'd better not clamp it while we're gone.'

The nightclub was empty of living people, although Toshiko could smell their presence in the humidity of the atmosphere: sweat, stale tobacco, cheap aftershave and cheaper perfume. The overhead lights had been turned on, and their glare transformed what had probably been something high-tech and impressive in the near-darkness into something that Toshiko felt was rather tawdry. Not her kind of place. She wasn't really sure what her kind of place was, but this wasn't it.

A long bar took up most of one wall, stocked with hundreds of upside down bottles of spirits, beer taps and drink dispensing hoses left limp across the bar. The surface of the bar was translucent acrylic, and it was lit from beneath. When the overhead lights were turned off, it would form the major source of illumination in the club, but now it just served to highlight how much the walls needed a new coat of paint.

The central area was reserved as a dance floor. It was scuffed by too many pairs of feet, and stained by years of spilt drinks, but none of that would have been evident with the lights off. Scaffolding hung from the ceiling, and spotlights hung from the scaffolding, fitted with motors so they could rotate and pan around, randomly picking dancers out of the crowd. Elsewhere, tiny video cameras could follow the spotlights, transmitting their images to flat-screen monitors that were located around the walls.

Tables were scattered around various platforms on different levels separated from one another by chrome rails and steps.

'Nice place,' Jack commented as he strode in. 'I wonder who did the decor for them. I might just have them redo the Hub in the same style.'

'What, with a bar?' Owen asked.

'Or maybe I'll just get Laurence Llewellyn Bowen to come in and put swags of velvet and stencilled oak leaves everywhere,' Jack continued. 'Just for a change.'

'Swags?' came a voice from the doorway.

'"Swag" – an ornamental drapery or curtain that hangs in a curve between two points. There's a proper word for everything, you know, and a lot of them are falling into disuse. I'm thinking of making it a Torchwood rule that every conversation has to include at least one word that nobody else knows. Thanks for turning up, by the way. How was dinner?'

Gwen walked into the club. 'What little I had of it was great. Hi Owen. Hi Tosh.'

Owen nodded once, then glanced away. Toshiko gave her a friendly smile.

'What have we got?' Gwen asked.

Jack walked over to the bar and pulled himself smoothly up until he was standing on it, looking down on the team. 'A quick recap. Tosh has been tracking an intermittent energy surge of a frequency and modulation that doesn't match anything in use on Earth at this point in time. She triangulated it to this area of Cardiff where some suspicious deaths had just occurred. The two seem linked, so I've thrown the local coppers out, allowing us to take a look around. I can't imagine that aliens living in Cardiff would choose to come *here* for a night out – there are clubs nearby that cater far better to the discriminating traveller – so I suspect that someone here was human and was dabbling with something they shouldn't have been in possession of. Swag, in fact, which is a word also used to mean "stolen goods".'

'Where are the bodies?' Owen asked.

Jack looked around. 'There's a couple of overturned tables over there,' he said, pointing. 'The smart money says that's where the bodies will be. Remember, we suspect that the deaths are due to some kind of alien tech, so keep an eye out for it. Someone may have taken it away, of course, so we also need to check the bodies for identities and any clues.'

'And also remember that the whole thing might be a coincidence,' Gwen added, 'and the person who had the alien tech, if there was alien tech, left when the fight started rather than get involved.'

'Let's get started,' said Jack. He jumped down from the bar and led the way across to a low plateau some ten feet above the dance floor, accessible via a set of stairs.

Jack was right. Sprawled across a clutch of tables and chairs that had been pushed apart and overturned were five bodies. Young men, all of them. There was a lot of blood, stark on white T-shirts, and a lot of broken glass. Looking at them, it struck Toshiko that sleeping bodies still had a certain amount of muscle tension pulling the limbs into distinct shapes. Dead bodies lost that tension. They just lay there, like carelessly thrown rugs.

'Owen?' Jack prompted.

'Don't touch anything if you can help it,' Gwen said quickly. At Owen's questioning glance, she added: 'There's still a police investigation that needs to occur. We only take stuff that's not from this Earth, and we leave without disturbing anything. Like the Country Code, only a lot weirder.'

Bending down between the bodies, Owen quickly checked them over. Toshiko admired the rapidity with which his hands and eyes operated: so similar to the way that she checked over technological devices she had never seen before. A combination of knowledge, skill and instinct. Owen was an exceptionally good doctor.

'The wounds are nothing out of the ordinary,' Owen said. 'Standard contusions and stab wounds mainly, with the occasional knuckle-shaped bruise and one punctured eye caused, I suspect, by a broken bottle. Just your usual Wednesday night in Cardiff. No laser burns, no strange bite-marks made by non-human teeth, no sign that the life force has been sucked out of them.' He grinned. 'I suspect the only sucking they were in for tonight was the home-grown variety.'

'I've got a couple of knives,' Gwen added. 'Two are still being held in the corpses' hands, one is half-under one of the bodies. They're nothing special: basic folding knives, available at any camping shop or school playground.' She systematically checked through pockets for ID cards, credit cards, anything that might tell the group who the kids were. 'I have a Craig Sutherland,' she said, 'a Rick Dennis, a Geraint Morris, a Dai Morris, presumably related, and an Idris ab Hugh. I'm working on the theory that we have three local Welsh lads and two students at the Uni, probably fighting over some girls. How often have we heard that story before?'

She straightened up, still holding the various cards she had taken from their pockets. Cards, Toshiko realised, they would never be needing again.

'Over to you, Tosh,' Jack said. As she knelt down next to Owen and prepared to search amongst the bodies for anything else, anything that shouldn't have been there, she noticed Jack walk over to join Gwen. His hands were thrust deep in the pockets of his greatcoat and there was a strange look on his face.

'They could have grown up to be anything,' he said. 'Scientists who might have invented the first practicable star drive, allowing humanity to escape an increasingly overcrowded and polluted Earth. Artists who could have encapsulated the human spirit in sculptures and paintings and forms yet to be invented, but which would have lasted for millennia. Politicians who might have brought peace to the Middle East. Or, if nothing else, they might have been happy, with partners and kids and barbecues on a Sunday afternoon. And none of that will happen now. They've been erased from the world for the sake of a few harsh words and the chance of a snog with the wrong girl.'

'Some lads would risk anything for a snog with the wrong girl,' Owen said, straightening up and wiping the blood off his hands with a Kleenex. 'Not me, of course,' he added, catching the way that Jack, Gwen and Toshiko were looking at him. 'But some lads I met. Once. Er... anything else, boss?'

Toshiko removed a small scanner from her pocket, about the size and shape of her thumb but matt-black and with an antenna on top. Switching it on, she swept it back and forth across the bodies, waiting for it to *beep*. If it did, then something in the area was transmitting somewhere in the electromagnetic spectrum.

Nothing.

Replacing the scanner, she took out another little device. This one was no larger than a lipstick, but a lot heavier. Again, Toshiko scanned it back and forth over the bodies. If there was an active power source of any kind there, it would vibrate.

Still nothing.

Something was nagging at Toshiko. Something wasn't quite right with the bodies. One of them was hunched over, protecting something. Gently, she eased a hand underneath his chest and tried to take the boy's weight so she could turn him over, but her angle was wrong and she couldn't get any purchase.

Seeing what she was doing, Owen bent to help. He took the body by the shoulders and tipped it backwards, allowing Toshiko to reach beneath it and retrieve the object that the boy had in his hand.

She brought it out slowly, reverentially, and as Owen eased the body back to the ground Jack and Gwen gathered around Toshiko, eager to see what she had found.

It was a metallic object, the size of a paperback book, but ovoid in shape and heavier than its size indicated. The colour was the first thing that struck Toshiko: a deep lavender which looked like it was the colour of the metal itself, rather than an enamel or a paint. The object was criss-crossed with raised ribbons of metal, and the ribbons broadened out at random intervals to encircle what looked to Toshiko like buttons. At the broad end of the object there were three irregular holes, perhaps cable sockets, and the other end, the narrower end, was different in texture, like ceramic rather than metal, but still the same shade of lavender.

'Is it an iPod?' Owen asked. 'It is, isn't it? It's the latest one.'

'It's not an iPod,' Toshiko said quietly. 'Look at the size of the buttons. They're designed for smaller fingers than any teenager has. And the layout is ergonomically wrong for an entertainment device. And, of course, there's nowhere to plug your headphones in.'

'Ever seen anything like it before?' Jack asked.

'I'm not sure,' she replied. 'I have a feeling it's similar to some of the items we have in the Archive, but let me take it back to the Hub and I can tell you everything there is to know about it.'

Jack nodded. 'I know you can.' Looking at the other members of the team, he said, 'Anything else before we leave? Remember, this is the last chance we get. After this, the police get to walk all over everything.'

They all shook their heads.

'Then let's go.'

The fresh air outside hit Toshiko as they left the club. The police were still holding back from entering, although there were some dark glances cast their way as they walked toward the Torchwood SUV.

The four of them climbed in and, within moments, it was as if they had never been there.

From the wall-wide window of the Boardroom, Captain Jack Harkness looked down at the central atrium of the Hub, and at his team.

His team. *His* team. He still felt a burning pride whenever thought of them in those terms. The three of them had confronted one of the most terrifying things any human being could confront – the knowledge that not only were they not alone in the universe, but they weren't even terribly important – and they had dealt with it, quietly and with grace. And now they worked together, each bringing their own particular skills to the party, to keep the world safe.

To prepare for the moment that Jack was privately dreading – the moment when it all started…

Over to one side of the Hub, Toshiko was using a hyperspectral scanner to investigate the interior of the device they had found at the nightclub. Jack already knew roughly where in the galaxy it had come from – he had quite a lot of background knowledge that the others lacked – but he wasn't going to give them any clues. Partly that was because it would mean giving something away about himself, and he was wary of doing that. Partly it was because he didn't know what the device was for. His knowledge was fragmentary, superficial. But metaphorically filleting alien technology and picking the bones out – that was what Toshiko did best.

Toshiko worried him. Although she was at the heart of the team, she didn't realise it. She felt that she was remote from the rest, off to one side. Perhaps it was her Japanese heritage showing through, perhaps it was just natural diffidence, but Jack viewed it with some concern. Beneath that reserved exterior, he suspected there was a supernova of emotion, and he didn't want the resulting explosion to damage the team.

Near Toshiko, Owen was at a lab bench, testing samples scraped from the device for traces of DNA, or any of the myriad other complex biochemical substances with which alien life forms transferred their genetic information. Owen's skills were literal versions of Toshiko's metaphorical ones; he filleted alien bodies and picked the bones out of them – when he could. And he patched the team up when things went wrong – which they did. Often.

Owen worried Jack too, but for different reasons. Where Toshiko was locked down, Owen was wide open. Things affected him too much, and he let everyone know about it. Jack had no idea what Toshiko got up to in her spare time – if she got up to anything – but Owen was an open book. The first fifteen minutes of any day consisted of him reciting everything he'd got up to the night before: every drink, every sexual encounter, even – until Jack had put his foot down – every bowel motion.

And then there was—

Hang on. Jack quickly scanned the Hub. No sign of Gwen. She should have been applying her analytical police brain to the fight in the nightclub, trying to work out what evidence they had, and where they could go next to work out where the device had come from. He knew she was annoyed about being pulled out of her dinner with the boyfriend, but he hoped she hadn't left to go back…

'Missing someone?'

Jack abruptly stopped looking down into the Hub and refocused his eyes on the reflections in the glass in front of him. And there she was, Gwen, standing in the darkness at the back of the room.

'Been there long?'

'Don't you know?'

'I know I seem omniscient – actually, I try hard to cultivate the image – but I don't know everything. How's the investigation going?'

She moved further into the room. 'I'm going to have to make some enquiries tomorrow – friends, relatives, workmates. Someone might have seen one of those lads with a new toy, something high-tech that they didn't recognise. I can't do it from here, that's the problem. As my old tutor at Hendon used to say: "There's no substitute for bodies on the ground."' She winced. 'Sorry, that wasn't the most tasteful thing to say, given the circumstances.'

He smiled. 'You're forgiven. Just don't do it again. Any other discoveries down there?'

'Tosh believes that the device is part of a whole batch that arrived on Earth some time back in the 1950s. We've got twelve or thirteen items already in storage, confiscated from various places around South Wales. One even made it as far away as London. Apparently, the Torchwood team there had it in *their* archives, until...' Her voice trailed away. She hadn't been in the team when Torchwood London had been laid waste, but Jack knew that she was sensitive to the fact that the others didn't like to talk about it. 'Anyway, it was destroyed. Tosh is trying to find out if there are any design elements that the items have in common, something that might shed light on what this thing does.'

'What do the other items do?'

Gwen shrugged. 'That's apparently the problem. They've been archived without anyone doing any serious analysis on what they are or what they do. Owen thinks that they're the interstellar equivalent of Apostle Spoons– all part of a set: a collection of stuff. Decorative, rather than practical.'

'He may have a point.'

Gwen looked around the Boardroom. 'You know, *you* could do with some stuff to brighten this place up. You should start a collection of your own.'

Jack indicated the Hub, behind and below him. 'I have you lot,' he said. 'That's enough to be getting on with.'

'Look, it's quiet now, and there's nothing I can do until tomorrow. Can I get back to my meal, please? Even if it's just for the mints?'

'I'll see you tomorrow,' Jack said and, as Gwen left the Boardroom, he turned and gazed out of the window again, back down into the depths of the Hub.

The meal was long finished and, by the time Rhys had drunk two cups of coffee, he had worked out that he wouldn't be seeing Gwen again that night.

Which, he thought, as he gazed across the table at Lucy's bright, open face, wasn't necessarily the worst thing in the world.

The restaurant had filled up to overflowing and then gradually emptied again whilst he and Lucy ate. And while they talked. In fact, it seemed like they'd never stopped talking, even though Rhys seemed to have eaten all of his own food and what was left of Gwen's as well. Now the white tablecloth was spattered with various sauces, the metal platters were piled up to one side, and the hot towels had cooled down some time before.

'Don't take this the wrong way,' he said, 'but I can't believe you stay as thin as you do and eat so much. I'm going to have to live off watercress for a week to make up for this.'

'I never used to be able to,' she replied. 'It's these tablets. They've really changed my metabolism.' She smiled. 'I can't believe how much fun this has been,' she said, gazing into Rhys's eyes. 'I really needed this, especially tonight. Thanks.'

'Hey,' he said, 'I enjoyed myself too. I'm only sorry...'

He trailed off, and Lucy made a sympathetic face. 'I guess it must be hard on you, with Gwen suddenly going off on urgent business all the time. I wouldn't have thought there was that much serious crime in Cardiff. I mean, you never really get to hear about it, do you?'

'Not often,' Rhys admitted. 'I used to listen to the local radio stations every night when Gwen was called out, just in case there was a report of a bank robbery, or a raid on some crack den, or something. Just in case she'd been hurt, you know? But there never was. Closest I ever got was a nutter on a phone-in show talking about UFO sightings. He had a thing about them. It worried me for a while, the fact that every time Gwen was out working, I'd listen to the radio and he'd be on, at two in the morning, talking about UFOs. Then it occurred to me that he was probably doing the same thing on the evenings when Gwen *wasn't* out working, but I was fast asleep and couldn't hear him.'

'You don't sleep when Gwen's out working?'

He looked down at the tablecloth. 'I get lonely when she's not there,' he said. 'Pathetic, isn't it?'

'I think it's rather sweet.'

He looked up at Lucy, not really thinking about what he was doing, but when his eyes met hers a sudden shiver ran through him. Part of him wanted to look away, but part of him wanted to keep holding on to her gaze for ever. He ended up looking away, then looking back to check what she was doing, and when he found that she'd done the same he blushed. And so did she.

Her eyes were brown, flecked with green, and her lashes were startlingly thick. Freckles were sprinkled across her cheeks and the top of her nose. Her mouth looked soft. He could see the tip of her tongue touching her teeth.

'She never talks about what she's been doing,' he said suddenly, surprising himself with the words. 'Which kind of worries me. I know it's all meant to be a big secret, and I guess there's some security reason why she can't tell me the details of what she does, but I wouldn't mind if she just gave me the highlights. "Hey, I abseiled down into a white slave trade convention tonight!" Or "Someone fired a machine gun at me and ruined my nice white blouse!" But she never says anything. Just "God, I'm tired." Every night.' He laughed bitterly.

'Look,' he said, 'this is… ah. Shit. Shall we go? It's getting late.'

Instead of replying, Lucy reached out across the table and put her hand over his. He felt a jolt run through him. 'I'd like to help,' she said softly. 'You've been so good to me tonight, and I'd like to make things better for you. If I can.'

'I'll get the bill,' he said. He could have sworn that he sent his hand a message that it should pull itself out from underneath hers, but somehow the message didn't get through, and his hand just stayed where it was.

And, thanks to the immutable laws of cosmic irony, which Rhys believed in as much as he believed in anything spiritual, that was the perfect time for Gwen to walk back into the restaurant.

THREE

Owen was whistling again.

At least, Toshiko assumed it was Owen. Jack was in his office, doing whatever it was that he did up there, Ianto was out in the little Tourist Information Centre they kept as a back entrance and Gwen had left, Toshiko assumed, to return to her interrupted meal with her boyfriend. It was just Toshiko and Owen in the central atrium of the Hub, and she wasn't the one who was whistling.

And if she *had* broken the peace and calm of the Hub at night with something as crass as whistling, it would have been soft and mystical, not an out-of-tune whine which wandered up and down several octaves apparently at random.

She tried to block it out by concentrating harder on the alien device on the table in front of her. There was something about the lavender colour and the smooth curves of the metal that made her think of Japanese art: the surface was incised in patterns reminiscent of formal calligraphy, and the colour was reminiscent of her father's favourite Hokusai etchings. It wasn't from Earth, of course. Her brain was just looking for comparisons, connections, similarities. But it was oddly comforting, compared with the harsh, hard-edged technology she usually ended up examining.

Toshiko had started off by using a microwave imager to get a picture of what was inside the shell. And that's how she thought of it: a shell protecting something delicate, vulnerable. The image she got was fuzzy, in shades of green and blue, and so she had turned to an ultrasound scanner, using the vibrations from whatever was inside to map out the interior structure. The results had been ambiguous: there were definitely voids within the shell, separated from each other by denser areas, but it wasn't as clear as she had hoped. The transmission X-ray system which she had wheeled in, based on the kind of thing used in dental surgeries but with some significant improvements of her own, had just revealed a series of what looked like grey-white whorls and spirals that didn't really help.

And that whistling was driving her crazy. Tuneless, atonal, and yet strangely mournful.

She glared over at Owen, but he was sitting with his back to her, oblivious. He had his hands behind his head, and he appeared to be leaning back and listening to something on his headphones. Didn't he have any work to do? Didn't he have a home to go to?

Looking at the images from the three separate imaging systems that she had employed to no good effect, letting her eyes skip back and forth from one monitor to the next, Toshiko felt her mind teetering on the edge of revelation. It was as if there were something momentous sitting just beyond her reach: she knew it was there, but she couldn't find a way of getting to it.

Her eyes slid from the turquoise contours of the microwave image to the grey spirals of the X-ray, and she suddenly noticed a correspondence: a curve that started off in the microwave and then apparently stopped dead, but in fact continued on in the X-ray, appearing there out of a dark void. And once her brain had made that connection, others suddenly sprang out. How could she have missed them? There *was* a picture, there *was* a coherent whole, but not revealed through any one sensor. Working feverishly, she whipped the cables out of the backs of the various monitors and fed them all into a central image-processing server. It took her ten minutes, during which she was so busy she couldn't hear Owen's sad whistling at all, but when she had finished she had all three images being projected at the same time onto the same screen.

And there, revealed in all its glory, was the inside of the alien device.

And it was beautiful.

'What the hell is that?' Owen's voice said from behind her.

'It's a composite image,' she said without turning, 'formed by combining

34

the images from three separate sensors. By themselves, the sensors didn't have enough resolution to be able to map out the interior of the device – each one could see a bit of the picture, but it was only when I combined them all that I could see the whole thing.'

'Yeah,' Owen said, dubious, 'but what the hell *is* that?'

'I don't know,' Toshiko said simply. 'But it's beautiful.'

The image on the screen was a multicoloured structure in which there were no straight lines at all. What appeared to be a series of flat oval plates of different sizes were linked to each other and to a constellation of small spheres by cobwebbed connections, and behind it all were hints of a larger irregular mass.

'I was expecting wires,' Owen said. 'A battery, perhaps. Would a battery have been too much to ask? Circuit boards, maybe? Or am I being old fashioned here?'

'They're there,' Toshiko said, running her fingers gently across the screen, following the contours of the inside of the shell, 'but they aren't obvious. They follow a different design logic to the one we're used to.'

'How do you mean?'

'The devices we humans build tend to follow some simple rules,' she continued, confident now that she was talking about the things she loved. 'Wires carry current, but the current heats the wires up, which means that resistance increases and the current drops, so we make the wires as short as possible. That way we don't lose too much power. The heat needs to dissipate, so we separate components as much as we can in order to allow some circulation of air. We use transistors to switch the current in different ways, and capacitors to store it up and discharge it in big chunks. But what if some alien devices were designed with a different set of rules? What if art was more important than power conservation? What if symmetry was more important than efficiency?'

'That's mad. Isn't it?'

Toshiko shook her head. She couldn't take her eyes off the screen. 'Look at it, Owen. Really look at it. What do you see?'

'A mess.' He moved closer, screwing his eyes up as he concentrated. 'No, wait. OK, it's still a mess.'

'Relax. Don't try to look *at* the screen: try to look beyond it.'

'What, like those dot pictures? I could never get them.'

'Try.'

'OK.' There was silence for a few moments. Toshiko could imagine Owen screwing his face up like a small child. Perhaps his tongue was even poking out between his lips. 'Oh. Oh shit. Is that what I think it is?'

'What do you see, Owen?'

He sighed deeply. 'This can't be right, but I think I can see a *face*. Inside that piece of tech. A fucking *face!*'

As soon as Gwen walked into the Indian Summer, she knew that something had changed.

It wasn't just the fact that the place was almost empty and the waiters were standing around with tea towels, waiting for the last few diners to leave: it was more the fact that Rhys and Lucy appeared to be holding hands and staring deep into each other's eyes.

A farrago of feelings bubbled up within her, rooting her in the doorway. Her legs seemed to be operating independently from the rest of her: they simultaneously wanted to run across to the table so she could slap their silly faces inside out, turn and stride out of the restaurant in a massive hissy fit, and collapse on the floor. Part of her felt like she wanted to be sick. Another part was telling her that it was all a massive misunderstanding, some trick of perspective that made it look like their hands were touching when they were actually miles apart on the table.

Rhys's face, when he turned his head and saw her in the doorway, put paid to the 'trick of perspective' theory. His eyes widened, and she saw – she actually *saw* – the colour drain from his face. He pulled his hand out from underneath Lucy's and the girl looked surprised for a moment. Then she turned her head to follow Rhys's horrified gaze, and she saw Gwen in the doorway.

And she smiled.

Gwen was surprised to find that a sudden flush of anger was powering her legs to carry her across the restaurant to the table. For a moment, when she arrived, she wasn't even sure what she was going to say. Rhys, on the other hand, seemed pretty sure that he wasn't going to say anything until he knew what tack she was going to take.

'I don't mind you eating my food,' she said to Lucy. 'But don't think you can do the same to my boyfriend.'

Rhys, to his credit, smiled, although it was a cheesy, uncomfortable grin. Lucy's face creased into an exaggerated look of concerned horror. 'Oh!' she said. 'I can see how it looks, but no! No, I was just telling Rhys about the problems I've been having with *my* boyfriend.' Her gaze dropped theatrically to the table. 'It's been terrible. Rhys was just comforting me. You're lucky to have him. He's very sensitive.'

Gwen was torn. On the one had, she didn't believe a word of it. On the other hand, she wanted to. Partly because, after the events at the nightclub, she just didn't have the energy for a fight. And partly because, if she and Rhys ended up having a heart-to-heart about the state of their relationship, lots of stuff was going to come spilling out. She just about had the moral high ground now, and she didn't want Rhys to feel that he had a genuine grievance.

So she decided to do something that was, she had realised during her time with Torchwood, a defining human characteristic. She was going to pretend she hadn't seen anything.

'Sorry,' she said. 'It's been a long night. I need to get to bed. Lucy, can we put you in a cab?'

'It's OK,' she said, forestalling Rhys who had opened his mouth to make some gallant offer to walk her home, or offer her use of the spare room for the night. 'I parked round the corner. I'm OK to get back.'

She got up, and put her coat on. Looking at Rhys, she said, 'Thanks for letting me talk. I needed someone to listen. See you in the office tomorrow?'

'Er... yeah. Goodnight.'

And with that, she headed for the door. Rhys, to his credit, didn't watch her elegantly skinny arse wiggling in her too-tight jeans as she went. Instead, he turned to Gwen and said something that gained him several brownie points in her eyes, and saved him from a night on the couch.

'I feel like a man who's just been pulled back from the edge of a cliff.'

'You know, you really don't want to be thinking about "going down" right now. Even in passing.'

He laughed, and it was a genuine laugh, not a forced one done for effect. 'Gwen—' he started.

'Rhys, we don't have to talk about it. We really don't.'

'There's nothing to talk about,' he said. 'Which is probably why we need to talk.'

They moved toward the door together with the kind of sub-telepathic harmony that partners get after a while. 'Lucy is cute—' he continued.

'You mean "hot".'

'No, *you're* hot. She's cute. And she's got some real problems with her boyfriend. He's doing heroin, and he's stealing her stuff to pay for it. And she's never sure what kind of mood he's going to be in when he gets home, which is becoming more and more infrequent. She's been reaching out for sympathy, and I just happened to be there. That thing with her holding my hand – I didn't know she was going to do it, and I was trying to work out how to get my hand back when you walked back in. I'm really sorry it happened. So – are we OK?'

Gwen reached out to take his hand. 'No, we're not OK, and it's my fault. I'm never home. I don't spend enough time with you. And when we are together, it seems like all we do is argue. Rhys, I don't want it to be like this. I love you, and I don't know how things got like this.'

He squeezed her hand as they left the restaurant, walking into the humid, petrol-scented air of Cardiff's city centre. Behind them, the waiters set to work like worker ants, clearing the restaurant in record time. 'I love you and you love me. That's what's important. Anything else is a trivial problem that we can sort out with enough chocolate and massage oil.'

'Rhys, I *really* love you.'

'I know. Oh, by the way – is it OK if Lucy comes to live with us for a while?'

Owen gazed, fascinated, over Toshiko's shoulder. 'That *can't* be a face,' he breathed. 'I mean, it just *can't*. Can it? Tell me it can't.'

But it was. At least, it was something approximating a face. Not even as close as the Weevils got, but the same basic shape, the same proportions, the same general relationship of features.

Toshiko was whistling to herself: a tuneless lament that grated on his nerves. He tried to ignore it, and process what his eyes were telling him.

As a biologist – or, rather, as a trainee doctor with a solid knowledge of human anatomy – Owen had assumed that life on other planets would follow a completely different course from life on Earth. Not that he'd thought about alien life on a regular basis before he joined Torchwood, of course, but it was the kind of thing that occasionally bothered him in those stretches of time, late at night, somewhere between the fifth bottle of San Miguel and the tenth, when his mind could raise itself from thinking about sex and consider some of the deeper mysteries of the world. Evolution meant that everything from bilateral symmetry to five fingers and five toes was the result of random mutation that, by sheer fluke, conferred a slight advantage over other random mutations, which meant that their possessors would have a slightly greater chance of not dying, and therefore a slightly greater chance of passing their mutated genes on to their offspring. And that advantage was entirely down to local conditions: the chemistry of Earth, the geology, the weather, the predators, everything. Take any alien planet – assuming there were such things – and any or all of those conditions could be different. And that meant other, different, random mutations would confer a slight advantage, and get passed on. Radial symmetry might be the preferred design option: an entire ecosystem of creatures that looked like starfish, perhaps, with eight, or ten, or fifteen arms. Or no symmetry at all: protean creatures with eyes located at random locations all over their bodies. The chances of two arms, two legs, two eyes and all the rest occurring as a random evolutionary outcome on an alien planet were infinitesimally small.

At which point, Owen usually stopped thinking about evolution, and random mutations, and alien life, and started worrying about whether he was going to get the chance to pass his own genes on that night.

Since qualifying as a doctor, and then later joining Torchwood, Owen had discovered that the basic human form was more like the norm across the universe than the exception. Not exclusively – there were creatures out there that were about as far from human as it was possible to get – but there were more beings that could pass for human in a dark alley than not. Which, for a biologist like him, raised the question: why? What was it about the universe that favoured a human-like design?

And now, as he looked at a picture of a form of life probably never even seen before by humanity, encoded somehow into a series of alien electronic circuits, all those late-night undergraduate thoughts came back to haunt him.

That lonesome whistle was really beginning to grate on his nerves. He wanted to say something to Toshiko, to suggest that she shut up, but Owen worried about the way Toshiko reacted to things sometimes. She internalised a lot. Not like Owen, who let everything out as often as possible. She pondered. Brooded. He didn't want to say anything that might make her withdraw even more. It wasn't that he cared, particularly, but she was a key part of the team. Owen didn't want to be blamed if she went over the edge.

The face that looked back at him and Toshiko from inside the alien device was differently proportioned to humanity: shorter and wider, something like a hammerhead shark. There were two eyes – at least, there were things that might have been eyes – placed at extremes of the head. A vertical slit right in the middle of the face could have been a mouth, or perhaps a nose. Or something completely different. The image finished at the neck, but Owen would have bet a lot of money on the probability of there being arms and legs somewhere beneath the head, all joined up with a central torso.

Scale was impossible to ascertain – that head could have been the size of a house, or the size of a microbe – but Owen was pretty sure that if you put the alien being and him side by side they could have looked each other in the eye.

'So is that all this is?' he asked Toshiko. 'Just a portrait? A snapshot of the wife?'

'No,' she said quietly, still studying the image on the screen, moving her finger across it as she talked. 'This is a functioning device. There is a power source just there: some kind of battery, I think. And I believe this area over here to be an amplifier, although I'm not sure what is being amplified. Judging by the way the circuits are routed, some kind of energy is being detected *here*, and the amplified version is transmitted *here*. The picture of the creature is a side effect. Something incidental to the primary function.'

'Incidental?'

She shrugged. 'Have you ever seen cheap radios shaped like…' She paused, casting around for an appropriate analogy. 'Elvis Presley! Or David Beckham!'

'No,' Owen said quickly. 'Never. I've never seen a radio shaped like David Beckham, and I've certainly never owned one.'

Toshiko glanced back over her shoulder at him, and her expression was disbelieving. 'I understand they were unaccountably popular, once,' she said. 'The circuitry works no matter what shaped case it's in. The shape of the case is a decoration. And that's all this is – a decoration. An incidental addition.'

'But with Elvis Presley radios, the decoration is on the outside. This image is on the inside. In the circuitry itself. It *is* the circuitry. Who was it designed for?'

'Perhaps it was a joke,' Toshiko said. 'Something the designer put in that they knew nobody else was ever going to see.'

'Or perhaps the race that the designer belonged to had some kind of X-ray vision. Perhaps everything they designed had a picture inside, rather than outside.'

'I suppose anything is possible,' Toshiko said. 'Look, Owen, may I ask you something?'

'Yeah, what is it?'

'Could you please stop whistling?'

That took him by surprise. 'I'm not whistling. I thought *you* were whistling.'

'I am not the one who is whistling. I assumed it was you. It is the kind of thing you would do. That, and singing. And breaking wind.'

'Tosh, I promise, I am *not* whistling.'

'You might be doing it without realising.'

'So might you.' He took hold of her shoulder. She tensed under his grip. 'Turn around. Come on – turn around.'

She turned on her stool, but for some reason would not look him in the eye.

'Tosh – look at me. Am I whistling?'

Her gaze rose to his mouth. 'No, Owen,' she said. 'You are not whistling.' Her face tensed as realisation caught up. 'But I can still hear whistling.'

She was right. Owen could hear that low keening noise as well, a mournful threnody that threatened every now and then to break into a tune but never quite made it. The kind of noise someone might make if they were working, concentrating on something, half-remembering a tune.

'Gwen's gone…' he said.

'And Jack is in his office, and we wouldn't be able to hear him from there. And besides,' she added, 'he does not whistle. Not ever.'

'Well if it's not you, and it's not me, and it's not Gwen, and it's not Jack…' He left the rest unsaid, but he gazed into the darkness at the edges of the Hub. 'What about Ianto? Is he still out the back in his little cubby-hole?' he asked, thinking about the interface between them and the rest of the world. The man who acted as gatekeeper and general office manager for Torchwood. 'Does he ever whistle?'

'I have never heard Ianto whistle.'

'Then the wind? Tell me it's the wind.'

'It's the wind,' Toshiko said, but she didn't sound convinced.

'It's not the wind,' Owen said. 'It's one of my big complaints about this place – no breeze. I keep telling Jack we need air conditioning.'

He nodded towards the dark depths of the Hub. 'Do you think we should…'

Toshiko nodded. 'I think we should. Definitely.'

Together, they moved away from the brightly lit central area of the Hub, and into the shadowy outer areas. As far as Owen was concerned it was like moving backwards in time. In the centre, the high-tech equipment and bright lights, not to mention the metal-backed waterfall that continued on down from the Basin above, gave the Hub a twenty-first-century feel despite the brickwork and the remnants of old pumping equipment. But as they moved further away, along one of the many curved tunnels that led away from the centre, the crumbling masonry and the massive, curved arches always made Owen feel like he was passing back through the twentieth century and into the bowels of the nineteenth. The architecture made him wish he was wearing a top hat and tails. Jack the Ripper should be prowling around there somewhere. Prostitutes in frilly knickers should be showing their wares on the corners.

'I think we're going the right way,' Toshiko said, and she was right. The whistling was getting louder, like an AM radio searching for a signal.

They turned a corner, and as they saw what lay ahead the whistling suddenly stopped.

It was the area where they kept Torchwood's occasional unwilling guests. A series of archways had been closed off with thick armoured glass, forming isolated cells. Riveted steel doors at the backs of the cells gave access to a connecting corridor. It was where the Torchwood team kept any visitors who really shouldn't be allowed to wander around. Wander around the Earth, that was, not just the Hub.

At the moment, the cells only had one inhabitant.

It was a Weevil: a hunched, muscular shape with a brutal, deeply incised face that could pass for human in the half-light of a Cardiff alley or the corridor of a crumbling tenement. A cannibalistic life form that – no, not cannibalistic, Owen corrected himself. Weevils weren't human. Carnivorous, yes, but not cannibalistic, although sometimes, looking at them, it was difficult not to think of them as some kind of human sub-species. Owen had often seen things that looked *less* human than the Weevil here coming into Casualty late on a Saturday night. This one had been captured by Jack and the team about the same time that Gwen had joined them. At first, they hadn't been entirely sure what to do with it, but as time went on it had become first some strange kind of mascot and then just part of the furniture.

The Weevil turned to look at them as they slowly approached the armoured glass barrier that separated them. It was crouched at one side of the cell: almost kneeling. Its head had been bent, and its arms extended almost ritualistically. Now, seeing them, it slowly straightened up to its usual ape-like stance and stared at them with deeply set, piggish eyes.

'Surely…' Toshiko started, then stopped.

'It must have been,' Owen said. 'I mean, I've never known the Weevils to whistle, but there's nothing to say they can't. I mean, if jackals can laugh then Weevils can whistle, right?'

'Right…' Toshiko didn't sound convinced.

They turned away and started to walk back towards the Hub.

And, behind them, the whistling started up again. Sad. Mournful. Alone.

* * *

Torchwood, her mobile read. Again.

The sky outside the window was pale, ethereal, marbled with nascent, nacreous cloud. The air that gusted in was fresh and cool. It was morning, but it wasn't the bit of morning that Gwen liked to see.

Rolling over, she found herself gazing into Rhys's slack, sleeping face.

People seemed so different when they were sleeping. Layers of experience sloughed off. Masks slipped away. What was left was the innocent core of the person. The child within.

She loved Rhys. That was a fact – unarguable, undeniable. And yet, there was something missing. The constant and surprising sex, the discoveries about the other person, the peaks and troughs of feeling – they had all faded away, eroded by time and experience into a comfortable emotional landscape of slight hills and minor valleys. It was like they had started off in the Scottish Highlands and were now living in Norfolk. Emotionally speaking. Gwen would never even consider living in Norfolk for real.

What did you do, when passion turned to friendship? When you knew each other's bodies so well that a voyage of discovery became more like a trip down to the shops? When the kind of orgasms that made you want to scream and rip the sheets became less important to you than a good night's sleep?

Oh God. Were they drifting apart? Were they splitting up?

'You'd better go,' Rhys said, his eyes still shut. 'If that thing goes off again it might wake me up.'

'Sorry, love. I thought—'

'Don't worry,' he mumbled. 'Talk later. Sleeping now.'

She rolled out of bed and dressed quickly, fresh underwear beneath some clothes that she found thrown down by the side of the bed. By the time she left, pausing in the doorway to take a last look at him, Rhys was buried beneath the duvet and snoring.

Outside, the birds were singing. The air was cool against her skin, as if freshly laundered. The smell of the trees – earthy, complex, indefinable – filled her lungs.

A second message had come through to her mobile while she had been getting ready, giving an address on the outskirts of Cardiff. She drove, deftly and fast, through quiet city streets, her mind deliberately blank. She didn't want to think about the man she was leaving behind – or the man she was driving towards.

When she arrived, at one of Cardiff's older districts – warehouses built in solid brick, a Victorian gothic church incongruously set across the street – the Torchwood SUV was already there: a black shape with curved edges, almost alien in itself.

Jack was standing in front of one of the warehouses. A smaller opening in the massive wooden plank door, all peeling green paint and rusty nails, stood open. Toshiko and Owen were getting their equipment from the SUV, and bantering quietly while they did so.

'Twice in one night,' Gwen said as she approached. 'I wish this was some kind of record, but it isn't.'

'We're not on the clock,' Jack replied, without apology. 'We're racing it.'

Together they went inside. It took Gwen's eyes a few moments to adapt. Shafts of light penetrated through holes in the warehouse roof, picking out the dusty air like spotlights in an abandoned theatre. The ground was flat concrete: empty of all but a few scraps of wood, a mangled bicycle and a body, curled up in a fœtal position.

Gwen and Jack approached the body together. At first, Gwen thought it was a man with dyed hair, dressed in a heavy and bloodstained overcoat, but as she drew closer the discrepancies began to win out over the similarities. The body was too bulky, the skin too coarse. And that ruff of yellow hair on top of the scalp…

'It's a Weevil,' she breathed. 'And it's dead.'

'Even Weevils die,' Jack said. He knelt down by its side. 'And they deserve the same kind of respect from us as anything else that dies. And that also means that, if they die before their time, then we need to find out how and why. We owe them that much, as a fellow life form on this Earth.'

Gently, he eased the creature over, and Gwen caught her breath. The Weevil's face had been eaten away. *Literally* eaten away: Gwen could see the gouges left by teeth in the gritty skin of the cheeks. The fingers had been chewed away as well, as had half the skin of the neck.

'What could have the strength to kill and eat a Weevil?' Gwen asked. 'Another Weevil?'

'They don't eat their own kind,' Jack said. He sounded sad. 'They're a surprisingly gregarious species. And besides, those tooth-marks are too small. Weevils have teeth resembling gravestones. And no orthodontists. Whatever had a go at this one had small, regular teeth.'

Gwen heard a sharp intake of breath from behind her. Turning, she saw Owen and Toshiko standing side by side, holding their equipment cases and staring at the body.

'It knew,' Toshiko said. 'Somehow, it knew.'

'It was mourning,' Owen confirmed.

'Make sense,' Jack said. 'Who knew? Who was mourning?'

'The Weevil back at the Hub,' Owen said. 'Somehow, it *knew* that another Weevil had died!'

Something scuffed in the darkness on the far side of the warehouse. In response, something else moved over near the door. Jack reached into his pocket, but didn't take his gun out. 'I think,' he said, 'that the pallbearers have arrived. Tosh, Owen – get your cameras out and grab as many photographs as you can.'

'How did they *know?*' Owen asked, glancing around nervously as he fumbled in his case.

'How did the one back in the Hub know?' Jack replied. Keeping his body still, he let his gaze sweep from one side of the warehouse to the other. Gwen followed his gaze. Behind her she could hear clicking as Toshiko and Owen clustered around the dead Weevil, taking their photos. Nothing was moving on the margins of the warehouse, but she could have sworn that some of the pencil-thin beams of sunlight that criss-crossed the dusty space were blocked in places where they had shone brightly before. Blocked by things that were not moving. Not yet, anyway.

A smell drifted across the open space towards them: thick, acrid, choking.

'Time to go,' Jack said. 'We've outstayed our welcome.'

The four of them edged slowly towards the door, leaving the Weevil's dead body behind them, spread-eagled on the harsh and unforgiving concrete.

'Are you sure they'll let us go?' Gwen asked.

Jack had moved so that his body was between them and whatever was in the darkness. His coat swirled around his body, the light from the doorway casting his shadow solidly across the floor. 'I'm not sure of anything in this world,' he said, 'but I think they have other things on their minds right now. Let's leave them to their grief.'

They left, and the Weevils did not follow them. All that Gwen heard as they climbed into the Torchwood SUV was a mournful whistling, coming from inside the warehouse.

FOUR

Rhys took a deep breath, braced himself, and looked in the mirror.

God. It wasn't a pretty sight. The morning sun streaming in through the bathroom window cast a harsh light across his face, shadowing it in all the wrong places and showing up bumps and odd little creases that he didn't even know he possessed. He hadn't shaved for a couple of days, thinking – if he'd thought about it at all – that it lent him a reckless, Colin Farrell vibe but, combined with the baggy skin under his eyes, it just made him look like a down-and-out who'd been sleeping in the rain for too long. The skin of his cheeks and temples was gritty, and he could have sworn that the flesh on his neck – the red-rashed, chicken-skin flesh on his neck – was looser than he remembered. Jesus, was he getting jowls! He *was*, he was actually getting jowls!

Rhys shook his head in disbelief. When had all this happened? When had he gotten old? The last time he'd taken a good look at himself he'd been young, fit and carefree. His eyes had been bright, his skin clear and his stomach as flat and as hard as a butcher's slab.

But now...

He looked down, knowing he wasn't going to like what he saw. And he was right. The bulge of his beer gut wasn't anywhere near big enough to hide his feet, but it was getting to the point where he'd have to take polaroids of his wedding tackle so he could remember what it all looked like.

Was this what Gwen saw whenever she looked at him? He groaned. No wonder she spent so much time out at work. He was a mess.

They'd had a long conversation, on the way back from the Indian Summer. It was probably the most serious conversation they'd *ever* had, apart from that hesitant, 'Are you on the pill?' 'No – do you have any condoms?' exchange the first night they met. They'd started off talking about Lucy, and how Rhys reckoned she needed a safe place to stay. Gwen had ducked the issue, making some sarcastic comment, and then she had started talking about the two of them and where they were going with their lives. Rhys was worried that she was winding herself up towards saying she wanted children, but fortunately her thoughts hadn't got that far along the road to the future. She was just worried they were drifting apart. The spark just wasn't there any more. He'd agreed, more because she was talking and he needed to throw in the occasional 'Yeah' and 'I know' to show that he wasn't thinking about something else, but looking at himself in the mirror now he had a pretty good idea *why* they were drifting apart.

When was the last time they'd been out to a gig? When had they last gone clubbing? When had they last spent money on something frivolous, something that wasn't for the flat or the car or dinner?

Somewhere along the way, they'd lost the fun.

He was turning into his father, that's what was happening.

Taking a deep breath, he began running through a list of all the things that would have to change in the flat. Radio 2, for a start. That would have to go. He'd found himself tuning to it more and more, while cooking food or tidying up, but despite the catchy tunes and the humorous banter of the presenters, it would have to vanish from the radio's memory. Radio 2 was the kind of thing he remembered his dad listening to. It wasn't called 'easy listening' for nothing. Radio 1 from now on – or, even better, one of the cutting-edge broadcasters that had sprung up with the advent of digital radio. Something radical. Something that would make him feel young again.

The fridge would need some clearing. Get rid of all the milk and replace it with skimmed, for a start. Or, even better, that soya stuff. The bread would have to go: no more cheese on toast of an evening. All that pasta in the cupboard was now surplus to requirements. And he'd go out later and get lots of fresh fruit and vegetables. He and Gwen could revolutionise their eating habits overnight. No more takeaways, no more Indian restaurants, just salads and healthy living.

No more takeaways. No more Indian restaurants.

And no more beer.

That would be the killer, but that was what had led him to this state in the first place. He let his hand caress his belly. You're going to have to go, my son. We've had some fun together, you and I, but if I need to sacrifice you to keep Gwen then that's what I'm going to do.

A gym? They were expensive, and having now taken a long hard look at himself in the mirror, Rhys was reluctant to let anyone else see him in this state, sweating and panting on a rowing machine. There had to be another way. Football? Perhaps he could get together with a few mates and form a team, enter one of the amateur leagues. The daydream made him smile for a few moments, before reality came crashing in. How many men did he see on Sunday mornings down the park, running around a pitch for a few minutes and then stopping, hands on thighs, gasping for breath? Football didn't seem to be doing them any good.

And then he remembered a snatch of conversation from the previous night. Lucy, talking about a diet clinic, and how the weight had just melted away from her. Something herbal, she'd said.

That was it. When Rhys got into work, he'd get the address of this diet clinic off Lucy, and he'd make an appointment.

The future suddenly looked very bright. Gwen didn't know it, but Rhys intended to become a new man, just for her.

'So which one of us is Ant, then?' Owen asked. He spread the photographs out across the metal surface of the autopsy table, sliding them around as best he could until he had a two-dimensional representation of a dead Weevil, life-sized, made out of A3 close-ups.

'Which one's the straight one?' Jack asked. He was prowling around the darkened balcony of the forensic lab like a tiger.

Owen thought for a moment, then swapped the photographs of the left and right hands over. 'They're both straight. Or they're both funny, depending what you mean by "straight".'

'Are you sure?'

'I'm positive.' He stood back, admiring his handiwork. He had to admit, in the absence of a real Weevil corpse it wasn't at all bad. If he half-closed his eyes, it almost looked as if there was an actual body on the table. Not one that he could cut open, of course, but one he could examine minutely if he wished. Toshiko had offered to take several different digital images of the same areas and turn them into a 3-D virtual image, but there was something about the physicality of the images that appealed to him. It was a bit like looking at X-rays. The images were about the same size.

'All right, which one's got the most charisma?'

Owen thought for a moment. 'Actually, they both look like Chuckie dolls.'

'Chuckie dolls?' Jack asked, still moving.

'Evil plastic children's toys turned serial killers.'

'I must've been away that week. Jeez, you take a few days off with the flu and you miss an entire invasion attempt. I hope you guys wrote it up for the record.'

Owen glanced up at him to check whether he was serious or not, but this was Jack, and it was impossible to tell. He might have been serious; he might have been joking. He might have been both at the same time – Jack was like that. 'Er… yeah, we wrote it up. Ianto has all the Chuckie dolls preserved in the Archive. Ask him about it.'

Jack was behind Owen now, looking down at the Weevil image. 'Ant or Dec? Ant or Dec? Remind me – why are we choosing sides?'

'For when these photographs get out on the Internet and we have to pretend that we faked them in order to discredit the whole thing. Like in the film.'

Owen could hear the shudder in Jack's voice. 'Jeez, I'm not going through that again.'

Owen looked up at him. 'What – you were involved with that? Faking the Roswell footage?'

'No, I meant I don't want to go through seeing the film again. That's two hours of my life I'd rather have dedicated to gargling rhino dung.'

'Have you ever—'

'Don't go there.'

'Watch me backing away.' Owen walked around to the other side of the table and took a closer look at the Weevil's half-eaten face, then tracked down the neck to the chest. It was hard to make out, but there were structures half-revealed through the tears in the flesh that bore no relationship to ribs. This was going to require a lot of careful study.

'What about cause of death?' Jack asked.

'Little to add to what you spotted back at the warehouse. Something chewed on its face, neck and chest. The tooth-marks are clear on the flesh and on the bone – or at least what passes for bone in Weevils. I can do a plaster cast and a quick computer animation to tell you what kind of teeth, but I'm guessing it has to be something really quite frightening in order to subdue a young Weevil and chew its face away.'

'Young?'

Owen nodded. 'Barely out of its teens, judging by the size. If you put this one next to the one we have down in the cells, this would definitely be the lesser of two Weevils.' He glanced up at Jack. 'OK, moving on. The initial attack was quick, but I think it severed a major blood vessel – or the next best thing in Weevils. It bled out, while its attacker was still chewing away.'

Jack looked sceptical. 'There wasn't much blood at the warehouse.'

'I know. I think the attacker drank most of it as it gushed out.'

'You can tell that just from an examination of the body?'

'No,' Owen admitted, 'I just have an active imagination.'

The police station was simultaneously familiar and alien to Gwen as she walked through the largest of the open-plan offices, surrounded by police officers busy filing reports and making calls, separated from each other by shoulder-high dividers. Familiar, because she had spent a couple of relatively happy years there, walking its institutionally painted corridors, smelling the bacon butties all the way from the canteen to the interview rooms, putting her street clothes in her battered grey locker at the beginning of every shift and getting them out again at the end. Alien, because it was all behind her now. She'd moved on. Grown up. It was like coming back to school after you'd left: you suddenly noticed all the little things you'd been used to before – the cracked paint, the battered corners on the corridors where trolleys of files had bashed into them, the coffee stains on the carpets. And everything seemed so much smaller, and so much drabber.

'You've got a nerve, showing your face around here!'

She turned, startled.

'Mitch?'

'Surprised you remember us, now you're running with that Torchwood mob.'

She grinned. 'I couldn't forget you. We shared chips at three in the morning too many times for that. You've shaved your moustache off. You looked better when you had it.'

Jimmy Mitchell didn't return the grin, or the banter. His face was set in a scowl that brought his heavy eyebrows together in a dark line and put a crease in the centre of his forehead. 'Don't try and sweet-talk me, Gwen. We know you removed evidence from the crime scene, and all we get told by the bosses is that we should proceed with the case with whatever evidence we have left.'

'I promise you this, Mitch – whatever we took was incidental to your case, but vital to ours.'

'Can I have that in writing?'

'Bugger off.' She smiled, to show there were no hard feelings. 'What's the story on the nightclub deaths, then?'

Mitch shrugged. 'Looking like a self-contained thing. Five lads got into a fight and inflicted fatal wounds on each other. We've got all the weapons, including the broken bottles. Only thing is, we don't know what they were fighting about. There were video cameras all over the club, relaying pictures to screens inside so the clubbers – narcissistic shits that they are – can see one another, and the management record everything just in case of trouble, but there's nothing there to give us any clue. One moment they're talking; the next minute they're fighting; then they're dead.'

'Can you run me off a DVD copy of the video footage?'

He thrust his chin out pugnaciously. 'Only if I can see whatever your people removed from the club.'

'No way.'

'That's the deal. Take it or leave it.'

Gwen thought for a moment. 'See, but not touch or take.'

He nodded. 'I just need to make sure it's not something we need to worry about – drugs, guns or stuff.'

'It's not. But I'll bring it anyway. That café round the corner – the one that does the espresso strong enough to stand your spoon up in? Three o'clock?'

Mitch's face relaxed slightly. 'Look, kid – I know you've done good for yourself. Whatever Torchwood is, it's got high-level cover. You people must be doing a phenomenal job. Whatever you hear, whatever we say, it's not personal, OK? It's just…' He paused, groping for the right word. 'It's just jealousy, I guess. You turn up in your fancy car, with your fancy clothes, and you waltz into our crime scenes like you're better than us.'

'But isn't that the same way you treat the Police Support Officers?' Gwen asked.

'Yeah, but we *are* better than them. What's your point?'

'No point. Can I have that DVD now?'

'I thought we agreed on three o'clock!'

'That was for the thing we took out of the club. I may as well take the DVD now, as I'm here.'

'You don't change, do you? You're still a chancer. Wait here.'

He was gone for ten minutes, and while she waited Gwen read through the various Health and Safety bulletins that were pinned to the dividing boards. When Mitch returned, he was empty-handed.

'I've set it up in the audio-visual suite. You can watch through it once, then take a copy with you. And you'll have to sign for it.'

'OK.' The AV suite in the police station was high-quality: she would be able to zoom in on images, enhance details, and do most of the tricks that she could do back at Torchwood, with the added benefits that she'd get a little privacy – which was sorely lacking in the Hub – and foster a little more trust between her and her former colleagues in the police.

The AV suite was just a darkened office with a widescreen LCD TV and a rack containing various bits of video equipment: a region-free DVD player, VHS, Betamax and U-matic recorders, a tape recorder and a CD deck, and even a laserdisc player for some bizarre reason. The lads probably thought it took LPs. The idea was that it should be able to replay any recordable media the police took in as evidence, although Gwen remembered them once being foxed by an archive of illegal phone intercepts made, for reasons known only to the suspect, on 8-track tape.

The DVD was sitting on top of the rack, a silver disc in an unlabelled black box. She slipped it into the machine and called up thumbnails of the eight chapters it contained. The disc had been pre-edited by Mitch or his boys: one chapter for the pictures from each camera that had caught the incident as it swung back or forth. It took her forty minutes to go through every chapter twice, at the end of which she knew three things.

It was Craig Sutherland who had brought the device along to the club.

He was demonstrating it to his friend Rick by pointing it at something or someone out of the camera's field of view.

And, seconds after Craig had demonstrated it, Rick had smashed a beer bottle on the nearest table and lashed out at a passing youth, slicing his face from eye to chin, leaving a gaping, bloody gash, horrifying even on the grainy video footage.

The rest was tragic and inevitable. The youth's friends weighed in, arms rose and fell, blood spattered the nearby tables and walls. Gwen timed the action: from beginning to end, it took twenty-three seconds. It was a Grand Guignol of unimaginable savagery from kids, just kids, who had been talking and drinking peacefully just a few moments before.

It wasn't her job. Not technically. It was up to the police to investigate the deaths, ascribe guilt and innocence and close the case. She didn't live in that world any more.

But it was clear from the video footage that nobody else was involved. It was the closest thing to an open and shut case she'd seen for a long time, except for motive. And motive would get lost along the way. The deaths would be blamed on drugs, or cults, or gangs, or something. Once the police knew they weren't looking for anyone else, they would wind the investigation down. Only Torchwood would know that the entire event, all five deaths, were due to kids using, or misusing, a piece of alien technology.

Toshiko was down on the firing range.

It was a darkened room, about fifty feet long and thirty wide, starkly illuminated by striplights suspended from an arched ceiling of old red bricks. A flat counter ran across the room at waist height, ten feet from the nearest wall. Partitions divided the bench into sections at which the Torchwood team would stand when they were conducting their regular firearms training, or when one of them was testing some suspected alien weapon they had found. On the other side the room was empty. The far wall contained a set of Weevil-shaped targets, some singed by laser fire and proton blasts, one still soggy from the time Owen had fired an alien fire extinguisher at it by mistake.

Toshiko was alone in the firing range. Alone, apart from two white mice.

One of the mice was in a small perspex cage on the bench, just in front of Toshiko. It was cleaning its whiskers with almost obsessive care. The other one was in another small perspex cage on a table in front of one of the distant targets. It was running up and down, sniffing at the corners and seams of its cage, stretching up to check the holes in the top.

Also on the bench, clamped in place so its longitudinal axis pointed towards each of the mice, was the lavender-coloured alien device.

Toshiko had two video cameras, one on each side of the room, recording her every move. One was set for long shot, the other for zoom. Jack wouldn't miss anything... in case her experiment went wrong.

Somewhere in the Archive, there was a section devoted to the records left behind by other Torchwood members; ones who had been carrying out experiments, just as Toshiko was. Ianto had showed her where it was, once upon a time. Videos. Photographs. An ancient daguerreotype. And one scratchy old wax cylinder that, Ianto told her, contained a man's voice talking very calmly up to the point when he suddenly let out the most God-awful scream that Ianto had ever heard.

Toshiko had no intention of only being remembered for the record of an experiment gone wrong. And even if she was, she wouldn't be remembered for a scream. She would be remembered for the longest, loudest, most unexpected stream of profanities ever recorded by Torchwood.

Using a laser pointer, she lined the alien device up carefully with the two mice: one just a few inches away, the other across the room. She was pretty sure that she had the thing aimed the right way: the overlaid images she had taken of the inside were ambiguous, but she had enough experience of analysing alien technology to know the difference between a transmitter and a receiver, no matter how many light years away they had been fabricated.

The mouse in the far cage was starving. Toshiko hadn't fed it for several hours, and she could tell by the way it was climbing the sides of the cage that it was desperate for food.

'I'm probably going to regret asking this,' a voice said from the doorway, 'because when I ask similar questions of Owen I get some rather disturbing answers, but what are you doing in here with two white mice and an alien device?'

Toshiko looked around. Ianto was standing in the doorway.

'I'm trying to confirm a theory,' she said. 'I think this is an emotional amplifier. I think it can actually transmit emotions over long distances.'

'And you're trying this out with mice, which are not, as far as I know, renowned for their emotions.'

Toshiko smiled. 'Hunger is an emotion,' she said.

Ianto entered the room and glanced at her experimental set-up. 'So one of these mice is hungry, and the other one isn't? And you want to see if you can project the hunger from one to the other?' He raised his eyebrows, looking at the small plate Toshiko had put to one side. 'Left to myself, I would have picked cheese. I notice you've gone for the rather more unusual chocolate-smeared-with-peanut-butter option.'

'I've worked with mice long enough to know that cheese is a cliché born of old *Tom and Jerry* cartoons,' she replied.' 'If you really want to tickle a rodent's taste buds, you want peanut butter and chocolate.'

The mouse on the bench beside her wasn't paying much attention. It had spent the past hour gorging itself on food. Now it just wanted to clean itself up and sleep it off.

'Right,' she said. 'Everything is set up.' She took a last look at the video cameras, to check the right lights were on, and then moved across to the device.

'Based on the interior structure,' she said to Ianto, 'the button that activates the device is here.' She indicated a wider section in one of the raised ribbons that criss-crossed the device. 'In fact, there are two buttons: one to activate the power and a separate one to operate the receiver and transmitter combination, placed far enough apart that a careless finger can't accidentally touch them both together. It has to be deliberate – first one button, then the other, and probably within a set period of time.'

Toshiko picked up the piece of peanut butter-smeared chocolate and slipped it through a hole in the top of the nearest perspex cage. It turned as it fell, landing sticky side down. The mouse in the cage glanced at it incuriously, and went back to cleaning its whiskers.

Toshiko pressed the first button on the device, and then the second one.

The ribbons along the side of the device glowed with a subtle apricot colour. Toshiko stepped backwards so that the video cameras could get a better view.

The mouse in the container on the far side of the firing range didn't react. It kept on climbing the sides of its cage, desperate to get at the food and satisfy its hunger. The nearest mouse, however, sat bolt upright, ears pricked, whiskers pointing forward eagerly. A sudden blur of motion and it was on the chocolate, tearing at it with tiny teeth, turning it over and over with its paws, wolfing down big chunks of the peanut butter. It was acting as if it was starving, as if it hadn't eaten for hours.

Toshiko reached out to touch the power buttons again. The apricot glow faded away.

The mouse rocked back from the chocolate. It brought its paws up in front of its tiny nose in an almost comical double-take, seemingly surprised at the peanut butter that was smeared across them. Convulsively it began cleaning its whiskers all over again. The chocolate lay, ignored, where it had fallen.

'Point definitively proven', Ianto said, impressed.

The area was mostly office blocks with wide glass frontages and lobbies that were all rose marble and lush tropical plants. Few cars passed by, and those that did were either chauffeur-driven, high-end hire cars or lost. No bus routes came that way: there was too much risk of hoi polloi getting in. Any old Cardiff pubs that had survived the blitzing and rebuilding of the area had been gentrified into wine bars or gastropubs catering for the office workers of a lunchtime. No chance of an eighty-year-old bloke with his dog nursing a pint of mild and bitter all night while watching a game of darts, Rhys guessed. The entire place was probably like a ghost town come nine o'clock.

A board in the lobby of the block that Rhys had entered contained a list of all the companies that occupied the offices. Half of the block appeared to be empty: an indication of the way businesses were being priced out of Cardiff by increasing rents.

A uniformed man, sitting at a rose marble desk that seemed to have been extruded from the ground rather than carried in and placed there, was giving him a curious stare. Rhys scanned the list, looking for one name in particular.

Each floor seemed to be devoted to a different company: Tolladay Holdings, Sutherland & Rhodes International, McGilvray Research and Development... collisions of surnames and generic phrases that didn't tell you much about what the companies did. There were probably people working for them who weren't entirely sure either.

And there it was. The Scotus Clinic. Twelfth floor.

Rhys took a deep breath. This was it. Once he booked in at the security desk, there was no going back.

He wanted Gwen to notice him again and, if Lucy's story of extraordinary weight loss was anything to go by, then this was the way to do it.

Nodding to the guard, he walked into the elevator and pressed the button for the twelfth floor.

He could do this.

He knew he had it in him.

FIVE

'So what have we got so far?' Jack asked.

They were back in the Hub. It was late on Thursday afternoon, and he'd called a council of war, pulling everyone back from whatever they were doing. In Gwen's case that had been interviewing the friends and relatives of the dead boy, Craig Sutherland: a depressing process, combining one part grief with four parts suspicion, to which she had become depressingly familiar during her time with the police and thought she had managed to escape when she joined Torchwood. No such luck.

Jack was standing at the head of the Boardroom table, the LCD screen behind him showing a rotating Torchwood logo, providing a dramatic backdrop to his muscular frame: constantly changing and yet constantly the same, moving and seemingly at rest.

'Well,' Toshiko said, and looked around at the others, 'I could go first.' She was sitting there, legs crossed, arms folded carefully in front of her. 'I have been working on the alien device, and I have discovered what it is. Or at least, I believe I have determined a part of its function.'

'I'll bite,' said Jack. 'What is it?'

'I haven't completed my tests yet, but I believe that it is an emotional amplifier. It can detect emotions some distance away and amplify them locally, or detect them nearby and amplify them at a point some distance away.' Seeing their blank faces, she continued: 'It works in much the same way as a loudhailer, for instance. That picks up quiet sounds and amplifies them so people can hear them a long way away.'

'Or a directional microphone,' Owen added. 'That picks up quiet sounds a long way away and amplifies them so you can listen to them.' He looked around the room. 'Not that I would ever try that outside Torchwood, of course. That kind of thing is wrong. Especially at three o'clock in the morning, when you think the girl across the street is having it off with her boyfriend. Completely wrong.'

'Moving rapidly on from Owen's dodgy moral sense,' Jack said, 'can anyone suggest what such a device might be for?'

Fidgeting, Owen said, 'I can think of one straight away. There might be alien races that communicate via some kind of short-range empathic sense. As they developed technologically, they might invent things that enabled them to communicate at longer ranges; let their friends know what they were feeling across the other side of the valley, or whatever. It's like an emotional mobile phone.'

'It's a theory,' Jack said. 'Tosh, what do we know about the construction of the device?'

'It's small, and built with a lot of artistry and care. More a piece of craftsmanship than a mass-produced item. I would deduce from this that the civilisation that built it puts great store by art and artisans. The internal circuitry serves two purposes: not only does it produce the emotional amplification effect, but it also contains a picture within its structure. An image. I believe it might be a portrait of the device's owner, or its designer.'

'What's the purpose of that?' Gwen asked. 'Bill Gates doesn't put his picture inside every computer he sells.'

'Doesn't he?' Owen asked, darkly. 'Has anybody looked hard enough?'

'I'm still trying to work out the purpose of the image,' Toshiko replied. 'But I will keep trying.'

'Do we know when the device arrived in Cardiff?' Jack asked. 'Or on Earth, if that's different.'

Toshiko shook her head. 'The external design of the device matches several others we have in the Archive,' she said. 'I am assuming they all arrived at more or less the same time, but I haven't tied it down any further than that.'

'Which raises the question: do we have all of the devices, or are there missing ones?' said Jack.

'There are symbols, incised into the circuitry,' Toshiko answered. 'They could be serial numbers. I'm attempting to determine whether they allow us to tell how many different devices there are, or whether they're just the alien equivalent of bar codes, scanned at the point of purchase. A price, perhaps.'

'OK,' Jack continued, 'we have the device, and we know what it does. Do we know how its last owner, its late owner, got hold of it?'

'My turn,' Gwen said. 'We identified who had it from the video footage in the nightclub. It was the kid named Craig Sutherland. He was a student at Cardiff University. I talked to some of his friends. He used to spend a lot of time in the junk shops, picking up old electrical devices and scavenging them for valves, transistors and other stuff. Apparently he had a thing for electronic music, and believed he couldn't get the right sounds out of digital instruments – synthesizers, computers and so on. He built his own analogue keyboards using old components—'

'Fascinating though this is,' Jack interjected, 'time flies. And if you've ever seen time flies, you'll know you don't want to mess with them. Big things, all covered in hair, wings the size of tennis rackets.'

'Time flies like an arrow; fruit flies like a banana,' Owen said quietly.

Gwen scowled, and looked away. *Don't encourage him*, she thought. 'I found a receipt in his room for something he bought at one of these junk shops,' she said quickly, before Jack could snap at Owen. 'Judging by the description, it's probably the alien device. It was part of a job lot of stuff. Tosh and I will go back to the shop and see if there's anything else there, but I think we can just put this one down to coincidence, rather than anything more sinister.'

Jack nodded. 'Agreed. Good work. But remember, the device caused five deaths. It's dangerous. Do we know what happened at the nightclub yet?'

'Me again,' Gwen said. 'Checking the video footage from the nightclub, I reckon young Craig was demonstrating the device to his friends. If you ask me – which you did – my best guess is that he'd worked out what it did, and was using it to chat up girls: finding out which ones were lonely, which ones were vulnerable, which ones were up for a shag – that kind of thing. They may even have been trying to project their own randy feelings across the room in the hope that it might influence some girl they were targeting.'

'Like a tuning fork inducing sympathetic vibrations in a wine glass,' Toshiko said, nodding.

Owen suddenly perked up. 'I could do with one of those.'

'You already have one of those,' Jack said. 'It's called "common sense". You ask yourself the question "Does she want a shag?" And your common sense chips in with the answer: "No, of course she doesn't. I'm unshaven and seedy. She would rather stick knitting needles in her eyes."'

'Moving on, before there's blood on the floor,' Gwen continued, 'the video footage is ambiguous, but my best guess is that someone walked across the beam: some local kids looking for a fight. The experiments Tosh did suggest that the device has quite a wide beam. Their aggression got amplified locally. Craig and his mate, Rick Dennis, suddenly got wound up. The emotions might even have got fed back to the local youths, who found themselves getting angrier and angrier. The whole thing just spiralled out of control. Someone made a comment, someone else threw a punch, and within moments there were knives out and beer bottles being smashed. They probably didn't even realise what they were doing.'

'Positive feedback,' Toshiko said. 'The device probably has some kind of safety cut-out to prevent that kind of unstable situation, but they just didn't know enough about the device to activate it.'

'All in all,' Jack concluded, 'raging hormones compounded by a badly understood alien device. If I had a nickel for every time that's happened around here…' He sighed. 'OK. Once Toshiko's finished her investigations, and once Toshiko and Gwen have visited that junk shop to check for other tech, we write it all up and file it all away. Case closed. Good work everyone. Now, what about the other thing – the dead Weevil? Owen?'

'I've concluded my remote autopsy, based on a close examination of the photos,' Owen said, straightening up. 'The creature exsanguinated – it bled to death. The wounds on its face and neck were almost certainly responsible. Someone or something had been chewing chunks of flesh from it, both before and after it died. Something quick and strong.'

'Another alien life form?' Gwen asked. 'Some kind of super-predator?'

'I'm not sure,' Owen said. 'I've done some sculptures of the tooth-marks, based on an extrapolation of what's in the photographs. You'd expect a super-predator, especially an alien one, to have large, sharp teeth, for ripping and tearing. What I've got looks remarkably like human teeth. Small incisors.'

'Human teeth?' Toshiko was shocked. 'You mean, a human being took down a Weevil with its bare hands?'

'Bare teeth,' Owen corrected. 'That's the way it looks.'

'I doubt that any of us could take a Weevil by ourselves,' Gwen said. 'Are we looking for a gang who hold it down while one of them has a feast? Or was it wounded, or sick?'

'I don't think Weevils get sick,' Owen said. 'They have an amazing physiology. They can digest almost anything, and their immune system is in some strange way an expansion of their digestive system into the rest of the body. Anything that gets inside their tough skin – bacteria, viruses, bullets, knives, stakes, whatever – gets digested. Rapidly.'

'Which doesn't answer the question,' Jack said grimly. 'What killed and ate this particular Weevil? If there's something out there that's rougher and tougher, even if it's human – *especially* if it's human – we need to know about it.' He turned to Toshiko. 'When we found the body, you said that the Weevil we have in captivity here in the Hub somehow knew that one of its compatriots had died. D'you really think that's possible?'

Toshiko shrugged. 'Owen and I were here last night, and the Weevil down in the cells started whistling. That's all we know.'

'They've never whistled before,' Jack said. 'Not that I've heard, anyway.'

'It was weird,' Owen said, shivering. 'Mournful.'

'Beware of ascribing human feelings to aliens,' Jack said. 'It's a classic mistake. They don't think like us, they don't feel like us, they don't react like us. It's hard enough working out what a cat is thinking, let alone something from another planet. Anthropomorphise at your peril.'

'That should be our motto,' Owen said. 'I'll get some T-shirts made up.'

'It's been a hectic twenty-four hours,' Jack continued as if Owen had said nothing. 'The alien tech thing is over, as far as I can see, so we can concentrate on the dead Weevil. With the autopsy over, there's no obvious plan of action apart from keep an eye on the situation, and intervene if we think there's something developing. The worry is that whatever ate the Weevil doesn't stop there. I doubt that the taste of Weevil is enough to keep a gourmet coming back for more. The nightmare scenario is that whatever this predator is gets a taste for human flesh and decides to move upmarket, preying on people in the city – and don't forget, there are an awful lot of those. So – I suggest everyone gets some rest until we have more to go on. Go home, get your heads down, and get ready for the next big bout of action.'

'Doctor Scotus – I have Rhys Williams for you.'

Rhys smiled at the twig-thin receptionist as she gestured for him to enter the office, wondering as he did so where on the spectrum of pleasantly plump to morbidly obese she was mentally placing him. She smiled back. Surely that meant he wasn't too far gone. Not compared to the other people she saw.

She was a good advert for the Scotus Clinic – thin and elegant, with blonde hair that shimmered in the light. Rhys smiled casually at her, and she smiled a professional smile back.

'Mr Williams.' The voice was deep and confident, with a veneer of good fellowship. 'Can I offer you a glass of water? I never offer tea or coffee, I'm afraid – the toxins they contain build up in the system, blocking the normal nutritional channels and preventing the breakdown of fat.'

'Right,' Rhys said, as the door closed behind him. He wondered what Doctor Scotus's opinion of eight pints of Murphy's Irish Stout was, and decided that he didn't want to find out.

Doctor Scotus was tall and reassuringly thin. He wore a black suit with a high, round collar, the kind Rhys wished he could get away with, and a shirt so white and uncreased that he might have put it on just moments before. He had blond hair, brushed straight back from his forehead, but a lock or two had escaped and hung over his eyes. He looked to Rhys to be about forty, but there was something about his healthily ruddy face that made Rhys wonder if he was actually a lot older.

'Nothing for me, thanks,' Rhys said, extending his hand toward Scotus. 'But thank you for seeing me at such short notice.'

'It's no trouble.' Scotus's hand was warm, hot even, but dry. 'Well, Mr Williams, please, take a seat.' He walked around the side of his desk, a massive slab of stone on top of an impressively architectural mass of wood. Apart from a laptop and a photograph in a frame, facing away from

Rhys, the desk was free of all clutter. A broad window behind him showed nothing but bright blue sky. 'Fifteen years of research has allowed me to develop an entirely natural process that works *with* the body, unblocking the nutritional channels and encouraging the toxins to drain away, taking the fat with them.'

'Sounds great,' Rhys said, looking at the chair in front of the desk. If it was a chair. It had no back, and looked more like a knot of pine with a padded seat and what might have been a knee rest. Gingerly, he slid into it. The knee rest took the weight of his body, stopping him from sliding forward. It was oddly comfortable, if undignified.

'How did you come to hear about the Scotus Clinic, by the way?'

'You were recommended by a… friend of mine.'

'What was this friend's name?'

'Lucy Sobel.'

Scotus's fingers danced across the laptop's keyboard. He gazed at the screen, and nodded. 'Ah, yes. Lucy Sobel. She responded well to our treatments. Very well. I presume you've seen her since?'

'Yeah.' Rhys shook his head. 'It's almost unbelievable. She used to be… big. Very big. Now she's…'

'Healthy,' Scotus said, 'and she will probably live for ten to fifteen years longer than she would have done before she came to see us. And those years will be good years. Years of mobility and clear thinking. It all links together, Mr Williams: heart disease, cancer, senility – all a result of the body becoming clogged up with fats and toxins. Material that it cannot use but has to carry around like a rucksack filled with rocks. My job is to remove that rucksack from your back and throw away those rocks.'

'Don't worry about the sales pitch,' Rhys said, 'I'm convinced. That's why I'm here.'

Scotus glanced at Rhys's body. 'To be frank, you are not in as bad a state as many of the people I see. You're probably two or three stone overweight. Regular sessions at the gym would probably shift that for you. And it would be cheaper.'

'Considerably cheaper,' Rhys admitted, looking away. 'But it's not that easy. I've thought about going to the gym, but I don't really get the time. Not on a regular basis. And…'

'And you are embarrassed,' Scotus said. 'I understand, Mr Williams. And I can help. I presume you were taken through the standard set of tests before you were brought to see me?'

Rhys shuddered, thinking back over the previous hour or so. The poking, prodding, weighing and measuring. The big pair of callipers that had pinched the spare tyre around his waist, measuring how much fat there was. The things he'd had to hold and push and pull to check his muscle mass. The tube he'd had to breathe into to see what his lung volume was. And all by professional young men and women who hadn't even made eye contact while they were talking to him. 'Oh yes,' he said. 'I was taken through them.'

'Good. It's important that we calibrate your physical attributes before we start the process.' He moved the mouse slightly, gazing at the screen on his desk, and clicked a few times. 'Let me just see what the results are. Body mass index… weight… height… lung capacity… Oh my.' He sneaked a quick glance at Rhys. The sunlight streaming in through the window behind him highlighted what looked like a halo of stray blond hairs around his head. They seemed to be waving gently in the breeze, although the window was closed. Scotus reached beneath his desk. Rhys heard the sound of a drawer sliding out. 'The good news is that, according to your physical profile, you will react well to the treatment. You have not yet travelled too far down the wrong path, and you should find the weight leaving your body rapidly, with no side effects.' His hand reappeared above the surface of the desk, holding a small blister pack. He slid it across the desk towards Rhys. The pack contained two tablets, each about the size of a large mint. One of the tablets was yellow; the other was purple. Printed above the yellow tablet was the word 'Start'. Printed above the purple tablet was the word 'Stop'.

'Does it come with instructions?' Rhys asked.

Scotus laughed. 'At least you've retained your sense of humour,' he said. 'I appreciate that. Too many people come through that door having lost all hope. They sit there, grey and dull, pleading with me to help them. You, on the other hand, still have a spark.' He gestured towards the blister pack. 'You take one tablet, with water, when you want to start losing weight, and the process will start. You take the other tablet when you have achieved the weight you find most aesthetically pleasing, and the process will stop. It really is that easy. You don't have to avoid anything, like alcohol or drugs, but I would advise some changes in your dietary patterns if you wish the weight to stay off after you've taken the second tablet. My receptionist will provide you with a diet sheet when you leave.'

'How does it work?' Rhys asked. 'I'm assuming... some kind of steroid?'

Doctor Scotus shook his head, and Rhys was struck again by those thin wisps of hair that seemed to float around his head like a halo. 'Ah, trade secret, I'm afraid. The Scotus Clinic needs to protect its intellectual property rights in our revolutionary dietary treatment. It's a cut-throat business, Mr Williams, and I do not intend that our competitors get a jump on us. Suffice it to say that they are a combination of plant-based esters and sterols distilled from a rare orchid that I discovered in the upper reaches of the Zambesi river. The orchid has yet to be classified by science.'

'You're an explorer?'

Scotus reached out for the framed photograph on the desk in front of him, and turned it around so that Rhys could see it. 'I was, once,' he said. The photograph showed a young man with long blond hair in a light khaki jacket and trousers. He was squinting, as if staring into the sun, and his face was glossy with sweat. Behind him, the background was a patchwork of different hues of green: leaves, vines, bushes, an explosion of plant life.

It took a few seconds for Rhys to realise that the man in the picture was Scotus. He looked only a few years younger than he was now, but he was at least twice the weight: his jacket and trousers were straining to contain the flesh inside, and his face ballooned out into a series of curves: cheeks, chin, forehead, all fighting for space on his skull.

'My mission is to make people thin,' Scotus said, 'and my reputation is your guarantee. You've seen, from your friend Lucy, that the tablets work.' He paused for a moment. 'I couldn't help but note from her records that the address we have for Miss Sobel is wrong. Do you know if she has moved recently?'

'She moved in with her boyfriend,' Rhys replied, 'but I think she might be moving out soon. Is there a problem?'

'No problem.' Scotus smiled reassuringly. 'It's part of our regular follow-up process. We wanted to check that she was happy with the weight that she had lost. We do offer a money-back guarantee, you know.'

'That's good to know.'

'Do you have Miss Sobel's current address?'

'I'll get her to get in touch with you,' Rhys said, cautiously. He thought he'd better check with Lucy first that she was happy with her address being given out.

'Of course, she works with you, doesn't she? Which reminds me – I forgot to ask. For the records. Where is it that you work?'

Rhys gave Doctor Scotus the name and address of the transport and shipping company, wondering why he felt faintly uneasy about it. Perhaps it was the eagerness with which Scotus typed the address into his computer, a half-smile on his face. Eventually, the Doctor looked up.

'Thank you, Mr Williams. It's been a pleasure meeting you. The tablets are yours – please feel free to call if you have any questions, or need any advice. You can settle up with my receptionist on the way out: we accept all main credit and debit cards. It's a one-off payment – no ongoing commitment required. And, as I said, we do offer a no-quibble money-back guarantee. So far, nobody has taken advantage of it.'

'Thanks for your time.' Rhys reached out to shake Doctor Scotus's hand.

He could feel Doctor Scotus watching him all the way to the door.

'All right – what is it?' Mitch said, weighing the alien technology in his hand.

'It's not a gun,' Gwen said, 'and it's got nothing to do with drugs.' She took a sip from her cappuccino. They were both sitting in a small Italian-run café not too far away from the police station. Mitch had a large mug of milky coffee in front of him. He'd asked for a strong white coffee several times, getting louder and louder, until Gwen translated it into a *venti latte* with an extra shot. The world was changing in ways that people like Mitch found it difficult to keep up with.

'I'd already worked both of those out,' Mitch said. His face still looked naked to Gwen, without that bushy moustache he used to have. 'The question is: what *is* it?'

'Some kind of games platform is the best we can come up with,' Gwen lied smoothly. 'We think one of the kids built it himself. You can see the design is completely different from anything Microsoft, Sony or Nintendo are putting out. It's possible that the fight started over this, but it's much more likely it started over a girl, or drugs, or something.'

Mitch grunted, still weighing the smooth, lavender-coloured object in his hand. 'So why are Torchwood hanging on to it?' he asked eventually.

'We think it might contain some proprietary software. We need to download what it contains and check who the owner is.'

'And that's what Torchwood does?' Mitch said, his face expressing his disbelief. 'Investigates copyright theft?'

'It's a big problem,' Gwen said, evading the question. 'Lots of new software and Internet start-ups in Cardiff.'

'All right. Keep us informed, luv. Did the video footage from the nightclub make sense?'

'Just about,' Gwen said. 'I could see the device clearly, but not what they did with it or what they were saying. But it's all grist to the mill. Thanks for making that copy for me.'

Mitch drained his *venti latte* in one go. 'Warm milk,' he complained. 'They always make it with warm milk, these days. Tastes like something from a kids' nursery. Look, I've got to get back. There's a briefing on. Keep in touch, and if you ever want to come back…'

'Thanks, Mitch. I appreciate it.' She watched him weave through the closely packed tables. He'd been a colleague, and she hated to take advantage of him.

She turned her attention back to the device on the table. An emotional amplifier, Toshiko had said. Something that took emotions and boosted them.

She and Rhys could do with a bit of boosting. Everything between them seemed trivial these days. Where was the grand passion they had started off with? When they made love, it was comfortable, nice, friendly. When they argued it was as if they just didn't have the energy any more.

Gwen ran her hand across the blistered surface of the device. She should be getting it back to the Hub before Jack realised she had taken it. She'd had a good reason, of course, and Mitch had learned nothing from it about aliens, or about Torchwood – but Jack frowned on Torchwood staff taking alien technology out of the Hub once it had been booked in.

And yet…

Gwen wondered what it would be like to make love with this device amplifying every feeling, every caress. What would an orgasm be like with this device accentuating the rush of sensation? What would it do to her? What would it do to Rhys?

Would it, could it, save their relationship?

She slipped the device into her handbag.

She was sure Jack wouldn't miss it for another few hours.

SIX

The further one went from the central atrium of the Hub, the darker it got. Toshiko had been walking for fifteen minutes now, along tunnels lined with damp red brick liberally scattered with circular blemishes of yellow fungus. Lights had been attached to the ceiling at some stage in the past – by Ianto perhaps, or by one of his predecessors – and linked by cables. They cast a strong orange light in a perfect circle underneath them, casting long shadows from the small blemishes in the brickwork, and leaving pools of darkness halfway between each pair of lights. For Toshiko, walking along the tunnel was like walking through an eternal sequence of rapid sunrises and sunsets, days and nights in rapid succession, leading her either forwards in time or backwards as she moved: she wasn't sure which.

It was a peculiar fantasy, and Toshiko wasn't normally prone to fantasies. She considered herself a rationalist. Physics was all there was, as far as Toshiko was concerned: everything, in the end, came down to the movements of molecules, of atoms, of elementary particles and, ultimately, quantum energy twisted into multi-dimensional loops and strings.

She and Owen often had this argument, late at night, when there was nobody else around in the Hub. Owen tried to persuade Toshiko that her belief in quantum physics, loop theory and superstrings was itself a faith, given that she couldn't actually buy them off eBay (and, as far as Owen was concerned, everything he needed in life could be bought online or obtained from a bar). In response, Toshiko logically proved to Owen that biology – the science he had spent his life following – didn't exist, being partly biochemistry, which was just a branch of chemistry, and partly classification of forms, which was just stamp collecting. And chemistry itself was just a branch of physics because it depended on how atoms and molecules interacted. Owen got really tetchy when she got to that point in the argument, and either put his headphones on and turned the music up loud or just stalked off in a huff. And that left Toshiko feeling like she had lost the argument, because the last thing in the world she wanted was for Owen to stop talking to her, and that was something that physics just couldn't explain.

Openings in the brick walls on either side of her provided glimpses of large, brick-lined chambers, some containing piles of crates and some row upon row of metal shelving filled with anonymous boxes. It was the Torchwood Archive; Ianto's domain, where the various bits of alien technology that Jack and the team had found, confiscated or otherwise obtained were now stored. Not for any particular purpose, but just to keep them out of the way.

A shadowy figure stepped from an opening ahead of her, and Toshiko stopped dead, putting a hand to her mouth to suppress a sudden scream.

Gwen lit the aromatherapy candle in the centre of the dinner table. Sandalwood and cedar-wood: that should set the right mood, if the search she had done on the Internet before popping out to the shops meant anything at all.

As a thin trail of smoke drifted up towards the ceiling, she stood back and looked at the table. The sweet white wine was open and cooling in the ice bucket, the good cutlery – the stuff with the beech-wood handles which hadn't come out of the cupboard since Rhys's sister had come to visit the year before last – was on the table and the food was cooking gently in the oven. Chicken breasts marinated in lime juice and orange juice, then wrapped in Parma ham and left in an oven dish on gas mark 4 for three-quarters of an hour. The smell was making her salivate already, and the food still had a quarter of an hour to go. The asparagus was in a dish, ready to pop in the microwave when the chicken was ready, and she even had a little parmesan to crumble over the asparagus when it was cooked. It didn't matter that Gwen thought parmesan smelled like puke and asparagus made her pee smell terrible; Rhys liked them, and this was all for him.

She crossed the room to the light switch and turned the lights down, just a little bit more, then went across to Rhys's pride and joy, the stereo stack system that he'd bought, piece by piece, from an audio specialist in Cardiff, and set the CD going. The Flaming Lips burst from the speakers in a fanfare of confusion. Quickly she pressed the stop button and selected something quieter from the rack. Suzanne Vega; that should do. As the strains of 'Luka' drifted across the room she allowed herself to relax. Just a little bit.

Just two things left. One of them was Rhys.

She had texted him earlier, and told him he needed to be home by seven p.m. He'd texted back saying that he was in the centre of town on a job, but he'd be back on time. It was five to seven now, and she was beginning to get a little edgy.

Which reminded her. The alien device. She didn't want to be edgy when that was switched on. Closing her eyes, she took a deep breath and held it, then let it out gently, visualising her tension flowing out of her with the breath. It worked: she could feel muscles that she didn't even know were tense letting go and she could feel her fingers unclenching.

She had put the alien tech beneath the candle, in the middle of the table. She wanted it somewhere central, and that was the best place. It even looked like something decorative, albeit something one might buy from a seaside craft shop to remember a holiday by, rather than pick out of an Ikea catalogue. For a while she had thought of hiding it in the room, or beneath the table, but that had seemed wrong. Having it in plain sight somehow made her feel like she wasn't actually manipulating Rhys's feelings without him knowing.

Of course, explaining to Jack how wax had spilled on it was going to be tricky, but she had until tomorrow to think about that.

Gwen quickly ran her fingers over the blister-like controls on the ribbon encircling the device. Gwen had been listening carefully when Toshiko had been demonstrating the device, and she was sure she remembered what to touch in order to get a generalised amplification of emotion within a few feet of the device. All she had to do was think sexy thoughts, and hopefully

Rhys should pick up on them. His sexy thoughts would echo back to her, and with luck they might not even get to dessert. Which was a shame, because she'd prepared a coffee crème brûlée, just in case. Well, she'd bought a coffee crème brûlée at the supermarket at least, and it had been expensive. Well, they were on a two-for-one deal, but it was the thought that counted.

Gwen took another deep breath. Was this right? Was she doing the right thing? In the short time that she'd been with Torchwood she'd seen what happened when people took alien devices home and tried to use them. It rarely ended well, and Jack came down hard on anyone who tried – but this was her and Rhys. This was their future. Jack didn't understand, he didn't have a life of his own, as far as Gwen could tell, but if Gwen lost Rhys then she would have lost the one anchor she had to the real world. Despite the risks, despite the danger, she had to try.

Things between her and Rhys weren't exactly *bad*, they just weren't *good*. They weren't the way she remembered them being, when they first met and fell into bed. The sex wasn't the 'wild, sweaty, so desperate for deep penetration that clothes got ripped' kind any more. It was more the 'it's been a week and we really should have a romp even though we're both knackered' kind. And that was only one step from the 'let's not bother, eh?' kind.

A horrible thought occurred to Gwen. The definition of getting old was that you'd already made love for the last time in your life, but you hadn't realised yet.

At which point, just as she got into the wrong frame of mind, she heard Rhys's key in the lock.

For a moment, all Toshiko could see, illuminated by the orange ceiling lights of the tunnels, was the bulky, stooped shape of a Weevil. Then her eyes adjusted and she saw that it was Ianto. Only Ianto, wearing a suit and looking like he belonged there, in the darkness, underground.

Physics. Light and shade, and the electrical reactivity of cells in the eyes. That's all it was. Keep telling yourself that.

'Ianto?' Her voice was shriller than she would have liked. 'What are you doing down here?'

He glanced casually back into the shadows behind him, and then turned back to Toshiko. 'I'm… auditing the Archive,' he said carefully. 'The records from the early years of Torchwood are pretty vague. I try and get down here as often as I can and correlate the contents of the boxes with the files we keep in the Hub. You'd be surprised at the stuff I've discovered we have but don't know about, or don't have but think we do. There's stuff here going back to 1885. I was just checking the chamber we have set aside for the remnants of Operation Goldenrod. Were you part of that?'

She nodded, remembering with a shudder the sheer chaos of Operation Goldenrod. It had been before Gwen had joined them, when Suzie was still part of the team. Toshiko had been working for forty-eight, perhaps seventy-two hours, on a hugely complex piece of alien technology that kept reconfiguring itself while she worked, but what she remembered, above all else, was the people that had been melted together during sexual congress by Goldenrod; their flesh joined, teratological monstrosities that Owen had to try to separate surgically leaving, for the most part, deformity and death behind him.

Ianto raised an eyebrow. 'And what about you, Tosh? What are you looking for down here?'

'That device we recovered from the nightclub – I think it's part of a set. According to the files, we have several more of them in a box.' She waved vaguely down the tunnel. 'Down there somewhere. Tunnel sixteen, chamber twenty-six, shelf eight, box thirteen.'

'Ah.' Ianto took her by the elbow and guided her back down the tunnel, the way she had come, away from the chamber where he had been working. 'You've come too far. It's a little confusing, down here. Let me help you orientate yourself.'

They walked back, Ianto holding Toshiko's elbow all the way. Something made a noise behind them, a movement, a scuffling, but when Toshiko turned her head she couldn't see anything. And Ianto didn't turn his head.

It was a rat. Just a rat. That's what Toshiko told herself.

'This chicken is delicious. What did you do with it?'

Gwen smiled. Suzanne Vega was still playing softly in the background, the alien tech was glowing a soft amber, which had surprised her but fortunately blended in with the candle, and Rhys was wolfing everything down with an enthusiasm she hadn't seen for ages. 'Nothing, really. I just marinated it for a while.'

'There's nothing "just" about that. It's inspired genius. And it certainly makes a change from the usual pasta in sauce.' He took another sip of his wine. 'We used to eat like this a lot,' he said reflectively. 'We used to cook together, remember? We'd buy a recipe book and go through the recipes, one by one. Sometimes they were great, and sometimes they were… well, not so great… but they were always interesting.'

'Remember the turkey with chocolate and chilli pepper sauce?' Gwen giggled.

'Which might have worked if we'd read the recipe properly and used dark chocolate instead of milk? I remember.'

'Give us some credit, we were drunk.' She wasn't sure if it was the wine or the alien tech, but she was feeling like she was slightly out of control now as well. Or possibly she and Rhys were synching together, so in a sense they were both controlling each other. Whatever: it was a nice feeling.

He was laughing now. 'What about the Brie wedges in breadcrumbs?'

'Which we left in the deep fat fryer for so long that the Brie just melted away and all we had left were these breadcrumb shells that tasted faintly of cheese!'

'What was the silliest thing we ever cooked?' Rhys asked. He reached out a hand and placed it over the back of Gwen's hand in a gesture of familiarity that took her breath away momentarily, it was so unexpected.

Gwen smiled at him, catching his eye for longer than they usually managed these days. 'The pork, paprika and pears, when the pears just cooked down to this porridge-y mush?'

His gaze locked with hers. 'No. No, I think it was the Cuban lamb. The one where the recipe said we had to marinade it in Coca Cola before barbecuing it.'

'Oh! Oh!' A sudden memory made her eyes widen. 'Surely it was the peanut butter and apple soup?'

Rhys nodded. 'Yes! Oh God, didn't we do that for a dinner party?'

'Rebecca and Andy came over. You found the recipe in a vegetarian cookbook. You were so proud of it.'

'And it was so thick and stodgy that none of us actually wanted our main course.' His fingers curled around her hand, touching the soft palm, stroking down to her wrist. 'Oh, Gwen, when did we stop having so much fun?' he asked softly.

She sighed. 'When I got a promotion, and you got a promotion, and we both ended up working silly hours just so we could get together enough money to pay the bills and take an exotic foreign holiday, once a year, just to keep ourselves sane.'

'Looking back, we may have made the wrong choice, somewhere along the line. No promotion, and a week in Criccieth every August. How does that sound?'

'It sounds like hell. Have you ever been to Criccieth?'

Rhys looked down at the remains of his chicken. 'Lovely though that is, I'm not sure I could finish another mouthful.'

'You usually clear your plate. What's wrong?'

He shrugged, avoiding her eyes. 'I thought I could do with losing a few pounds.'

Gwen reached out and placed her hand over his.

'I wouldn't complain,' she said, 'but that doesn't mean I don't find you shaggable just the way you are.'

Gwen could feel a slight tugging in her hand, as if Rhys subconsciously wanted to pull her towards him. Or was it subconscious? There was a slight curve to his lip, a certain glint in his eye, that sent a tingle through her, from her head to her toes but lingering somewhere around her middle. She could feel her nipples getting hard, rubbing against her dress. 'Er, you know I did dessert?'

'Get thee behind me, temptress.'

'I was rather hoping to have you behind me,' she said, enjoying the way his eyes widened.

'We could always bring the dessert with us,' he said, teasingly. 'I could lick it off your… stomach. And your breasts.'

'It's crème brûlée,' she breathed. 'I need to caramelise the sugar.'

Rhys stood up at the same time Gwen did.

'The way I'm feeling right now,' he said, pulling her towards him, 'heat isn't going to be a problem.'

As Gwen felt his fingers spread themselves through her hair, pressing her lips hard against his, she in turn pressed herself hard against him. They stumbled together towards the bedroom, not even noticing the amber light that pulsed in time with their heartbeats, from the dining table.

Tunnel sixteen, chamber twenty-six looked exactly like the twenty-five chambers that had come before it and the fifteen that Toshiko had overshot by: a red-brick arch in a red-brick tunnel, water trickling down and etching the mortar away, small patches of fungus spread across the walls. Toshiko hoped that they were good, old-fashioned Earth funguses, and not spores of something alien that were patiently eating their way into the walls. She hoped that the rats that she heard scurrying in the darkness sometimes really were rats, and not tiny things with many legs and many eyes that had snuck in along with some of the alien technology they had found. She had nightmares occasionally that something was growing, deep in the bowels of Torchwood. Something alien. Something bad.

Toshiko shivered. They were just dreams, provoked by some of the strange things they did and saw in Torchwood. They weren't real. They weren't backed up by observation, or evidence. By science.

She looked around, trying to work out where they were exactly, in relation to Cardiff geography. The Hub was directly beneath the centre of the Basin, but now they were probably some distance away, somewhere under the Red Dragon Centre, if she didn't miss her guess. How much of Cardiff rested on Torchwood's tunnels? How many ways in or out were there?

'Here we are,' Ianto said, stopping by a stack of metal, bolt-together shelving. 'Shelf eight, box thirteen.' He indicated a box at eye level: an ordinary plastic box – more of a crate, in fact – institutional grey in colour, half a metre along each edge.

There was nothing written on the box, apart from what looked to Toshiko like a random string of alphanumeric characters. She couldn't work out how Ianto had got to the right box so quickly. In fact, she couldn't work out how he had even got to the right chamber, given that there was no way of telling them apart. She gave him a sceptical look.

'I have a system,' he said, affronted.

Together they pulled the box off the shelf and lowered it gently to the floor. It was about the weight of a portable TV. Funny, she thought, how they kept comparing alien devices to ordinary things, like iPods and portable TVs, as if they were just different examples of the same thing. But they weren't. They really weren't.

The box was sealed with tape. Ianto ran his thumbnail around the edge of the lid, splitting the tape in two.

'Do you need me for anything else?'

She shook her head. 'No. Thanks for helping me find the stuff. I might have been down here for days looking for it, otherwise.'

'Helpfulness is my middle name.' He looked down the tunnel, towards where Toshiko had seen him earlier on. 'If there's ever anything else you need down here, let me know. I can find it for you much quicker than you can find it yourself.' And with that he walked off, back towards the Hub, walking fast and not looking backwards.

Dismissing Ianto from her mind, Toshiko reached down and pulled the lid off the box.

Afterwards, when all passion was temporarily spent, when they were lying with Gwen diagonally across Rhys's chest and with his hand cupping the heaviness of her breast, with the sweat and the moistness of their bodies cooling on their skin, the silence between them was the silence of lovers who didn't have to say anything, not lovers who couldn't think of anything to say. Gwen had climaxed twice: once quietly, biting her lip, while Rhys touched her with insistent gentleness, and once again gasping, hips raised, while Rhys moved deeply within her. Rhys had climaxed once, crying out like a man who had just run into a brick wall, the sweat trickling down his face and dripping onto Gwen's shoulder blades. Now they lay there, on the same bed where they had made love so many times before, trying to incorporate this latest time into the story of their lives.

'That was incredible,' Rhys said. He was still breathing heavily. '*You* were incredible.'

'You weren't too shabby yourself.'

'Don't expect me to recover any time this week. You've used me up.'

'I could go again. Just give me a few minutes.'

He shook his head. 'It's no good. I'm finished. You go on without me.'

Gwen laughed quietly beside him, her breast moving gently in his hand in time with her laughter. He felt himself stir. Perhaps he could manage one more time. Once he'd caught his breath. And had a piss.

'I need to go to the bathroom,' he said. 'I'm exhausted. Drained. I need vitamin pills. Lots of vitamin pills. In fact, I may just try to dissolve as many of them as I can in a glass of water and drink it.'

Gwen giggled, and rolled off him. He rolled in turn to the edge of the bed and stood up. His clothes were strewn across the floor. Responding to a half-formed thought provoked by the mention of pills, Rhys reached down and burrowed in his pocket for a moment. There, wrapped in a piece of tissue paper, was the blister pack that he had been given by Doctor Scotus that afternoon. Closing his fingers around the pills, he looked down at himself, at the curve of his stomach, at the way his thighs flattened out against the mattress. Gwen still loved him, but if he wanted to show her that he loved her then he needed to do something dramatic. He needed to lose that weight.

Padding to the bathroom, he was already pushing the 'Start' pill from its blister as the door was closing behind him. The pill was larger than he had realised, spherical and a mottled yellow. He popped it into his mouth and swallowed. The pill stuck in his throat for a moment, as if fighting to get out, then a wash of saliva carried it down.

As he returned to the bedroom, the night air cold against his naked skin, thoughts of the pill led Rhys to think about the Scotus Clinic, and that in turn led him to think about Lucy, who had given him the Clinic's address. His brain wasn't editing his thoughts properly: he was feeling tired, in a good way, and still turned on. That's why he suddenly said: 'So have you thought any more about Lucy coming to live here?' He listened to the words coming out of his mouth with horrified fascination, knowing exactly what kind of reaction they would provoke but unable to call the words back. 'Just for a while,' he added, weakly.

Gwen's head popped up from the tangle of sheets on the bed. 'If that's a joke,' she said, 'it's in really poor taste. What's the matter – one woman in bed not enough for you?'

The candle back in the dining room was flickering a deep crimson, casting dancing shadows across the hall and around the bedroom, illuminating Gwen's incredible breasts with a bloody wash of colour. Although part of Rhys's mind knew that he'd stepped into a minefield and he ought to back out rapidly, by far the greater part felt a sudden and brutal surge of anger, a dark wave that washed over him, knocking rationality off its feet and leaving something older and nastier behind. 'For Christ's sake,' he snapped. 'She's just a *friend*. Do you want me to write it down for you to make it easier to understand? Or shall I just text you the details, since you seem to pay more attention to whatever appears on your mobile than anything I say?'

The light from across the hall was flickering faster and faster, casting Gwen's ribcage into stark and ugly relief. 'Fuck you if you can't understand that I don't want another woman in my flat. And fuck you if you can't handle the fact that I have an important job. I guess simpering Lucy the simple secretary is more your type!'

Gwen sprang to her feet and jumped off the bed, clutching the bed-sheet to her chest. For a moment, Rhys thought she was going to push him out of the bedroom, but instead she sprinted past him and into the hall. The door slammed shut behind her, but not before he had seen, in the insane pulsating light, the expression on Gwen's face.

And beneath the rage, which he had been expecting, which he was feeling, there was something else.

There was horror.

Nestled together inside the storage crate were a collection of rounded objects, each about the size of a small piece of fruit. No two were identical, but they were all alike, and they were all similar to the object that was currently sitting on her workbench. It wasn't easy to tell, in the orange light that drizzled down from the overhead lamps, but their colours seemed to run the gamut from aquamarine to rose: nothing too bright or too dark, all pastels, all colours that would look good in a nice restaurant or bar. Relaxing colours. Their surfaces were blistered, but the blistering looked as if it was part of the design, not the result of extreme heat or extreme cold. The blisters were all the same size and the same distance apart, and they formed bands, or ribbons, around the objects, with areas of plain material

– some kind of ceramic, she thought – between them. They looked to Toshiko like controls of some kind.

Each object was different in shape from its brethren. Some were long and thin, some were short and squat, and some consisted of globules all massed together.

There was a sheet of paper in the box. It had slipped down between the objects and the box wall. She fished it out. For a moment she thought it had been printed in an old-fashioned typeface, then she noticed that the paper was yellow and stiff, rumpled slightly by dry conditions in the way that old newspaper often got. The typeface was literally that – the note had been typed. By hand. On a typewriter.

It was a list of the objects: brief descriptions and colours, enough to be able to identify them uniquely. And there was a paragraph about how they came to be in Torchwood: two of them had been discovered in what was believed to be an alien life-craft ejected from a crashing spaceship, found in an archaeological dig on an Iron Age site near Mynach Hengoed in 1953; five had been bought as a job lot in an auction in 1948, provenance unknown; and one of them had been transferred from an earlier Torchwood box dating back to 1910. They had all been put together in the Archive based on a similarity of appearance, and the function of none of them had been discovered.

The paper was signed in a bold hand; the ink faded by the passing of years.

Beneath the signature was the name of the person who had signed these objects into the Archive, along with the date.

Captain Jack Harkness. 1955.

SEVEN

Friday morning arrived unwillingly in the city; dragging itself into existence with reluctance, grey and dull, sluggish and tired. The traffic moved as if drugged; the drivers slow to use their accelerators and brakes, slow to react to traffic lights or pedestrians on crossings. A haze seemed to hang damply in the air, coating the sides of the buildings and making people's faces look as if they were covered in sweat, even though they were wearing thick coats. The pigeons huddled together for comfort, unwilling to fly for longer than it took to find a new space to land in. Even the water on the sculpture in the centre of the Basin trickled more slowly than usual. The heat and frantic activity of the past few days had ebbed away, leaving a muddy estuary of apathy behind it.

The mood in the Hub was equally funereal, as far as Gwen could tell. Toshiko looked as if she had worked all through the night again: she didn't speak unless spoken to, and hardly even then. Owen's hair was pointing in all the wrong directions and, although he'd left and come back, he was still wearing the same clothes, and he hadn't shaved. Only Jack was cool and crisp, moving through the still air like a predator; a faint crease of worry between his eyebrows.

Gwen waited until Jack was talking to Owen before slipping the alien device back onto Toshiko's desk. Toshiko looked at it blankly for a few moments, then glanced up at Gwen with an unreadable expression on her face.

'Did you get what you needed from it?' she asked.

'I got what I deserved,' Gwen replied, and turned away.

She couldn't stand to be in the Hub with the others; the silence was too intense. Instead she wandered off, down one of the tunnels she rarely used. Her footsteps echoed off the red brick as she walked, the *tock tock tock* of her heels matching the *drip drip drip* of water somewhere off in the darkness.

Jesus, how had it all gone so wrong so quickly?

She had meant for the alien device to have boosted the affection between her and Rhys, cementing the relationship between them, repairing the cracks that had developed over the past couple of months. Instead, it had driven a wedge into those cracks and levered the two of them apart. Stupid, stupid, stupid. She should have guessed that the device would amplify *any* emotion. After all, nothing is ever completely perfect. Even the most loving conversation contains the seeds of argument; the skill is in just nurturing the seeds you want and letting the rest stay fallow. The device just amplified whatever it was fed, with no selection, no discrimination. A momentary flash of irritation on her part had translated itself into anger for Rhys, which had then echoed back into a ferocious rage sweeping through Gwen's body. She had run out of the bedroom as quickly as she could, knowing she had to turn the device off before she slapped Rhys, or he hit her. She could feel it coming, like the prickling you got before lightning struck. They had been seconds away from violence, perhaps seconds away from one of them killing the other. And what terrified her the most wasn't that proximity to violence; it was how it had always been there. The alien device hadn't created it: only accentuated it. You couldn't amplify something that didn't already exist.

Alongside love, lay hate. That was what Gwen had to come to terms with.

She had slept on the sofa that night, wrapped in a sheet, the rage that had burned within her keeping her warm until it drained away and left her shivering and silently crying. She had showered early and left the flat before Rhys had woken up – assuming he had slept at all, and not just lain awake in their bed staring at the ceiling.

She needed to text him. She needed to call him and talk, but she needed to text him first to prepare the ground, because if she called him now she didn't know what he was going to say.

Perhaps it was all over. Perhaps they had already broken up, in his mind, and she didn't know it yet. Perhaps she was suddenly single.

Her blind footsteps had carried her far away from the Hub. She walked past Owen's medical area, and the firing range. She walked past the entrance to the long platform that extended parallel to a set of metal rails which vanished into a black tunnel; the terminus, Ianto had once told her, of an underground railway system that linked the Torchwoods together, although she had suspected then that he was joking in that straight-faced way Ianto had. She walked past the archives into which Ianto placed the various alien devices Torchwood had confiscated over the years. She kept walking until she was deep into territory that she had never seen before.

A sudden wave of coldness passed over Gwen, raising goose flesh on her arms. She looked up to see an opening in the tunnel wall on her left. Light began to ripple on the ground, just within the arch of the opening; a deep, violet light. Entranced, she entered.

Inside the doorway was a large, open space where the walls were punctuated by glass sheets fronting tanks full of water. The room was heavy with darkness, and even the scant violet light that oozed from the tanks was just a minor variation of the darkness. She waited for a few moments for her eyes to become acclimatised then she walked further into the centre of the room and looked more closely at the tanks.

They were full of nightmares.

The things that were in the tanks were fish, but not the kind you'd want to see on your dinner plate. Some of them were translucent, with organs and bones clearly visible through their skin. Others were covered in what looked like black armour, or mottled grey flesh that looked unhealthy, diseased. They all had mouths that were too large for their bodies, or eyes too large for their heads, or no eyes at all. One tank contained a nest of slowly writhing, fleshy worms about the thickness of her leg, bright red in colour, with holes at their ends that were less like mouths and more like gaping rips in their flesh.

Floating, half-deflated, in their tanks, the creatures looked like God's rough sketches for what he was going to populate the oceans with later.

'Where the hell in this universe did these monstrosities come from?' she breathed.

'The Pacific Ocean,' said Jack, behind her, making her jump. 'The Atlantic Ocean. The Indian Ocean. Pretty much any ocean you care to name on this planet.'

'But – but I assumed they'd come through the Rift, like everything else we deal with. You don't see these things on ice in the supermarket.'

'They live too deep. The pressure down in the ocean trenches is immense. It could turn a polystyrene coffee cup into a hunk of stuff the size of a small coin. If anyone could fish that deep – which they can't – and could bring one of these fish to the surface – which, I stress, they can't – the things would just explode. The difference between the pressure in their bodies and the atmospheric pressure around them would just be too much for their skins to take.'

'But – why are they here in the Hub? What's the point?'

'I don't know,' Jack admitted. 'They were here when I arrived. Somebody's little aquarium of freakish fish. I think whoever put them here was trying to make a point that there are stranger things in the Earth's oceans than slip through the Rift. They could've just written it on a Post-it note: I would have got the message. This thing is kinda like overkill, if you ask me.'

'Who feeds them? Who looks after them?'

'I think Ianto does it. Either that or it's automated. The real trick is how the pressure and coldness of the ocean depths is maintained in those tanks, and I guess that technology *is* something that came through the Rift. We couldn't build tanks like this on Earth now.' She heard, rather than saw, him shrug. 'Hey, maybe the whole aquarium is some kind of alien tech that was confiscated by Torchwood, and the fish just came along with it.' He paused for a moment, then went on, quietly. 'You took that alien device that we recovered from the nightclub, didn't you? You took it out of Torchwood.'

Rhys looked at himself in the mirror, and he didn't like what he saw.

He was haggard and pale through lack of sleep, and there were dark circles under his eyes. His hair felt lank. Sleep had evaded him for most of the night; too many times to count he'd half got out of bed to go and talk to Gwen in the living room, but he'd just fallen back, unable to form the right words. Each time the flat had creaked he'd thought it was Gwen coming back to bed, but he was always wrong. He'd already phoned in sick, but the sickness wasn't in his body – it was in his soul.

He had come within moments of lashing out at Gwen, backhanding her across her face. Her beautiful, wonderful face. And moments after the best sex they'd ever had, as well. He had no idea that he was capable of violence like that, but the rage had just taken control, escalating from nowhere into a hormonal storm that had hijacked any rational thought. He'd had his share of fights, of course – brawls outside pubs when some drunken yob had yelled one insult too many, fights on football pitches after questionable tackles, one memorable thrashing he'd inflicted on a drug-frazzled would-be mugger in an alleyway where he'd gone to have a piss – but he'd never thought of himself as a fighter. He'd never been consumed with the need to see blood, to split someone's face open. Not before last night.

He knew that he needed to talk to Gwen, to try and repair some of the damage that had occurred, but he didn't know how. He didn't know what words to use. She was the talker, the thinker, in the relationship. He was the intuitive one, the one who went with his feelings.

And look where that had got him.

What did one do in circumstances like this? Flowers? He could have them delivered to her workplace, but he didn't even know where she worked any more.

Perhaps he could just text her. Just one word – sorry. See if that worked.

And what if it didn't? What if she was already phoning around to find a new flat to move into? What would he do then? He wasn't even sure he could survive without Gwen in his life. She had intertwined herself into his very existence to the point where the thought of being single again was like the thought of losing an arm, or an eye.

Should he have proposed to her? Did she want kids? They'd never really talked about that kind of thing before. Conversations about their future usually revolved around which area of Cardiff they wanted to move to, and whether stripped pine floors and chenille throws over the furniture were too naff for words.

He felt lost. He felt as if he was drifting in uncharted and deep emotional waters in which strange fishes swam.

But on the bright side, he realised, looking at his stomach in the mirror, he was definitely looking slimmer.

He ran his hands across his stomach in disbelief. Surely that pill couldn't have started working already? Where would the fat have gone? It didn't just evaporate, and he couldn't remember having taken a dump since he'd taken the pill. But there was definitely more muscular definition there, and the swags of flesh that bulged out on either side of his belt when he got dressed – the things that Gwen referred to as 'love handles'– weren't as pronounced as they had been.

Jesus, that pill was worth the money.

And with that thought came another – he was hungry. In fact, he was ravenously hungry. Despite all of his well-meant mental promises to cut down on the carbohydrates, eat his five-a-day ration of vegetables and fruit and drink a litre of water between sunrise and sunset, he was hungry.

Rhys's legs carried him out of the bathroom, across the hall and into the dining room before he even knew what was happening. The remains of dinner from the night before were still there, the clearing-up delayed first by rampant sex and then by their vicious argument. The chicken was dry; the asparagus limp; the Parma ham darker and hard. Despite that, Rhys shovelled them into his mouth, savouring the taste of the orange and lime marinade. His jaws worked like crazy, masticating the food into a pulp so he could swallow it down. All thoughts of his stomach were forgotten now, blurred and overlaid by the need to satisfy his raging hunger.

He'd finished his portion now, and started on Gwen's. Raising the plate to his lips he scraped the food into his mouth with a fork. The flavours blended in his mouth: asparagus, salty ham and the citrus tang of the chicken. It was gorgeous. It was heaven.

And it wasn't enough.

Gwen had mentioned dessert, and Rhys stumbled into the kitchen area in search of it. He found it in the fridge: two ceramic pots containing a creamy vanilla custard, just waiting for sugar to be poured over the top and to be shoved under the grill to caramelise. Bugger the sugar: he grabbed a spoon from the draining board and scooped the sweet, creamy stuff into his mouth. Finishing the first, he started on the second. Within moments, it was gone.

Rhys stood there in the kitchen, stark naked, with the juices from the chicken and the asparagus trickling down his chest and the remains of the crème brûlée plastered around his mouth, and he wasn't thinking about his appearance, he wasn't thinking about his diet, he wasn't even thinking about Gwen.

He was thinking about the rest of the food in the fridge.

Gwen closed her eyes and sighed. Jack didn't sound angry, and somehow that was worse. Somehow, it meant that he had expected her to do it all along. 'I borrowed it so I could get some information from a police contact,' she said. 'He didn't touch it, and he didn't get anything from it. As far as he was concerned it was just a piece of decoration, but I managed to get the video footage from the nightclub in return.'

'Enterprising. Risky, but enterprising. What else.'

'And then… then I took it back to my flat. I thought if Tosh was right, and it was an emotional amplifier, then I might be able to test it out. I could see whether it made Rhys and I… more connected. Happier.' It felt like a betrayal, just telling Jack this. Not a betrayal of him and Torchwood; a betrayal of her and Rhys.

'I'm guessing that it didn't work.'

She paused, listening to the distant bubbling of the pumps that kept the aquarium going, watching the blind, incurious eyes of the deep sea fish. 'It didn't work. It just made things worse. I understand why the fight took place in the nightclub now. I understand why those kids died. It was just trivial stuff that escalated out of nowhere.'

'But we already knew that,' Jack said softly. 'Tosh worked it out.'

'Yeah,' Gwen said, 'but there's a difference between knowing and *understanding.*'

'Where is the wisdom we have lost in knowledge?' Jack quoted softly. 'Where is the knowledge we have lost in information?'

'T. S. Eliot?'

'Damn. I thought it was A. A. Milne.'

Gwen laughed. It was such a typical Jack comment.

'Which one: *When We Were Very Obscure*, or *Now We Are Philosophical?*' she asked.

'Ever read about those tribes in South America or on the Pacific Islands, back in the 1950s, just when long-distance air travel got started? After generations of nothing much happening, they suddenly started seeing things in the sky – big white birds that flew higher than anything else, and flew in lines straighter than anything found in nature. Sometimes the tribes just couldn't cope with this visible demonstration of something unnatural, and they just disintegrated. Sometimes they worked the aircraft into their own religions, worshipping them. But they never stayed the same. Never ever stayed the same. Even if their witch doctors, or shamans or local wise men told them to ignore the big white birds, and called them into their huts whenever the birds passed overhead, the wise men knew. And that knowledge changed them. We all get tempted, from time to time,' he continued. 'That's what the Rift does: it presents us with an infinite conveyor belt of consumer goods and cuddly toys that we're just not ready for. We have to be strong, and put them to one side.'

'I already knew that,' Gwen said, almost talking to herself.

'But now you understand it,' said Jack. He walked forward, into the aquarium, and stood beside her. She could feel his closeness in the darkness, his warmth, his solidity. 'These fish live so far down in the depths of the ocean trenches that only the faintest trickle of light can ever get to them. They live in almost perpetual night-time. They either have no eyes at all, or they have eyes that can amplify a handful of photons to a point where they make a coherent picture. But here, in this aquarium, we shine a light on them so we can see them. It's a faint light, sure, but it's more radiation than they probably get in an entire lifetime. And it burns them. It blinds them. Just so we can see them. It's as if something alien landed here on Earth but couldn't see us, or our buildings, or our landscape, without flooding everything with gamma rays. Forget the fact that it would kill us: they couldn't see without it.'

'I understand the analogy,' Gwen said, 'but I'm missing the point.'

'The point is that we can't observe without interfering. We shine a light into the darkness, and it alters things. Small things, big things, things we may not even notice. But we can't stand apart from it. Everything we see, we change. Even here in Torchwood. We think we can stand away from the alien technology and what it does to people, but we're people too. We can't investigate without becoming involved. And we shouldn't be able to. All we can do is be strong.'

She could see what he was getting at, but she wasn't going to give him the satisfaction of acquiescing to his point, despite the guilt she still carried within her. 'Very profound,' she said.

'Oh, hey, it's not mine. Some guy named Heisenberg said it first.'

'Heisenberg? Didn't he brew beer?'

Jack shrugged. 'In principle, yes,' he said. 'But it's uncertain.' He gazed around. 'Every now and then I feel like I ought to close this thing down, but where would I put the fish and the tube worms and stuff? It's not like Cardiff Aquarium has the resources to look after them. This isn't an aquarium any more; it's a retirement home for deep sea creatures.' He sighed. 'Come on – every time I come down here I leave feeling that a massive order to the local sushi bar is in order. Let's tell Owen that the wasabi paste is just a mild kind of green tomato sauce.'

'He'll never fall for that again.'

'Oh, he will. You don't know Owen as well as I do.'

Jack gestured for Gwen to precede him. She looked around the aquarium again. The various creatures that floated in the tanks – incurious, in pain – ignored her leaving just as they had ignored her arrival.

'I think there's one more thing these creatures can teach us,' she said.

'What's that?' Jack asked.

'They survive under extreme pressure. They've found a way to adapt and survive. I'm not sure we've learned that lesson yet.'

They walked away, back towards the Hub, towards life and light.

Behind them, the violet light faded away, leaving darkness behind.

'I thought you were ill,' Lucy said. 'They said you phoned in sick this morning.'

Rhys tried to put a pained expression on his face. It wasn't hard: he'd only had a couple of hours sleep, and every time he turned his head it felt like his brain was lagging behind by a few seconds. 'I felt a bit off, this morning,' he said weakly.

'Hangover?' She smiled, taking the sting out of the words. If Gwen had said that to him, he'd have automatically been bristling at the suggestion, whether it had been true or not. Which should, he reflected, tell him something about the state of their relationship.

'Sadly, no,' he replied. 'I think it was something I ate.'

He'd asked Lucy to meet him in a juice bar near where they worked, guessing that with her new figure she wouldn't want much more than a rhubarb and beetroot smoothie, or whatever they served in those places. She surprised him by suggesting they met up over a pizza at a local Italian-run restaurant. She surprised him even more by ordering a large Venetian with extra toppings.

'Look,' he continued, 'I need to ask you something, but first you have to promise not to tell anyone.'

She put on a serious face. 'I promise. Cross my heart and hope to die.'

'That weight-loss clinic you went to – the Scotus Clinic? I went there too.'

Her eyes widened in surprise, and her gaze quickly flicked down to his abdomen. 'But you don't need to lose weight.' She looked down at the tablecloth. 'You've got a great body.'

'You haven't seen me naked,' he said, then blushed furiously when he realised what he had said. 'But seriously,' he went on before she could say something like, 'I'd like to', which might lead to all kinds of problems, 'I wanted to ask you about that pill they get you to take. Have you had any side effects?'

'Actually, now you come to mention it, there have been a few.' She waved vaguely at the half-eaten pizza in front of her. 'I'm eating more than I ever did, but the weight is still falling off me.'

She was right. When she had walked into the restaurant heads had turned. Her figure was stunning, and her slimness meant that her breasts were truly amazing. And she was dressing to show them off, which she had never done before. Rhys's reaction had been immediate and physical when he saw her.

'I guess it's something to do with the effect of the tablets,' she went on. 'They must alter the way your metabolism works. Your body must be able to process the foods and just take the stuff that you need, letting the rest just flow away.'

'You make it sound so lovely'

She laughed, and it was a musical sound. A sound he wanted to hear more of.

'There is something else,' she said. 'My stomach – it felt really tender for a few days after I'd taken the pill, but it settled down. I'm feeling great now.'

'And you're looking fantastic.' There, he'd said it out loud now. 'Have you taken the second tablet yet?' he asked quickly, before she could react.

'Not yet. I keep meaning to, but… but I'm scared that I might start putting on weight again, so I keep putting it off.' She looked at her watch. 'Oops. I should be getting back. It's all right for you – you're off sick. Some of us have to work for a living.'

Rhys paid the bill. They walked out of the restaurant together.

'Thanks for lunch,' she said. 'This was great. We should do it again.'

'I'd like that,' Rhys replied, and felt the sharp edge of guilt slicing through his heart. 'I'd like that a lot.'

There was an awkward moment as they both stared at each other, half-smiling, each waiting for the other one to do something. Eventually Lucy leaned up and kissed his cheek. 'I hope you feel better soon,' she said, and turned to walk away.

Rhys watched her go, admiring the way the creases in her tight – but nicely tight, not horribly tight, they way they had been once – jeans flickered diagonally bottom right to top left and then bottom left to top right every time she took a step. It was hypnotic. Mesmerising.

Which was why, when a white van that had been cruising along the street suddenly swerved towards her, the side door sliding open, and when the man with the shaven head who had been walking along beside her suddenly turned and pushed her towards the opening, Rhys saw the whole thing.

Lucy screamed. Heads turned, but nobody did anything. Everyone else seemed hypnotised, mesmerised, but for all the wrong reasons. Rhys felt like he was watching something on a stage: he was the audience, they were the actors; he shouldn't interfere. Then she turned towards him with terrified eyes, and he found himself rushing forward, a snarl forming on his lips. 'Oi! Leave her alone, you arsehole!' he yelled. It took five steps to reach the tableau, by which time Rhys was running, and the force of the impact when his right arm pistoned up from somewhere below his waist and connected with the shaven-headed man's nose caused blood to spray in all directions and pain to lance right down to his shoulder socket. The man fell backwards. Rhys grabbed Lucy from where she was teetering on the edge of the van and pulled her back onto the pavement. The van pulled off fast, slowing only slightly for the shaven-headed man, his face all scarlet and wet apart from his insanely angry eyes, to roll in. The door slid shut and the van accelerated away, vanishing around a corner within moments. He could hear the squeal of its tyres for a few seconds more.

'My hero,' said Lucy as she clutched at his arm.

'My God,' said Rhys. 'What the hell was that all about?'

EIGHT

Gwen held the mobile in a hand that was suddenly nerveless and trembling.

New Message read the tiny LCD screen. *Read now?*

She looked around the Hub: at the desks and the LCD terminals; at the brick walls and the pillars; at the water sculpture and the big glass windows into other areas; at Toshiko, head down and working on a whole pile of alien devices that looked like the one they had recovered from the nightclub, and the preserved hand that floated in a specimen jar. How the hell could she get a signal this deep underground when all she had to do in some parts of Cardiff was turn around and she lost her signal?

She was prevaricating. The entire shape of her future life depended on this message.

At least, she thought it did. She and Rhys: she had assumed they would just keep on going, but it had been just that – an assumption. They hadn't really talked about it. She hadn't really considered it in any detail. Did she want them to get old together? Did she want Rhys to be the father of her children? Did she actually want children? Big, big questions that she'd never really made the time to consider. In the way that young professionals do, she had just shoved the Big Life Questions to one side and lived her life one day at a time. Big Life Questions, like mortgages and life insurance, were something for adults to think about. And, despite the number of times she'd told Rhys to stop acting like a child, she still didn't think of herself as an adult. Not really.

She was still prevaricating. Convulsively, her thumb closed on the Y button before her thoughts had a chance to catch up and cancel the action.

Sorry. Really really sorry. If yr still tlkng 2 me, pls call. I stll wnt us 2 b 2gther. R.

Bloody typical. Even at a time like this he couldn't avoid using text-speak.

But the annoyance was another form of prevarication. Gwen let it wash away from her, waiting to see what she felt when it left. And what she felt was relief. Sheer relief. They were still a couple. Thank Christ, they were still a couple.

Owen walked into the Hub, coming from the direction of the armoured glass cells where they kept living alien specimens whilst they decided what to do with them. Jesus, she was hardly one to hold the moral high ground, was she? And it was her unauthorised and unwise use of the alien device that had excavated these undercurrents within the relationship. Best to just cover them up and keep going. Big questions could wait until she and Rhys had *both* grown up a bit.

She selected *Options* and then *Call back* on the phone's menu, then watched the LCD screen, almost hypnotised, as it dialled Rhys's mobile back. She had to force her hand to raise the mobile to her face.

'Gwen?' He sounded scared and far away.

'Rhys, look, I'm so sorry.'

'Me too. Can you forgive me?'

'Can you forgive *me*?'

'Can we just exchange forgiveness?' he asked; 'cancel everything out and get back to where we were?'

'Let's do that.'

'Well…' Rhys was thinking: she knew the sound of that silence. 'When I say "back where we were", I mean before the argument but after the hot sex. Is that OK?'

Gwen smiled, and turned away from Toshiko and Owen, shielding the mobile with her hand. 'That's exactly where I'd want to leave it too. But leave it in a "pick it up later at that point" sense. But hey – where are you?'

A pause. 'I'm just outside that Italian restaurant near work.' There was another pause: not so much a thinking pause, but a working out how to

98

say something pause. 'Look, Gwen, you are the only girl for me. I love you totally and completely, right?'

'There's a "but" coming. I can feel it.'

'But someone tried to abduct Lucy.'

Gwen suppressed the desire to say 'You were having lunch with *Lucy*?' That wouldn't have helped. And besides, she could tell from Rhys's voice that he was contrite. And that he still loved her. Instead, she said: 'Has she reported it to the police?'

'Yeah, but as we didn't get the licence plate of the van and we couldn't describe the guy it all got a bit inconclusive. We ended up reporting it to your old partner, Andy, by the way. I don't think he likes me at the best of times. He wasn't helpful.'

'I'll have a word. Hang on – what van? What guy?'

'A van pulled up by the side of the road and some guy tried to shove Lucy into it. I hit the guy and pulled her back. The van just drove off.'

'Wow. Are you OK?'

'Bruised knuckles and swollen ego. The former will heal; the latter may take some time.'

'Is this connected to Lucy's boyfriend? The drug addict?'

'Lucy says no, but I'm thinking yes. He wasn't the guy who tried to shove her in the van, but I'm wondering if it's some kind of thing where he owes someone some money and they try to kidnap Lucy to make him pay up.'

'Sounds like it.' As words started forming in her brain, Gwen felt her face twisting into a grimace. There was an obvious conclusion to this, and she just didn't like it. 'Rhys – has Lucy got anywhere else to stay?'

Rhys's voice indicated that he'd already got to where Gwen was going, but he wasn't going to say it first. 'She can't go home, and I don't think a hotel is a good idea. She's in a bit of a state.'

'Other friends?'

'Nobody else she knows well enough to impose on.'

'Family?'

'South Shields.'

'Rhys – setting aside any arguments that we may or may not have had recently... I think Lucy should come and stay with us for a while. Until this whole kidnap thing is sorted out.'

'I think that's a terrible idea,' he said. 'The trouble is, all the other ideas are worse. Gwen – are you OK with this?'

She drew a breath. 'If *we're* OK, then I'm OK with this. *Are* we OK?'

'We're OK,' he said, and his voice held both warmth and reassurance and love.

'Then she can move in. But she does her own laundry: I don't want to see her panties in the wash, OK?'

He laughed. 'OK. Love you.'

'Love you too.'

There was silence, as they both waited for the other one to disconnect. That hadn't happened to Gwen for so long she'd almost forgotten the tremulous feeling it produced. 'Are you still there?'

'Yeah. I really do love you.'

'And you. Let's hang up together. On a count of three, OK? One… two… three.'

They hung up.

Arriving back at the flat she shared with Rhys, Gwen was uncharacteristically nervous. Standing outside the door, keys in her hand, she found herself reluctant to actually open the door. Someone else was in their flat. Someone was trespassing on their privacy. And if Gwen went in, she was worried that she would suddenly feel like the intruder.

She could hear voices from inside, and part of her wanted to flatten herself against the door and listen to what they were saying. Another part told her how stupid she was being, but it didn't matter. Were they talking about her? Were they laughing? And would there be a sudden awkward silence when she entered?

Idiot. Gwen had quite cheerfully kicked open doors to drug dens and marched in, smiling and shouting instructions, and yet here she was, frightened to walk into her own flat. Get a grip on yourself!

Quickly, before she could stop herself, Gwen shoved the key into the lock, twisted it and pushed the door open.

Down the short hall she could see Lucy curled up in one of their armchairs. She looked, if anything, even thinner than the last time Gwen had seen her: thin to the point of anorexia. Her hair hung lankly around her face, and it looked like she'd been crying. Rhys was across the other side of the room, stretched out on the sofa. He looked tired, but as soon as he saw Gwen he beamed and bounced out of the sofa.

'Hi, kid,' he said. 'Come and sit down. Cup of tea? Glass of wine?'

'That sounds great.'

'What does?'

'A cup of tea and a glass of wine.' She reached up and kissed him as he slipped an arm around her waist, letting her bag slide to the floor. The kiss was meant to be a peck, but it turned into something longer, something that might have graduated to full-on sex if they hadn't had a guest in the flat.

'Hi, Lucy,' Gwen said, disengaging herself from Rhys. She was perversely pleased to see how their new housemate was overtly studying her fingernails.

'Hi,' Lucy responded. Her voice was pallid, toneless. She seemed to lack energy; hardly surprising, Gwen thought, given what had happened to her.

The side table by the armchair had an empty bowl beside it. Noticing the direction of Gwen's gaze, Rhys said: 'Lucy was hungry, after what happened. I cooked her some risotto. And bacon. And cheese.'

Gwen glanced over to the empty bowl on the floor beside the armchair.

'It would have been churlish not to have joined in,' Rhys added. His hand was fondling her buttocks through her jeans. She tightened the muscles to give him a little more encouragement.

Gwen was about to make a comment about Rhys and food, but bit the words off before she could say them. Partly it was because she desperately didn't want to start another row, even in the absence of the alien technology, but also it was because she realised with some surprise that Rhys's T-shirt wasn't being stretched by his incipient beer gut any more. It was almost flat. Almost strokable, in fact.

'You're looking good,' she said. 'I can see why muggers would be scared of you.'

Rhys beamed. 'I'll make that a *large* glass of wine and a *mug* of tea,' he said, and swaggered off into the kitchen.

'How are you feeling?' Gwen said as she slid onto the sofa opposite Lucy.

'Shaky. Nothing like this has ever happened to me before.' She winced. 'You must hear that all the time, in your job.'

'And I take it seriously every time. Don't worry – you're not a statistic. You're a friend.' *Of Rhys's,* she almost added, but decided it wouldn't be tactful.

'Your colleague didn't seem particularly interested.'

'Don't let Andy fool you. He's a really good police officer. Did you give him a description of the man who attacked you?'

Lucy nodded. 'As far as I was able. I didn't really get a good look. It all happened so fast.' Her face clenched suddenly, convulsively. 'Listen to me – I'm just talking in clichés!' Her face relaxed into a forlorn expression. 'I'm hungry,' she said plaintively.

'It's shock,' Gwen reassured her. 'It'll pass away. A good night's sleep will do you the world of good.' *And I'm talking in clichés too,* she thought.

'He was taller than me. Tea's brewing, by the way.' Rhys entered from the kitchen carrying two tumblers of wine. He passed one to Gwen and was about to hand the other one to Lucy when he noticed Gwen shaking her head. 'Shock?' he mouthed. Gwen nodded, and he smoothly took a drink from the tumbler as if it was what he had intended all along.

'You know these are whisky tumblers?'

'Don't get pernickety just because we have a guest.'

Gwen turned her attention back to Lucy. 'So, this man: taller than you?'

'And thinner, the bastard,' Rhys continued. 'And close-shaven around the scalp area.'

'How was he dressed?'

'You realise this isn't your case? You don't need to start an interrogation.' He smiled, taking the sting out of the words as he slipped onto the sofa beside Gwen. 'He was wearing those things that men wear that aren't culottes.'

'Cargo pants?'

'Yeah, I think that's it.'

'How do you know about culottes but not cargo pants?'

'Because you've got three pairs of culottes in your wardrobe that you haven't worn for years.'

'You go through the stuff in my wardrobe?'

'I don't go through it – I just know what's there.'

'You don't by any chance wear any of it, do you?'

Rhys shook his head. 'It wouldn't fit. Yet.' He stroked his stomach lovingly. 'Give it time.'

Lucy was looking back and forth between the two of them.

'Sorry,' Gwen said. 'Look, I know this is awkward for you, but Rhys has mentioned some of your history. Do you think this could be linked to your boyfriend?'

Lucy shrugged forlornly. 'I can't see Ricky getting it together for long enough to make a phone call, let alone arrange a kidnapping. And he's called in all his favours already to get more smack. I just don't see how he could be involved.'

'What about his friends?'

'He hasn't got any friends. Just people he knows. People he shoots up with. People he buys from.'

'Might *they* want to hurt you? Maybe use you to get Ricky to pay some of the money he owes them?'

Her expression crumbled. 'He wouldn't notice. He wouldn't care.'

Gwen was about to ask something else when her mobile bleeped. She reached for it with heavy foreboding.

'Torchwood?' Rhys asked, face and tone neutral.

'What's Torchwood?' Lucy asked.

'I'm guessing it's some kind of elite police group working in counter-terrorism,' Rhys went on. 'Something like that. Am I right?'

'Close enough,' Gwen said, picking up the mobile. The display just had the word *Torchwood*, followed by a postcode. Somehow, despite the fact that the LCD screen only had one font, *Torchwood* looked heavier, more menacing. 'Rhys – I…'

'I know.' He reached out and touched her hand. 'Go. Go and come back safely.'

'Thanks. I love you.'

'I love you too.'

She got up and walked out, not even bothering to change her blouse, because that's what happened when Jack called. It was never convenient and never negotiable, but it was always, always important.

As the door of the flat swung shut behind her, she could hear voices talking. Voices talking about her.

Driving through Cardiff, she checked the street map with one hand by the crimson glow of the setting sun. The reference took her down near the docks, to an area she remembered from her time in the police. A place where old newspapers went to die, where rusty cranes towered black and insectile against the sky, where it always seemed to be dark and it always seemed to be raining.

She parked and went in search of the team. She found Owen and Toshiko standing on the concrete jetty overlooking the turbulent black water of the river. The SUV was parked a few feet away, next to a warehouse made out of some kind of angular corrugated iron. Toshiko was holding a portable scanner of some kind. It looked like she had detached it from the car. Her face was underlit by ghostly red light.

'Well met by moonlight, proud Titania,' Owen said.

'I'm guessing there's a porn version of *A Midsummer Night's Dream* that you've seen,' Gwen riposted. 'It's the only way you'd get to know any Shakespeare.'

'I studied the play at school, if you have to know.' He sounded hurt.

'And?'

'OK, and there's *A Midsummer Night's Wet-Dream*, but I swear I haven't seen it. Not for years.'

Gwen just looked at him.

'You can't even get it on DVD,' he trailed on. 'I think they only ever released it on Betamax.'

'Where's Jack?' Gwen asked Toshiko.

Toshiko glanced up. Gwen followed her gaze.

Jack was standing on the roof of the warehouse, coat billowing out behind him. His gaze was beaming out across the water like a psychic lighthouse.

'How does he get up to those places?' Gwen muttered. 'If I try to follow him I just get out of breath, but he's as fresh as a daisy.'

'I think he teleports,' Owen replied.

'Floats.' Toshiko was looking at the screen of the scanner again. 'Anti-gravity devices in his boots.' She looked up to meet Gwen's eyes. 'I am joking, of course. He was there when we arrived.'

'Which leads to the very important question: what are we doing here?'

'There's some kind of activity in the Weevil population,' Owen said. 'Suddenly they all appear to be moving – lots of sightings across the city. We thought for a while they were tracking something, but Toshiko's analysed their movements, and she thinks they're *being* tracked. Something's got them spooked.'

'Something's got the Weevils spooked?' Gwen frowned. 'That's not a something I'd like to meet on a dark night.' She looked around in sudden realisation. 'On a jetty. By a river. Oh God, we're looking for whatever it is that's hunting the Weevils aren't we?'

'Whatever killed that Weevil we found the other day,' Owen said, 'is nasty. Very nasty. It's kind of the chief predator, and that's not something we want in Cardiff. So we're going to have to track it down, subdue it and take it back to the Hub. Without, needless to say, anyone noticing. And without getting attacked by the Weevils whilst we're at it.'

'And tomorrow,' Toshiko muttered unexpectedly, 'world peace and a solution to the Riemann Hypothesis.'

Jack was standing over by the edge of the wharf, although Gwen hadn't seen him move from the warehouse roof. Somewhere behind him, across the water, a spotlight was pointed towards them, outlining Jack in white fire, casting his dark shadow across the concrete and the tarmac and the weeds.

Gwen nodded towards the device that Toshiko was holding. 'What's that thing do, then?'

'It tracks Weevils,' Jack replied.

'I didn't know we could track Weevils.'

'I think—' Toshiko began to say.

'Owen tells me their body temperature is lower than humans,' Jack went on. 'They're not quite cold-blooded, but they're not far short. Toshiko figured out a way to use overhead infra-red imagery from military satellites to track anything of a certain size that's moving at a walking or running pace and has a lower than normal body temperature.'

'Assuming there aren't many penguins on the loose in Cardiff,' Owen added, 'and, let's face it, stranger things have happened – we should be able to sort out the Weevils from the chavs.'

'Excuse me—' Toshiko interrupted.

'If we can do that,' Gwen said, picking her way carefully through the words, because she knew that she was missing something, 'then surely we can clear the Weevils out. Save some lives.'

Jack shook his head; the light behind him magnifying the gesture into a dramatic shadow-play. 'They spend time indoors, and Toshiko can't track them there. And besides, I need to know how they move, how they live, how they breed, in order to determine their social structure.'

'And what good is that going to do?'

Toshiko looked from Gwen to Jack. 'Excuse me, but—'

'That way,' Jack continued, 'I can work out a way of getting rid of all of them for good. It's like snails. You can step on individuals from now until doomsday, but if you know they don't like moving across sharp objects then you can scatter crushed eggshells around the edges of your garden and they'll never come in again. I need to find the Weevil equivalent of crushed eggshells.'

'Will you all please stop talking?' Toshiko snapped. 'I have something to say!'

'Go ahead, Tosh,' Jack said. 'We're listening.'

'I'm detecting twelve signals which I believe are Weevils. They are all moving in the same direction, at roughly the same speed. Eight of them are either moving through the warehouses near us or moving across the roofs. The other four are moving beneath us. I think they must be in sewer pipes.' She paused, examining the scanner. 'There is a time-lag between the thermal signatures being detected by the satellites and this scanner receiving the processed signal, but I think all of the Weevils are now either here or they have passed us.'

'But if they've passed us…' Owen started.

'Then we are caught between them and whatever is chasing them,' Jack finished.

Something snarled at them from the end of the wharf.

NINE

Toshiko could smell the Weevils before she could see them: a rank odour, like the elephant house at the zoo. Whatever it was, it made her nose wrinkle and her eyes water.

The display on the sensor receiver showed that they were being flanked on three sides: two Weevils somewhere in, beneath or on top of the warehouse; three more that had to be climbing under the wharf or swimming in the bay if they were anywhere; and another three in the darkness behind them. All eight Weevils were moving fast. Toshiko glanced around, but she couldn't see any sign of them.

Was this how the victims of the Weevils felt? A moment's nervousness, a prickling on the back of the neck, looking around to see nothing, and then teeth sinking into the neck, tearing the flesh apart, shredding it. And then the hot splatter of blood on the face and the arms and the chest? And then darkness. Was that how it was?

'Spread out,' Jack said. 'Everyone get your weapons out. Owen – that means your gun, OK?'

Toshiko reached behind her and pulled the Walther P99 from the holster in the small of her back. The gun dragged her hand down. She felt wetness on the grip: oil, sweat, humidity – whatever it was, it made the grip slippery and the gun hard to hold straight. Long hours of training on the Torchwood firing range made her check there was a bullet primed and ready to go, and then made her click the safety off. The bullets were made of some alien alloy, and their noses had been hollowed out and filled with a

Teflon fluid. The entry wound was the size of a penny piece; the exit wound was the size of a dinner plate. They could take down an elephant – if one ever went rogue in Cardiff. With one shot. And Toshiko hated them. They were technology gone bad.

Owen had a Sig Sauer P226. He was holding it two-handed, sweeping it back and forth, tracking shadows and mist. Gwen had a Glock 17, pointing it straight up in the air. Both weapons, like Toshiko's Walther, had come from the Torchwood armoury. Jack had once told her that he liked having lots of different weapons around, just for variety. Jack, of course, was suddenly holding his usual ancient Webley pistol.

Something made her glance up towards the top of the warehouse, where Jack had been standing a few moments before. Where there had previously been a straight line, metal against starlight, there were now two dark lumps. Industrial-age gargoyles, silhouetted against the night. Faces like relief maps, all chasms and mountain ranges. Staring at the four of them. Staring unblinkingly with eyes that had seen alien worlds, alien suns.

'Jesus fuck,' breathed Owen. He had seen them too. No, Toshiko realised as she glanced at him – he hadn't seen them at all. He was staring towards the bay.

Toshiko turned slowly around. There, crouched along the crumbling concrete edge of the wharf, were three more Weevils. These ones were crouched, knuckles resting against the concrete. Their gaze, as they stared at the Torchwood team, was blandly curious. Their serrated teeth, wet with saliva, glinted in the meagre light. They were different from one another in size, attitude, expression, and yet they were the same. They were violence and death, incarnate.

'Be calm, people,' Jack said.

Owen snorted. 'As in, "Be calm. Be very calm"? I saw that film. It didn't end well.'

'What about Ianto?' Gwen asked. 'He's got the SUV. He can come and get us.'

'You mean, rescue us,' corrected Owen.

'I'm holding him in reserve.'

'What, you think something worse is going to happen?' Gwen snapped.

Toshiko glanced at the sensor receiver display. It was still showing two traces on the warehouse side, three traces on the bay side, and three traces behind them. Slowly, she glanced over her shoulder. The spotlights on the cranes shone through the latticework of their construction, illuminating the wharf in a lacy web of light. And also illuminating three shapes that might have been piles of rubbish, might have been scrap metal, or might have been Weevils cutting off their retreat.

'It already has,' she said.

'Weevils to right of them,' Jack declaimed. 'Weevils to left of them, Weevils in front of them. Boldly they rode, and well, into the jaws of Death, into the mouth of Hell.'

'Very poetic.' Owen's voice was scathing. 'Is that Eminem or Chris de Burgh?'

'They're not in front of us,' Gwen muttered. 'They're behind us.'

'Like a lot of things in life,' Jack said, 'it depends which way you're facing at the time.'

As if reacting to an inaudible signal, the Weevils behind them – or in front of them, Toshiko corrected herself – loped towards the group. She braced herself, bringing her gun up.

Gwen was tracking the Weevils on top of the warehouse as they broke their stony immobility and started moving along the line of the roof. Owen was doing the same to the Weevils over by the edge of the wharf. They were moving too. Jack was—

Jack was standing with his gun by his side. 'Relax,' he said. 'We're not at risk.'

'Are you willing to bet our lives on that?' Owen challenged.

'I *am* betting our lives on that.' Jack glanced around. 'Cos that's what I do. Look at them. They're treating us like some potentially dangerous obstacle in their path. Check it out, then go round it.'

'Like buffalo,' Gwen murmured.

'Love buffalo,' said Jack. 'Thanks for asking.'

Toshiko suddenly realised that the Weevils on the warehouse and on the edge of the wharf had gone, vanished into the night. The Weevils that had been behind them swept past, close enough to touch, close enough for Toshiko to smell them, and then they too were gone.

'Well, that was fun.' Owen lowered his gun. 'We should do that again some time.' His hand was shaking.

'Perhaps with more Weevils,' Gwen added. 'Eight didn't really do it for me. I reckon ten minimum.'

'Sixteen,' said Owen. 'Four each. That seems fair.'

Reluctant to join in, Toshiko bent to retrieve the sensor display unit. It had dropped from her hand at some stage during the confrontation, but she didn't even remember letting go of it. The casing was scraped on one corner, but otherwise the device was still working. Green and orange webs meshed themselves together across the screen: a display that looked like abstract art unless you knew what it represented. Rapidly, Toshiko assessed what was going on. The Weevils, represented on the display by knots in the meshed webs, were moving off along the edge of the bay, strung out in a rough ellipse. They were moving fast.

Jack was standing beside her, looking intently at her face rather than the display. 'Have they gone?' he asked.

'We're safe,' Toshiko replied.

'That's not what I asked. Have they gone?'

Toshiko shrugged. The distinction was meaningless to her. 'Yes, they have gone.'

Gwen had caught the edge of the conversation. 'Is that it then? Can we go home now?'

'Not quite yet.'

'Why not?' Owen asked. 'The danger's past. The Weevils have gone.'

'Yeah,' Jack said, 'but why did the hedgehog cross the road?'

'I don't know,' Owen shrugged. 'Why *did* the hedgehog cross the road?'

'Because it was stapled to the chicken.' Jack glanced back in the direction from which the Weevils had come. 'The point being, sometimes you do things not because you want to but because you're forced to.'

Owen and Gwen pivoted to look in the same direction as Jack.

'Hard to believe that anything could spook a single Weevil that badly.' Gwen bit her lip. 'Let alone eight of them. I can't imagine anything that eight Weevils couldn't handle.'

Jack was still gazing out into the darkness. 'Let's not forget that one of their kind was taken down and eaten by something prowling this fine city.

That kinda puts a damper on your day, even if you're a Weevil. They're a strangely gregarious lot, far as I can tell. I don't think they sit around the campfire toasting marshmallows – or whatever else they find floating down in the sewers – but the death of one of them has a strange effect on the others. I think they're truly scared.'

'Scared of what?' Owen asked.

'Scared of *that*,' Jack said, nodding his head towards a patch of darkness that seemed to have come unmoored from the night and was drifting along the side of the warehouse. 'Tosh – anything on the scanner?'

'Nothing,' she replied, tearing her gaze away from the moving shadow and checking the display. 'Whatever it is, it's not registering on here.'

'That means its body temperature is closer to human than the Weevils are,' Jack said.

'Or it hasn't got a body temperature at all,' Owen continued bleakly. 'It's cold-blooded. Or it hasn't got any blood. No blood. Bloodless.'

'Come on,' Gwen chided. It sounded to Toshiko as if she was trying to talk herself out of bleak thoughts, rather than Owen. 'You're a doctor. You saw the photographs of the dead Weevil. Whatever killed it had teeth. That means it has a mouth. That means it needs to eat. That means it… oh shit. I've run out of conclusions. You know what I'm trying to say. It's real, not some spooky *Scooby-Doo* ghoul thing.'

'Actually,' Toshiko felt constrained to say, 'the ghouls and ghosts and monsters in *Scooby-Doo* always turned out to be men in masks. Usually the caretaker.' She noticed Gwen's raised eyebrow. 'I liked Velma,' she said defensively.

'Yeah, which only goes to prove that you're not a true *Scooby-Doo* fan,' Owen said. He was still watching the patch of darkness as it hugged the corrugated metal side of the warehouse, moving slowly but inexorably toward them. 'The sixth incarnation of *Scooby-Doo*, dating to the early 1980s, had Scooby and Shaggy meeting up with real ghosts, vampires and all kinds of shit. Didn't you ever see *The 13 Ghosts of Scooby-Doo*? Or *Scooby-Doo Meets the Boo Brothers*?'

'Sadly, no.'

'Fun though this is,' Jack interrupted, 'I think we have a more pressing concern right now. Although I did think that *Scooby-Doo and the Reluctant*

Werewolf marked an absolute low in the output of the Hanna-Barbera studios.' He stepped forward. Toshiko expected him to raise his gun, but instead he left it hanging by his side. 'Hi,' he said brightly. 'We've kinda gone astray. What's the best way back to the Millennium Stadium from here?'

'I… I'm not sure,' said a tremulous voice from the darkness. 'I think I'm lost. Can you help me?'

'We can help anyone.' Jack's voice was confident, but Toshiko noticed that he wasn't moving forward. 'That's what we do. It's our *shtick*, if you like. Or our *raison d'être*, if you prefer. Do you want to step out into the light, where we can see you?'

'Are you all right?' Gwen called when the voice didn't answer.

'I'm hungry,' the voice said. 'I'm so very hungry.'

And then it was on them in a blur of limbs and clothing, crossing the concrete wharf between the warehouse and them before anyone could react. Its feet seemed to touch the ground once, twice, propelling it forward like a greyhound. Its limbs were just as thin, its face narrow and pointed.

It wore a silk blouse and large, silver earrings, Toshiko noticed in the frozen moment before it launched itself at her face, jaws impossibly wide, teeth strung with glistening strands of saliva. And its belt was probably Prada.

The thing's hands caught her right in the middle of her chest, but it was like being hit with a handbag. Toshiko stumbled backwards more through the shock of the impact than anything else. Whatever the thing was, it was light.

As she fell, she realised that the thing was snapping its teeth in her face, trying to rip the flesh from her cheeks. She held it off as best she could, but it was strong – much stronger than its size would have indicated.

Her head hit the concrete of the wharf. For a moment, concerns about teeth and body mass went flying. The number of stars in the sky suddenly doubled, tripled, and the sudden jagged shards of pain that tore through her head made her feel like it had come apart like a melon, leaving her brains steaming on the pavement. That would also explain why she couldn't think properly. Everything was muddy. Distanced. Small details occupied the entirety of Toshiko's mind – a moving point of light high in the sky that might have been an aeroplane or might have been a satellite; the sticky feel of blood matting her hair; the way the teeth of the thing that was attacking her had fillings in its molars. Porcelain as well, not the cheaper mercury amalgam that so many people had.

As the thing's teeth closed around her throat, Toshiko's last coherent emotion was despair.

The thing's teeth snapped shut, but not on Toshiko. Something had grabbed it and was yanking it away. It yowled, thin and angry. Limbs thrashed madly in all directions.

Hands were checking Toshiko over, from head to foot. Calm hands. Experienced hands.

'Owen,' she breathed.

'Stay still,' he said. 'I don't think there's any major damage but I need to make sure. Can you look left? Right? Up? Down? Good girl. How many fingers am I holding up?'

'Eight,' she murmured, wondering how he could get so many fingers on one hand, and how come she'd never noticed before.

'Divide by two,' he said.

'Oh – four?'

'That's right.'

'How's my Toshiko?' said a voice from behind Owen's head. A young, brash, American voice. Jack's voice, her brain told her after a slight delay.

'Skull's intact. Some contusions on the scalp; no indications of concussion, but I'll check for sure when we get back to the Hub. Arms and legs are OK – no sign of any fractures. All in all, nothing that a couple of aspirin and some rest won't cure. You see worse things in Cardiff city centre every night of the week.'

'You don't almost get your face eaten off by a crazy woman in Cardiff city centre,' Jack said, moving round in front of Toshiko.

'You do if you go to the right clubs,' Owen breathed.

He helped Toshiko to sit up. The world swirled around her, and she felt suddenly hot and sweaty. Saliva flooded her mouth.

'Not too fast,' Owen said. 'Breathe deeply.' He produced some pills from a pocket. They were loose. 'Take these – let them dissolve in your mouth. They'll help quell the nausea.'

Toshiko peered at the tablets. 'What are they?'

Owen glanced down at the palm of his hand. 'Whoops – not those.' His hand dived back into his pocket, returning with a couple more tablets, larger this time. 'These are the ones. Trust me – I'm a doctor.'

Dubiously, Toshiko nibbled the tablets from Owen's palm. The coating dissolved with sudden sweetness in her mouth, and was replaced with a chalkier, grittier taste. The world seemed to gradually swim back into focus: lights were brighter, she could see further and the sensation that she was about to throw up receded. Shakily, with Owen's help, she got to her feet.

Jack and Gwen were holding something down on the ground – something that struggled madly in their grip. 'Is that the thing that attacked me?' Toshiko asked.

'It is,' Owen said, still holding her arm. She didn't want him to let go. Not ever.

'But it attacked and killed a Weevil! Eight other Weevils were scared to take it on! How come Jack and Gwen can just hold it down like that?'

'Because Weevils don't have a pharmaceutical industry.' He frowned. 'As far as we know. Actually, they might *all* be qualified pharmacists.' He brightened. 'But a dose of carfentanyl works on them the same way it works on most living creatures.'

'What's carfentanyl?' Toshiko asked.

'It's an anaesthetic and sedative,' Owen explained. 'It has a quantitative potency approximately ten thousand times that of morphine. Usually it's used to sedate large animals. Very large animals. I've been wondering whether it would have any effect on Weevils but I've never had a chance to find out. Fortunately, I had some with me.'

He reached into his jacket pocket, frowned, moved his hand to a different pocket, smiled in relief and brought out a plastic tube with a nozzle on one end and a small trigger or lever about halfway up. A transparent window in the tube indicated that it was empty. 'Pressurised air syringe. Blasts drugs straight through the skin. Well, human skin, anyway. It just makes Weevil skin soggy.'

Toshiko moved closer to the writhing, hissing thing on the ground. 'How much did you use?'

'Everything I had. And it wasn't enough.'

Jack was straddling the thing's chest, holding its arms down to the ground. Gwen was kneeling on its legs. Toshiko moved to one side so that neither of them blocked her view of the creature that had attacked her.

It was a woman.

Actually, it was a girl. Late teens or early twenties. Blonde hair. Brown suede trousers, a white silk blouse and a leather jacket.

'*Hell!*' Toshiko exclaimed. 'I thought it was an alien creature!'

'No such luck,' Jack said, still trying to stop the girl springing to her feet. 'Owen – any more of that sedative stuff?'

'Used it all up.'

'Nothing at all left?'

Owen frowned, then reached into his jacket and pulled out another of the pressurised air syringes. This one was full of a yellowish liquid. 'Ketamine?' he asked.

'Don't mind if I do.'

Owen reached down, grabbed an arm, and pressed the trigger on the syringe. There was a sudden hiss, and the yellow fluid vanished from the tube. A few seconds later the girl's struggles subsided. 'That's my evening ruined,' Owen muttered.

'Look on the bright side,' Jack said, standing up. 'You've got a girl paralytic and you didn't even have to spend any money.'

The four of them gathered around the girl's body and gazed down at her. She was moving her head slowly from side to side, and her eyelids were flickering. There were stains on both the blouse and the jacket. Toshiko thought at first they were blood, but there were fragments of herb and crumbs mixed in. Tomato sauce? It looked like she'd been in a car accident with a pizza delivery boy.

Jack knelt down again, this time beside her. 'What's your name?' he asked gently.

'Marianne.' Her voice was coated with a patina of pain and worry. 'Marianne Till.'

'OK, Marianne, how are you feeling?'

'Hungry.'

'When did you last eat?'

'I'm always eating. I can't get enough food to stop the hunger.'

'What have you eaten this evening?'

'Chinese takeaway. Pizza. Some sandwiches I found in a bin.' She hesitated. 'A pigeon. Someone's dog. I tried to eat this guy who bought me a drink in a bar, but he ran away. There was blood on his face, and he was screaming. And... and I ate a kebab.'

'A kebab,' Owen muttered. 'That's just sick.'

'Don't worry, Marianne. My name is Jack, this is Gwen, and that's Toshiko and Owen. We're going to be your friends, and we're going to try and help you get over this.' Without turning his head, or taking his gaze away from the girl, he said to Gwen, 'Call Ianto. He's parked just around the corner. Get him to drive over here as quickly as he can. We have to get Marianne back to the Hub.'

Gwen stepped to one side and brought her mobile up to her mouth. While she was talking, Toshiko just stared at the creature. At the girl. At Marianne.

'She's so young,' Toshiko said. 'And so thin! How can she be that thin when she eats that much?'

Owen shrugged. 'Fast metabolism?' he said. He reached out towards her face.

For a moment Toshiko thought he was going to stroke her hair, but instead he reached around and felt the back of her head. 'Bleeding's stopped. You need to get that washed when you get back. I'll give you some cream.'

'Thanks.'

With a quiet rumble of tyres, the SUV pulled up beside them. Its black surface reflected the warehouses, the cranes, the wharf, defining the car's presence only by the way it distorted its surroundings. The driver's door opened and Ianto stepped out, leaving the engine purring. As usual, he was dressed in a three-piece suit and tie. His shirt was double-cuffed, secured by cufflinks. He even wore a tie pin. Sometimes Toshiko thought that he wasn't quite real.

'I hope I'm not too late,' he said calmly.

'Ianto, you're never too late and you're never too early.' Jack stood up and looked around. 'That's why we love you. Now, everyone, we need to

116

get this young lady back to the Hub and find out what's wrong with her. And just in case the various anaesthetics that Owen's injected her with start wearing off, I recommend that we immobilise her. Ianto, did you bring the cuffs?'

'I assumed you might be needing them.' He brought his hand up to show that he was already carrying the thin metal tapes that could be wound around a captive's wrists or ankles and, when pressed together, would meld into an unbreakable loop – unbreakable, that was, until they were irradiated with low-level microwaves, in which case they would revert back to their ribbon-like state. Toshiko had spent many months trying to determine how they functioned, without success.

Ianto passed the tapes to Gwen, who bent down and pinioned Marianne's ankles, and then her wrists. Ianto and Owen then picked Marianne up and placed her carefully into the back of the SUV.

'I hope we're not stopped by the police on the way back to the Hub,' Ianto said. 'Explaining why we've got a young girl tied up in the back could be tricky.'

Jack smiled. 'We'll let Owen talk us out of it. I'm sure he's had lots of practice.'

They all climbed into the SUV and drove back through darkened city streets to the Hub. Ianto used a device fixed to the dashboard that automatically set the traffic lights to green as they approached.

The trip was quick, but Toshiko found herself drifting into a reverie as they drove. The lights of the city elongated into ribbons of light that wound around each other in a psychedelic skein. She felt hypnotised. Anaesthetised, like Marianne. Part of her knew it was the shock of the attack and the after-effects, as her body reacted and then recovered, but the rest of her just wanted to curl up and let unconsciousness take her away. Let the darkness win, just for a while.

She woke as they were arriving in the Hub via the hidden vehicular entrance in the basement of the Bute Place car park. As she climbed from the car, Ianto went to fetch a trolley. Together they all manhandled Marianne onto the trolley and rolled her through the Torchwood tunnels towards the area of sealed cells where occasional guests were kept.

Still rubbing her eyes, Toshiko watched as Ianto and Jack carried Marianne into the cell, and Jack removed the metal tapes from her arms and legs while Gwen covered him with her automatic. Together they all backed out of the cell, shutting and sealing the entrance behind them.

At which point, Owen asked the question that had apparently been in everyone's minds. 'So – what do we do with her now?'

Jack grimaced. 'We need to work out what's happened to her. I don't know whether it's physical or psychological, but she's somehow developed this ravenous hunger that nothing can satisfy. Owen – we need to find some way of getting some blood from her that you can run tests on. Might be best to do it quickly, before the horse tranquillisers wear off. Make sure Ianto covers you. Check for anything that might explain her actions. Gwen – I need you to work on her identity. She said her name was Marianne Till. See if she's local, and if anyone's reported her missing. She also mentioned biting a man in a bar; see if that's been reported as a crime. I want to track her progress across the city. I want to track it *back* and find out where she started from. Tosh – I need you to work on non-invasive sensors that can give us a picture of what's going on inside her. Microwave, ultrasound, magnetic resonance imaging, X-ray… anything you can get to work at a range of six feet through an aluminium screen. I know it's a tall order, but we can't afford to keep sending people in there to conduct tests. They'll pretty soon become lunch. Which reminds me. Ianto – get on the phone to Jubilee Pizzas. We'll need a whole load of stuff. Just get them to load the pizzas up with whatever they have and keep them coming. Tell them we're having a party.'

Owen, Ianto, Gwen and Toshiko turned to leave. Jack remained, staring at the girl. As Toshiko walked away, she heard him say: 'Stay with us, Marianne. We'll get you through this.'

The last cell in the row was the one that contained their long-term Weevil guest. As Toshiko's gaze scanned across it her heart missed a beat. For a moment the cell looked empty, and she panicked, thinking the Weevil had escaped. Then she looked closer, and relaxed. The Weevil was still there, slumped against the wall.

The momentary relaxation was replaced by a deeper concern.

The Weevil was right up against the wall furthest from Marianne's cell, and its head was turned away. It seemed to be pressing itself into the brickwork. Toshiko had never seen it react like that before. It was scared. It was terrified.

What exactly had they brought into the Hub?

TEN

Morning arrived slowly, a tide of amber light washing up a beach. Rhys awoke in gradual stages, moving from deep sleep to wakefulness over nearly an hour, slipping backwards into dreams every now and then, but eventually managing to claw his way to consciousness, open his eyes and turn over to face the ceiling.

Morning and wakefulness were bleaching his dreams away. He tried to hold on to them, but all he got was shreds of emotion and tattered images. There was something about him being pregnant, he recalled: stumbling around the flat, huge and graceless, knocking things off shelves. That was a weird one. Even in his half-awake state he realised that he'd better not tell Gwen; the subject of kids had been avoided so far, and he wanted to keep it that way. And there were fragments of a story about a beanstalk or a vine that was growing faster than he could climb it, although he had a feeling that there was something disturbing at the top of the beanstalk that he didn't want to see. Maybe it was a giant. God alone knew what *that* dream was about. Gwen would probably tell him that it meant he felt he was committed to a path that he wasn't sure about. As far as he was concerned it meant he'd eaten too much cheese the night before.

The thought of cheese and the night before suddenly triggered a string of memories that he'd half-hidden from his conscious mind while he'd been asleep. Rhys winced, remembering that after Gwen had gone out he and Lucy had eaten dinner, then dessert, then had cheese on toast as a snack while they were watching *Newsnight*. And they'd put away two bottles of wine. God, and he was meant to be losing weight as well! The trouble was that he just felt so hungry all the time. Lucy wasn't helping; she could shovel the food away as fast as he could. And the tragic thing was that she stayed as thin as a giraffe.

Cautiously, Rhys let his hands slide down his chest to his stomach, expecting to find it distended with food. To his great relief, and surprise, it was flatter than he remembered it being since he'd left college. There was even a trace of muscle development beneath the fat. He let his hands rest there while a smile crept across his face. Whatever that pill from the Scotus Clinic had been, it looked like it might be working. Three cheers for Amazonian orchids!

Someone stirred in the bed beside him. Rhys turned his head, hands still resting possessively on his stomach. All he could see was a hump of duvet. No head on the pillow. No hair spilling out from the bedclothes. Panic suddenly swept over him. Gwen had left on police business before he had gone to bed, and he didn't remember her coming back. Please God, don't let it be Lucy in bed with him! Lovely though she was, and much as a primitive and unrepentant part of him wanted to shag her senseless, this was neither the time nor the place. Not in his and Gwen's bed, for Christ's sake! Not as things were sorting themselves out between them! Surely he couldn't have got that drunk?

Tentatively, he reached out beneath the duvet and found a hip. Judging by the way his fingers fitted into its curves, its owner was facing away from him. Gently he stroked it.

The warmth felt like Gwen, and the shape felt like Gwen, but it had been long enough since he'd been in bed with someone else that he couldn't quite remember whether girls all felt different in bed or if they all felt the same. He wanted to pull whoever it was towards him, turning them over so he could see their face, but if it was Lucy then he really didn't want to know. It would lead to all kinds of trouble.

He stroked the hip again. From nowhere, a smaller hand closed over his fingers.

'Tired,' said a sleepy voice. 'Got in late. Got to sleep.'

Relief sluiced through him like a waterfall. It was Gwen! Thank Christ, it was Gwen. That meant Lucy must be on the couch. And it was a Saturday as well, and he didn't have to get up and go to work. God was in his heaven and all was well with the world.

He slipped out from between the duvet and the sheet, trying not to disturb Gwen, and pulled his ratty old dressing gown on. It wasn't the kind of thing he wanted Lucy to see him in, but he wasn't going to pull his usual trick and wander around the flat naked while she was staying. That would have been disastrous. Cautiously, he pulled the door open a crack and peered out.

The living room was dark, but a thin sliver of light slicing through the gap between the curtains illuminated the sofa. Their spare duvet had been placed on the sofa so that one half of it covered the cushions and the other half curled up and over Lucy's recumbent body. A tousled mass of black hair and a fragment of pale forehead were all he could see of her. She had still been suffering from shock, the previous night; still reliving the bizarre attempt to abduct her. That primitive and unrepentant part of him wondered what she looked like under there; was she wearing panties and a T-shirt, or was she naked? Now that she'd lost so much weight, what did her body look like with no clothes on? What were the chances that she might turn over and snuggle into the duvet, revealing her naked back and her arse? Were her breasts really that phenomenal, close up?

He quickly changed mental channels. Creeping past the sofa he made it into the kitchen area of the flat, sorted out two mugs, then rinsed the metal percolator jug out, retrieved the ground coffee from the freezer, where Gwen insisted they stored it, and put three spoonfuls into the hopper on the machine. *Genuine Cinchona Coffee*, it said on the packet. Rhys hadn't got a clue whether that was meant to indicate quality or not, but it certainly tasted strong and rich. The coffee gradually dripped its way into the jug, releasing a gorgeous smell, dark and complex, pungent and spiky. He felt himself becoming more awake just breathing it in.

He poured a cup for himself and another for Lucy, adding milk from a carton in the fridge and being careful that the bottles of wine in the fridge door – depleted after last night – didn't clink when he shut it. Gwen sounded as if she needed to sleep; he could always warm a cup up in the microwave for her later on. She must have arrived back some time around sunrise, although that was becoming more and more the case these days.

Whatever Torchwood was, it was consuming her. Obsessing her. She'd never worked this hard before, not in any of her police jobs.

Or perhaps it wasn't the job. Perhaps it was this mysterious boss of hers. Jack. That was the name she'd mentioned from time to time. Perhaps he had some kind of hold over her.

Rhys carried Lucy's cup of coffee into the living area. Bending down, he placed it on the coffee table close enough that she could reach out and get it but far enough away that she couldn't accidentally knock it over. From where he was, he could see her clothes folded in a neat pile on the floor. Jeans. Blouse. Black lace bra, catch at the front, underwired. Rhys was no judge of size, but the sight made him feel breathless and warm. And there were a pair of trainers, sat demurely beside the clothes. Rhys had always thought of trainers as being big, clumsy things, but these were small, with pink and silver flashing. There was something so innocent, so girlish about them that he felt his breath catch in his throat. He'd never noticed Lucy wearing them before. He'd not noticed a lot about Lucy.

'Morning,' said a voice. He glanced up, startled, embarrassed. Lucy's face was about two feet away from him. She'd lifted herself up from the sofa slightly, shifting the duvet so that it fell away from her body from shoulder to thigh. The deep shadows made her body more erotic, more mysterious. He felt his heart skip a beat.

'Coffee's here,' he said, his voice cracking. 'I'll do breakfast.'

'I'm starving,' she said.

'What do you want to eat?'

She smiled, sleepily and suggestively. 'You?'

'Or bacon,' Rhys said quickly. 'Bacon and eggs do you?'

Lucy pouted, gazing up at Rhys from beneath heavy lashes. 'If that's all there is on the menu.' She tugged the duvet around her, sitting upright with that sudden switch from sensuality to practicality that, Rhys had noticed, only women could manage. 'And can I have lots of it? With toast?'

Rhys was about to straighten up when he noticed a dish on the side table that hadn't been there the night before. Sticky traces around the edge indicated ice cream. A sudden pain ran through his stomach, as if someone had grabbed hold and twisted. Ice cream. Sweet and cool, melting in his mouth and trickling down his throat.

Lucy noticed his fixed gaze, and misinterpreted what he was thinking. 'Sorry,' she said. 'I woke up during the night and felt like I needed a snack. I hope you don't mind…'

'That's OK,' he said. 'I was just wondering whether ice cream counted as breakfast.'

'Actually…' Lucy played with the edge of the duvet. 'I think I might have finished it.'

'No problem – I can always pop down the supermarket and get some more.'

'It's a good thing you didn't need to go to the loo or something while I was getting the ice cream,' she said, smiling at Rhys. 'I completely forgot where I was, so I ended up stark naked by the freezer, scooping ice cream out of the tub.'

The mental picture of Lucy, her beautiful body illuminated by the light from the freezer door, licking ice cream from her lips hit Rhys's mind. 'I'll… just get that toast on,' he breathed.

'What's the plan for today?' he called from the kitchen area as he slotted toast into the toaster.

'I guess I could try calling the police again, see if there's any news.'

'OK. Gwen said she'd make a couple of calls herself, see if any of her friends know anything.'

'Good for Gwen.' Lucy shook her head, black hair spilling across her bare shoulders. 'Sorry, that sounded bitchy. You've both been so good to me. I can't stay here forever, I know that, but I don't want to go back to my place just in case someone's there waiting for me. I guess I could look for another flat. I'll have to do it some time, anyway, just to get away from Ricky.'

'If you want a hand, I'll come with you,' Rhys offered.

'I'd appreciate that.'

The toaster *chunked* as the wire basket shot up. The smell of hot toast filled the kitchen.

Lucy's head snapped round. 'Actually,' she said with fake casualness, 'rather than let the toast get cold, I could just eat it now, while you're doing the bacon and eggs…'

* * *

Jack had called a council of war in the Hub.

'Exciting night, last night,' he said. 'Apparently Everton won against Liverpool – a giant-killing performance which puts them solidly on course for the Premiership. And, in the small print on page eight, I see we caught ourselves a little puzzle. Well done, by the way. I hope everyone is feeling refreshed and recovered after a good night's sleep.'

'What was left of it,' Gwen muttered. She was feeling woozy after having driven home through empty streets – which was fortunate, as she twice found herself driving along the white line in the centre of the road – and then having stumbled into bed past a recumbent and snoring Lucy, snuggled up on the sofa. And thank God she *was* on the sofa, and not in Gwen's bed.

'Toshiko,' Jack continued as if nobody had spoken, 'how's the head?'

'It's feeling fine, thank you,' Toshiko said. 'Owen stitched me up last night.'

'Stitched the *wound* up, I hope. Although I wouldn't put anything past him.' Jack turned to where Owen was glowering, off to one side. 'Owen: what did we learn from the lady's blood sample?'

Owen's mouth twisted in that little grimace that, Gwen had noticed, he made when he was stumped but didn't want to admit it. 'High levels of blood sugar and lipids, which you'd expect from someone who had eaten recently, and her cortisol levels were elevated, which indicates stress, like she'd been running or been in a fight. Apart from that, the blood work indicates she's in good health. If she was suffering from some kind of disease I'd be looking for a shitload of leucocytes, that kind of thing, but she's clear.'

'And she's human?'

'Sorry – didn't I say? Yes, she's as human as I am.'

Jack glanced over at Gwen. 'Do you want to take this one, or shall I?'

'Let's give him a free ride,' Gwen replied. 'I'm feeling generous.'

'OK.' Jack looked over at Toshiko. 'Tosh, I know you haven't had much time, but what's the odds of getting some kind of scan going of Marianne's insides. I want to see if there's anything there that shouldn't be.'

'Most non-invasive imaging techniques require the cooperation of the patient,' Toshiko replied, 'either willingly, because they want to help, or unwittingly because they are unconscious. I'm assuming that conducting a scan of this young woman is like X-raying a conscious tiger: you couldn't expect her to stay still, and you might lose your life if you tried. Ideally I would prefer her to be heavily sedated, but we saw last night how much sedative it took to even render her sleepy, let alone put her to sleep for any length of time. And I understand from Ianto that she recovered very quickly once she was left alone. So I'm still working on options for remote scanning. I may have to disassemble one of the scanners we have and reassemble it on either side of the cell. That counts as heavy engineering, and it won't happen quickly.'

'Any way of speeding it up?'

Toshiko shrugged. 'I could try something that doesn't require transmission techniques – single-sided X-ray, perhaps. The quality of the image would be reduced, but it might be quicker.'

'Go for whatever has the best chance of a quick win. Thanks Tosh. Ianto – what kind of mood is our guest in?'

Ianto stepped forward from the shadows at the back of the Hub. Gwen hadn't even known he was standing there. As usual, his bland face was set in a slight smile. 'Hungry. She has put away several pizzas so far, and still wants more. The more she eats, the less edgy she gets. Apart from that she is chatty, but confused. She doesn't know where she is or what's happening. I've given her the impression that she is being held in custody after an incident last night. I've also given her the impression that a drink she had may have been drugged with Rohypnol, which is why she can't remember anything and why she may have hallucinated some strange things.'

'Good work. That should hold it for a while. Gwen?'

'Marianne Till was reported missing this morning. Her mother said she'd gone out for a meal last night with some friends; the friends said she wandered off from the group early in the evening. She said she was feeling ill, and wanted to go home.'

'Not much chance of that at the moment,' Owen said. 'Mummy and Daddy would be on the menu within half an hour, followed by Granny, the dog and the next-door neighbours.'

'The police won't investigate,' Gwen continued. 'I've been in this situation too often before. Over two hundred thousand people are reported missing in the UK each year. Most of them return safe and sound within seventy-two hours, but there's still a couple of thousand who don't. Trouble is, the police won't actively look for these people unless they're exceptionally vulnerable or obviously the victims of a crime.'

'Looks like she's going to be staying for a while,' Jack said. 'Hotel Torchwood.'

'But her family are worried about her,' Gwen pressed on. She could hear the plea in her voice, but she couldn't help herself. 'Her mother will be crying her heart out, and she won't be able to stop. Her father will be punching the walls and the kitchen counter in sheer frustration. I've been there. I've seen it happen. They'll be printing off flyers with her photo on, and organising searches of the places she was last seen, more to keep busy than with any real hope that it will help. We can stop all that. We can ease their pain. All we have to do is—'

'Is what?' Jack asked. 'Tell them we have her, but we can't give her back? That'll sound like a ransom demand. Anything we do will attract attention to us. And, by the way, this is still meant to be a secret organisation.'

Gwen refused to be cowed by the patronising tone in Jack's voice. 'We could send them an anonymous message,' she said, voice dangerously quiet. 'Toshiko can fake anything. We can send them a message from her saying she's, I don't know, met an Italian waiter and gone off to get married in St Lucia.'

Jack stared at Gwen for a moment. She met his gaze without blinking. There was some kind of struggle going on between them in that long, level stare, a fight between compassion and action, perhaps. Gwen wasn't sure, and she didn't want Jack to think that she was challenging his authority over Torchwood, merely the way he sacrificed short-term battles in order to win the long-term war. But this time *she* intended to win.

'Tosh,' Jack said. 'Send an email message to Marianne's parents. Make it look like it's come from some Internet café on, oh, I don't know, Ibiza or somewhere. And make sure Marianne's booked retrospectively on a flight to Ibiza early this morning. Fake the emigration records, and see if you can't get her image on a security camera recording.' He looked back at Gwen. 'Happy?'

She considered a sarcastic reply, but Jack had compromised his plan for her, and he deserved to claim some kind of victory. 'Thanks,' she said simply. 'Her family will appreciate it.'

'And they won't be causing trouble by searching the streets for her,' Jack said. 'I get the distinct feeling it's not safe out there at the moment.'

Gwen frowned. 'What do you mean?' she said. 'We've got Marianne.'

'What makes you think she's the only one with a huge appetite out there?' Jack said. 'Which reminds me: Ianto, did you save those pizza crusts from her cell like I asked you to?'

'I did,' Ianto said. 'It wasn't easy. She was quite prepared to eat the entire pizza, crust and all, but I managed to get a few bits back using a long pair of tongs. She tried to eat the tongs as well, by the way.'

'Give the crusts to Owen.'

'Actually,' Owen said, 'I brought sandwiches in today.'

'And before you get round to eating them, I want you to match the shape of Marianne's tooth-marks in the crusts with the photographs of the dead Weevil you took. See if you can tell whether it *was* Marianne who ate its face off, or whether it was someone else.' Jack shook his head. 'This city seems to be full of women always wanting to bite people's faces off lately.'

'You can't eat that here!' Rhys exclaimed. He glanced up and down the aisle, hoping that none of the Asda staff were watching.

'It's food,' said Lucy. She was holding a half-eaten bagel up to her mouth. There were crumbs around her lips.

'It's not your food. Not until we've paid for it.'

'But I'm hungry. I'll tell the girl at the till that I couldn't help myself. As long as she scans the barcode in, it'll be fine.'

'But what if someone sees that you've eaten it before we get to the checkout?'

'Rhys, people do it all the time! Kids take grapes off the stalk, mothers feed biscuits to their babies! I once saw a bloke in a suit downing a can of Special Brew in the pharmacy section. At least I'm going to own up!'

Rhys shook his head. This shopping trip was turning into a nightmare. He and Gwen rarely shopped together – their schedules so rarely coincided, and when they did the last thing they wanted to do was spend quality time together in the tinned goods section of a supermarket – so when Lucy mentioned that she was feeling guilty about eating all their food and suggested popping down to Asda, Rhys was all for it. Either he or Gwen usually ended up shopping alone, more often than not at some ungodly time in the evening when normal people were at home and the only other people in the supermarket were late-shift workers and singles hoping to meet their soul-mates over a marinated salmon fillet at the fish counter. He kind of missed the cosy domesticity of arguing over whether to buy Cheshire or Wensleydale cheese, the comfort of debating the merits of virgin versus extra virgin olive oil. That's what he was hoping for with Lucy, but when she wasn't flirting with him she was throwing food into the trolley with gay abandon. All the major food groups were represented, as far as Rhys could tell. She'd chucked in a whole load of tropical fruit – mangoes, pineapples and some little spiky yellow things he didn't recognise – as well as a kilo bag of potatoes, three packets of risotto rice, several large bars of chocolate, an economy-sized tub of raspberry ripple ice cream, three bags of frozen lamb chunks and two loaves of wholemeal bread. And now she'd just ripped open a packet of bagels and started chewing away. It was like shopping with a five-year-old.

And the trouble was, looking at the pile of random items in the trolley was making him massively hungry, despite the pile of bacon, eggs, mushrooms and fried bread that he and Lucy had ended up sharing that morning. Gwen had joined them after a while, but all she had time for was some dry toast before she rushed out to work again. His stomach was suddenly all twisted up.

'Have we got any plan for all this stuff,' he asked, trying to distract himself, 'or are we just going to throw food at the frying pan and see what sticks?'

Lucy looked hurt. 'I was going to do a – a stew,' she finished lamely. 'Irish stew.' She gazed at the trolley as if she'd never seen its contents before. 'With mangoes. And stuff.' She gazed forlornly at the bagel in her hand. 'Rhys,' she said in a small voice, 'what's happening to me?'

'It's probably shock. You've been through a traumatic experience. I guess you'd expect there to be some after-effects. Maybe your mind is celebrating the fact that you survived a kidnap attempt unscathed by having a feast, or something. I don't know – I'm no psychologist. All I know is, it'll take a while before things get back to normal.' He reached out and took the bagel from her hand. 'We should make an appointment at the medical centre. Get you checked over.'

She shook her head violently. 'No. I'm fine. Really, I am.'

'OK, then let's get you home. Get some lunch inside you.'

'That sounds – Rhys!'

'What?'

For a moment he couldn't work out why he was having difficulty talking, and then he realised that he'd just taken a bite out of the bagel. 'Sorry. Come on – let's get out of here.'

Still masticating the chewy dough, he wheeled the trolley toward the checkout fast enough that Lucy only managed to throw one or two extra items in it. Getting it scanned and paid for was relatively painless, despite the look that the bloke on the checkout gave him when he came to the opened pack of bagels. Fortunately, Gwen had left him with the car, so they were back at the flat within ten minutes.

'Coffee?' he asked as the door closed behind them, 'or shall we unpack the stuff and get some food on?'

'Actually,' Lucy said, 'I want something else.'

He glanced back at her. There was a confident, dangerous look in her eyes. 'Look, Lucy, we need to—'

'No talking,' she said, and strode toward him, hips swinging.

His gaze kept flickering between her face, her incredible breasts as they swung from side to side and her crotch, a smooth Y-shape outlined in tight denim. How could something so close to a wet dream be just a step away from a nightmare? He put his hands up, unsure whether he wanted to push her away or pull her closer, crushing her to his chest. She kept walking, breasts pressing against the palms of his hands, nipples hard beneath the fabric of her blouse and that black, lacy bra that he remembered seeing beside the sofa that morning.

'I need you,' she moaned. 'I need you inside me, Rhys.'

And, turning her face up toward him, she leaned forward and sunk her teeth into his cheek, worrying the flesh before tearing a chunk away.

The last thing Rhys remembered was seeing his own blood, splattering across her cheeks like scarlet freckles.

ELEVEN

Owen could hear sobbing even before he reached the cells.

He stopped before he rounded the corner, and she saw him. It wasn't that he liked listening to women cry – although he'd experienced more than his fair share since he lost his virginity in a stationery cupboard at school when he was fifteen – it was more that he didn't want to see what any girl looked like when she was crying that hard. The sobs were racking, heaving things, and sobs like that in his experience were accompanied by snot and dishevelled hair and a general loss of self-respect. He liked women who were neat and tidy; at least, outside the bedroom.

When she showed no sign of stopping crying, Owen scuffed his foot against the floor. She didn't hear or, if she did hear, she didn't respond, so he did it another couple of times.

Eventually the crying stopped and, after a few moments when Owen imagined her hurriedly wiping her face, a small, scared voice said, 'Is there someone there? Hello?'

He walked nonchalantly around the corner as if nothing had happened. She was in the third cell along: a girl with blonde hair, matted now, and a face blotchy from crying and streaked with mascara. Still, at least she'd made an effort to clean herself up. She was still holding a tissue. Cardboard fragments lay scattered around her feet. Owen had a feeling that they were all that was left of the pizza boxes that had been stacked up in her cell earlier.

'Hallo, Marianne,' he said.

'Everyone seems to know my name,' she replied, 'but I don't know who anyone else is.'

'I'm Owen. I'm a doctor.'

She moved closer to the transparent barrier that separated the cell from the corridor. 'Am I ill? Is that why I'm here? I can't remember.'

'This is an isolation ward. We think you might have caught an infectious disease.'

She wasn't convinced. 'It looks more like a cell. A really old cell.'

'Ah. This part of the hospital had been closed down. We reopened it because of the epidemic.'

'But I thought I'd been drugged. The man who was here earlier told me someone had drugged my drink.'

'Yeah, that's right,' Owen said, thinking quickly. 'But we think whoever drugged your drink was infected with a tropical disease.' He racked his brain for the name of some remote illness, the kind of thing that GQ published ghastly colour photographs of under the heading '10 Diseases You Really Don't Want To Catch'. 'It's called Tapanuli Fever. Never been seen in the UK before. We're isolating anyone this guy came into contact with until we can get them checked over.'

'Is that why I'm so hungry all the time? Is that one of the symptoms?'

'Look,' he said reassuringly, 'the chances are you're clean, but we need to be sure. If we're wrong, it'll make avian flu look like a joke.'

'Avian flu *was* a joke. It never happened.'

'Yeah, but if it had, it would have been really serious.'

He took a deep breath. She wasn't your normal Cardiff city centre good-time girl, this one. Sparky. If he'd met her in a bar, he'd have been tempted to chat her up and take her back home. Well, back to her home. 'Look, do you know how many people died of flu in the great pandemic of the fourteenth century?'

'Sorry, I was crap at history,' she said. 'But I was really good at biology.'

'I bet. It was twenty-five million. About a third of Europe's population at the time. These things can spread faster than Crazy Frog ringtones if they're not checked.'

'And that's what you do?' She looked him up and down. 'Aren't you a bit young to be a doctor?'

'Aren't you a bit young to be hanging around in bars accepting drinks from strangers?'

'Point taken.' She sniffed. 'So what can I do to help? Apart from just hanging around in the cold and the damp?'

'I need to conduct an examination, but I can't come in the... unit... with you.'

'OK.' She started unbuttoning her blouse. 'You want me to take everything off?'

'Yes. No!' Owen took a deep breath. Tempted though he was, if Jack caught him getting a girl to strip off in the cells, he'd be out on his ear. It had been bad enough last time it happened; he'd never talk his way out of it again. 'No, I've got a kind of scanner thing. If I pass it through the food slot, you can wave it all over your body. It'll take readings which I can analyse later.'

'And it'll work through clothing? I don't mind taking everything off. You're a doctor, after all.'

God help him. 'Yes, it'll work through clothing. You don't have to take anything off.' *Although,* he almost said, *if it'll make you feel more comfortable...*

Owen reached into his pocket and took out his Bekaran deep-tissue scanner: slim and rectangular, with a lens arrangement set along one edge. It was essentially an ultrasound generator and detector, but Toshiko had modified it, reconfiguring the device to send its readings via wireless LAN directly to Owen's terminal. But he didn't really care *how* it actually worked. As far as he, or any doctor, was concerned, it fell under the general banner heading of 'shuftiscope' – a device that allowed him to take a shufti into someone else's body. Whatever a 'shufti' was. Something his dad used to say, as in: 'I'll just take a shufti at that washing machine.' Maybe Jack would know where 'shufti' came from. He was good with old words.

Owen knelt, and slid the device through the slot at the bottom of the door where pizzas had obviously been passed through to her. 'Here. It's switched on already. Just move it carefully along the outside of your clothes, as close to the skin as you can get. Try and make sure you cover everything.'

'OK.' She hesitated. 'Look, I don't want to seem critical, but if this is an isolation ward, and if I might be infected with something horrible, then why is that food slot left open? And why are there ventilation holes in this glass screen?'

Jesus. He was really having to work for this. 'Positive pressure in the corridor,' he said with as much confidence as he could muster. 'The airflow goes into the… unit… not out. So I'm safe.'

'Here goes,' she said with trepidation. Holding the device above her stomach, she began to move it up her body.

Sour metal.

That was the first thing Gwen smelled as she pushed open the door of the flat. Sour, hot metal, like a garage where car parts were being welded together.

It was a smell she knew. Almost an old, familiar friend by now. The first time it had pricked her nostrils had been at three in the morning in a house in Butetown, where an elderly man had patiently used a hacksaw to cut through his left wrist, all the way to the bone and beyond. Gwen hadn't seen the body – she'd been too junior for that, so she was just standing at the door, stopping anyone apart from the police and the coroner from going inside, but she remembered that smell, creeping down the stairs, and every time she smelled it now it put her back there, standing at the bottom of those uncarpeted stairs, listening to her colleagues trying to unstick the old man's body from the bath. The next time had been in a squat in Ely, when a doped-up kid had whacked her in the nose with the heel of his hand as he tried to fight his way past her. The bleeding had stopped within ten minutes, leaving her lips and chin crimson and sticky, but she still had that flat, metallic taste in her mouth the next day. The times after that – too numerous to mention. The places were all different, the cause was always the same.

Gwen knew blood when she smelled it.

'Rhys?' she shouted, slamming the door into the wall and rushing into the hall. 'What's happened?'

Not even listening for an answer, she kept moving towards the living room. Rhys wasn't there, but Lucy was crumpled on the floor, back against the sofa. Her alabaster forehead was marred by a massive bruise. By her feet, a spatter of blood marred the carpet.

'Gwen?' Rhys emerged from the bathroom, holding a tea towel to his cheek. The front of his T-shirt was bright red, the same colour as his neck, the same colour as the tea towel was turning where it touched him. 'Thank Christ you're back.'

She rushed to him and took his weight, feeling him lurch into her, supporting himself on her shoulders. 'You need to sit down. Come on, let's get you into the living room.'

Like competitors in some crazy three-legged race, they staggered together out of the hall. Carefully, Gwen let Rhys slip from her grasp, transferring his weight from her to the armchair, still keeping the tea towel clamped to his cheek. She stood over him, feeling like she'd come to a dead end, a junction where she wasn't sure which way to turn.

'I wasn't expecting you back,' Rhys murmured. His eyes were closed, his head resting on the back of the armchair.

'Obviously,' Gwen said. Her gaze clamped on Lucy, slumped on the floor a few feet away. She bent down to check the girl. Her pulse was strong in a throat that was so thin Gwen could see the throbbing of the blood in her arteries and the taut lines of the tendons distending the skin. She was unconscious, but breathing normally.

And there was blood on her lips: wet and smeared across her cheek. Gwen cautiously pulled Lucy's lower lip downwards. Her teeth were bloodied as well, the blood outlining the gaps between them.

'Rhys, what the hell has been going on here?'

'We went out shopping for food, and Lucy started acting strange.' Rhys kept his eyes closed as he spoke in a quiet, strained voice. 'We came back, and she started coming on to me. I thought she was going to kiss me, and I tried to tell her not to, but she suddenly launched herself at me and bit my cheek. I pushed her away, but she just threw herself at me again. I pushed her away again, and she stumbled back and went arse-over-tit over the coffee table, hitting her head on the arm of the sofa as she went. I think she's out cold. She's still breathing, at least. I checked that before I went to sort my face out. I was just about to ring you.'

'Let me look.' Gwen reached out to take the tea towel. It was cold and wet. For a moment she thought that Rhys had been rinsing it under the tap in the bathroom when she arrived, but as she took it in her hand she realised it was too bulky, too cold. There was something inside: a packet of frozen peas.

Cautiously, Gwen peeled the cold tea towel from Rhys's face. He hissed in pain, eyes clenched tight together. Strings of glutinous, clotting blood joined the towel to his face, but the damage wasn't as bad as she'd feared. The cheek was more or less intact, but Lucy's tooth-marks were clearly visible in Rhys's flesh. It looked like she'd relaxed her grip when he pushed her back, rather than tearing his cheek off. He would live.

'But why would she try and bite you?' Gwen asked. 'Apart from the obvious.'

'I don't think the obvious had anything to do with it. She was in a frenzy. The way her lips were drawn back, it was like a starving dog seeing a raw steak. I swear, Gwen, if she'd got a better grip she would have torn my cheek off and swallowed it whole, then come back for more. She would have eaten my entire face off if I hadn't stopped her.'

With a sickening lurch, Gwen realised that if things had gone slightly differently, if Rhys's reactions hadn't been quite so fast or if Lucy had come at him while he wasn't looking, Gwen might have come home to find him like that Weevil they'd discovered in the alleyway, his face all raw tissue and bloody bone.

What the hell was going on? What with that girl – Marianne – in the Hub, and now Lucy, it was beginning to look like some kind of bizarre epidemic was affecting Cardiff.

And affecting Gwen's personal life, as well. No matter how much she tried to keep the two of them apart, Torchwood and home were blurring together.

'We need to get you seen to,' she said.

'You make it sound like you're taking me to the vet's.'

'I wish! I was thinking more in the realm of tetanus shots. Antibiotics. Maybe stitches.'

'What about Lucy?' Rhys's eyes flickered open. 'We can't leave her here. She might be injured.'

'More to the point, she might wake up and start on the main course. Don't worry about her.' She reached for her mobile.

'Who are you calling? The police?'

She gazed at him, at his bloody face, at the sweat on his forehead. Her Rhys. The man she loved. The man she had almost lost because of her job. Because of the Rift, and the things that came through it.

'No,' she said. 'I'm calling Torchwood.'

'Bloody brilliant,' he sighed.

As the phone rang at the other end, Gwen walked into their bedroom. Rhys would be OK for a few moments, and she might need to say something she didn't want him to hear.

It was Jack who answered. 'Gwen? What's up?'

'Rhys has been attacked.'

'Transportation can be a cut-throat business, I hear.'

'This is serious. The girl who attacked him tried to eat his face off.'

There was a pause at the other end of the line. Gwen didn't know where Jack was, but she imagined him standing on a rooftop somewhere – perhaps on top of the Millennium Centre itself – gazing down at Cardiff Bay, watching the reds and blues and yellows of the city's lights reflected from the waves. Of course, he might just have been in his office in Torchwood, sitting with his feet up on the desk.

'I get you,' he said finally. 'The key words there being "face", "eat" and "girl". What do you want us to do?'

'The girl's name is Lucy. She's a friend of Rhys's. I've got to get Rhys to hospital. I need someone to come and take her away.'

'What kind of state is she in?'

'Unconscious.'

'Great – I'll send Owen. Stay where you are until he arrives.'

Jack cut the connection.

Gwen stared at the phone for a few moments, as if the mere sound of Jack's voice had charged it with some strange energy, then she put it away and went back into the living room.

Rhys was still sat in the armchair, clutching the freezing tea towel to his cheek.

Lucy wasn't there.

'Where the hell did she go?' Gwen exclaimed.

Rhys opened his eyes, puzzled, and looked at the patch of carpet by the sofa where Lucy had been crumpled. 'I dunno,' he said muzzily. 'I heard someone moving around. I thought it was you.' He looked sheepish. 'Sorry – I kind of zoned out there for a bit. I'm not used to this kind of thing.'

'I wouldn't want you to be,' Gwen said, heading into the hall. She'd left the door wide open when she came in and smelled the blood, but now it was pulled to. Lucy must have come to and made her escape. Gwen cursed herself. She should never have left Rhys in the room with Lucy, even if she thought the girl was unconscious! Either Lucy had been faking, or she'd come to while Gwen was on the phone to Jack, but either way she might have just leaped on Rhys and picked up where she'd left off, sucking his eyes from their sockets, or tearing his ears off. What the hell had she been thinking?

What she'd been thinking about, of course, was Rhys, and how hurt he was. Her normal police instincts had deserted her, faced with injury to a loved one.

'You were right,' Rhys murmured, breaking the self-destructive spiral her thoughts were descending into.

'Right about what?'

'Right about Lucy. About letting her stay here. *Definitely* a bad idea.'

Gwen laughed – more a hiccup than a proper laugh, but she felt the darkness recede from her mind. 'I wasn't anticipating anything like this, I must say.'

'What were you expecting, then?'

'I was—' She stopped, embarrassed. 'Look, I'd better sort that door out. We don't want her coming back.' She walked down the hall and pushed the door closed until it clicked.

'Come on – what were you expecting?'

'If you really want to know, I thought she was trying to get you into bed!'

'She was.' Rhys's voice was calm, flat, although it was the calmness of encroaching shock. 'I guess I was flattered. I guess I was even interested. But nothing happened, and nothing was ever going to happen.'

Gwen felt as if someone had poured cold water down her back. 'Why not?'

'Because I love you, and because I want to stay with you.'

'Despite… despite the fact that things aren't the way they were when we started seeing each other?'

'Or maybe because of that.' He shifted position slightly and winced. 'It can't always be like the first few days. Relationships change. People change. And so long as they change together, it's OK. I'll be honest, there's a part of me that wants things to be as exciting as they used to be. But there's another part of me that likes the snuggling up and watching telly together.'

'She's prettier than me. And she's a bloody sight slimmer than me too.'

She wanted Rhys to say that *she* was prettier than Lucy, that she was *slimmer* than Lucy, but she knew that he would have been lying, and if there was one thing she wanted at that moment it was the truth about what was happening to them.

'I have a feeling you're working with guys who are handsomer and slimmer than I am,' he said eventually. 'But nobody can keep trading up for better and better partners. Not if they want anyone to ever trust them.'

'Oh Rhys…'

'Oh bugger.'

'What's the matter?'

'I'm just wondering how the hell I'm going to shave around this for the next few weeks.'

'Where's Owen?'

Toshiko looked up from the screens that were currently displaying the output from the three work stations that she was running in parallel. 'I believe he is feeding the prisoner,' she said.

Jack was sitting in his office, separated from the rest of the Hub by a dusty glass screen. 'Is it my imagination, or is he spending a lot of time with that girl? It can't be healthy.'

Toshiko had been wondering the same thing, but she wasn't going to betray Owen. Assuming there was anything to betray. 'She *is* very hungry,' Toshiko responded. 'Owen has been diligent in supplying her with food. I think he's even been getting different takeaways so Jubilee don't get suspicious about the amount of food we're ordering.'

Jack was just a shadow through the glass. 'Tell him to come in here when he's back. I need him to go to Gwen's place.'

Toshiko got up and walked over to the doorway, concerned. 'Is everything all right with Gwen?'

Jack looked up from where he sat. His feet were up on the desk. A row of apples sat before him, lined up along the far edge. Some were green, some red, some a dusty grey. Some were large and some were small. They were all, however, recognisably apples.

'Her boyfriend's apparently been attacked by one of these women on the verge of a bulimic episode,' he said. 'They've got the girl there, unconscious. I want Owen to go across and bring her back. While he's at it, I want him to assess how much the boyfriend knows. We may need to do something about him.'

'Can I ask a question?'

'Just as long as it's not trigonometry. I'm shit at trigonometry.'

'Why have you got all those apples on your desk?'

Jack stared at Toshiko, then at the row of fruit.

'It's an experiment,' he said.

'What kind of experiment?'

'All of these things are apples, right?'

Toshiko shrugged. 'They would appear to be apples, yes.'

'Different varieties, yes?'

'Yes.'

Jack pointed at them, one after the other. 'St Edmunds Pippin, Mère de Ménage, Catshead, Ribston Pippin, Ashmead's Kernel, Mannington's Pearman, Lodgemore Nonpareil, Devonshire Quarrenden.'

'I'll take your word for it.'

'So what makes them apples? Why aren't they something else?'

Toshiko shook her head. 'I don't understand.'

'All these apples taste different from one another. They look different. They feel different when you bite into them. But they're all apples, and we know they're all apples. You know, there are pears that look more like some of these apples than the other apples do, but they're *not* apples: they're pears. But how can we tell the difference?'

'Jack, perhaps you ought to take a break.'

He sighed, and continued as if she hadn't said anything. 'So much variety. That's what I like about this planet. Thousands of varieties of apples, for no good reason. Same with pears. Problem is, they're dying out. People don't want grey apples, or small apples, or lumpy apples. They want their apples all the same size and all the same shade of green. Doesn't matter what they taste like. Give it another few years, and you'll only be able to buy Cox's Orange Pippins and Golden Delicious, and you'll be hard pressed to tell the difference between them.'

'I think—'

'It's like the Weevils. They're not human. The question is: why aren't they human? They eat like us, they wear clothes like us, and at night, with the streetlights behind them, they could be taken for human. In fact, I've seen people wandering the streets of Cardiff who look less human than the Weevils. So how is it we can make a distinction? And this girl downstairs – Marianne. She's human, but she eats like a Weevil. Which side of the line does she go?'

'Jack…'

He looked up, and there was something almost tragic about his face. 'Don't worry about me, Tosh. The apples are just a symptom of what's to come. I've seen the future, and it all looks and tastes the same.' The shadow passed, and he was the same old Jack that she had known ever since he tracked her down in London and asked her to join Torchwood. 'Sorry. Just me being stupid. Let me know if Owen turns up.' It was a dismissal, of sorts, and Toshiko turned to go. As she did so, Jack reached out, picked up the first apple in the line and took a bite out of it with a crisp crunch. 'Lemony,' he said.

Toshiko returned to her work station. She sat down just as Jack bit into another apple. 'Sweet, juicy, touch of mango.'

Filtering out the sounds of crunching from the office, Toshiko turned back to the screens. The first was showing the progress of the various viruses and worms she'd let loose on the Internet to create an electronic trail for Marianne Till, showing that she'd headed out for Ibiza when she was actually in the cells within Torchwood. It was basic work, and Toshiko didn't have to pay much attention to it after she'd started it off.

The second screen was just an array of flickering numbers. It was the raw processing of the ultrasound scans that Owen had completed on Marianne; data being filtered, filleted, massaged and stitched together into a coherent whole. It was taking time, but it looked like it was going to produce a useful set of pictures.

The third screen was the one that was taking most of her attention. It had nothing to do with Marianne Till, nothing to do with dead Weevils and nothing to do with sudden and spontaneous attacks of hunger. It was the interior of one of the almost biological alien devices that Toshiko had discovered, with Ianto's help, in the Torchwood Archive; sibling to the one that the Torchwood team had found at the scene of the deaths in the Cardiff nightclub.

The device was sitting quietly on the desk, focus of a number of sensors. It looked something like an over-inflated clover leaf: three rounded lobes about the size of an orange, but flattened, joined together, with a stalk hanging beneath the point where the lobes met. The stalk looked to Toshiko like a handle of some kind, giving her some more clues as to the size and shape of the hands that might have held it. Assuming it *was* a handle, and assuming that it fitted her hand in roughly the same way as it would the alien user, then one of the lobes would either project or receive energy of some kind, while the others might contain processing hardware, or energy cells, or something else.

Based on a cursory examination of the device, Toshiko had a theory that it projected an electrical charge at short-to-medium range. The device contained something like a low-power laser which, she suspected, was designed to ionise the air along a straight line. An electrical charge would then be projected along the ionised air, shocking anything at the far end. Perhaps it was a weapon, perhaps it was a sex toy; Toshiko wasn't sure. She wasn't sure she cared, either. What intrigued her at the moment was the suspicion that the device contained another hidden picture.

The image on the screen was similar to the one that Toshiko had generated from the interior of the other device: a patchwork of various images in different colours, all overlaid on top of one another. A line moved slowly down the screen, marking the point where her software was progressively refining the resolution of the picture by processing scans lasting many minutes. So far it was just a clash of colours with some indications of an underlying structure, a bit like an overhead photograph of a field where the shape of an old settlement could still be seen in the contours of the land, even though the stones themselves had long been buried. The circuits were there, but she would have to puzzle them out, tease out their edges, their connections, their mountings. But, like the previous device, she got tantalising hints of a picture behind the picture, an image that wasn't the circuit but was built from parts *of* the circuit.

And now, if she half-closed her eyes and let the pictures from the screen refract in rainbow shards from her long eyelashes, she could just about make it out. She could feel the strain in the muscles of her eyes, and her head began to ache as if a spike was being driven into her temples, but it was there.

A face, wider than it was high, with what might have been bulbous eyes at each end and a vertical slit of a mouth in the centre. But the image was slightly different. The head seemed to droop down at the ends, leaving the eyes hanging, and there were folds around the mouth.

It was older, but it was still the same alien face she had seen before.

Which meant that the devices were something more than just devices. They had a meaning over and above what they actually did.

But what the hell was it?

TWELVE

The Outpatients department of Cardiff Royal Infirmary was full of people. They sat there, arms folded, looking like they wished they had brought something to read with them. Magazines were scattered around, but they were all months out of date. Half of them were car magazines, the other half dishing the dirt on celebrity lifestyles. People would pick them up, glance at a page or two, then put them down again with a sigh.

Gwen wished she'd thought to bring her John Updike book with her. It was sitting beside the bed, cracked open to the page where she'd finished a chapter. She'd been trying to get back to it for a couple of months now – long enough that she couldn't quite remember how it had started or who some of the characters were – but life and Torchwood kept getting in the way. She could have scooped it up as she and Rhys left the flat, but she had bigger things on her mind. Like the trail of blood that Rhys was leaving behind him all the way to the car.

Rhys was reading a Dean Koontz novel. He'd read all of Dean Koontz's novels, and still kept them in the flat, even though he wasn't likely to read them again. Gwen had tried to read one, once, just to please Rhys, but she couldn't get past the first paragraph. At the time she'd thought the horror-based plots in which innocent people were menaced by dark forces beyond their comprehension too outlandish for words.

Now she thought them too tame. Funny thing, life.

She'd texted Jack with an update on the situation, and she hoped that they'd be out scouring Cardiff for Lucy. Looking around, she couldn't help but notice that most of the people in Outpatients didn't look as if they were injured. Rhys was definitely the person there with the most blood on him. A few were sneezing, and one woman had a rash of small red spots across her arms and face. There was one guy with his arm in a makeshift sling, and another with a bloody cut above his eye. No small children with their heads stuck in saucepans, which was a shame. Considering it was such a cliché, Gwen didn't think she'd ever seen it. *Carry On* films had a lot to answer for.

No drunks, either. It was still too early in the evening for that. Come midnight and the place would reek of beer and sweat. People would be slumped against walls and lying on the stained carpet tiles.

Beside her, Rhys was leaning back in his seat, eyes closed, tea towel still held to his cheek. It was maroon all over now, and sopping wet with the condensation from the pack of frozen peas.

'How are you feeling?' she asked for the hundredth time. She wished she could think of something more original, something sensitive and caring, but that was all that came to mind.

'Like a bit of an idiot, actually,' Rhys replied. His eyes were still closed. 'I'm going to have to make up some kind of story for work. I can't possibly admit that Lucy bit me. The jokes will never end.'

'You can't say that I bit you either. Nobody gives a love bite that big. And not on the cheek.'

He frowned. 'I read somewhere that there are more bacteria in the mouth than anywhere else in the human body. Is that true? Could I get infected just by being bitten?'

'If we ever get to see a doctor, we can ask him. But seriously, I think they'll give you an antibiotic shot. When I used to have to break-up fights and stuff in the police, there'd be lots of guys whose teeth had cut the inside of their cheeks when they'd been punched. The paramedics would always give them antibiotics in case the bacteria inside their mouths got into the wounds and started up an infection.'

'Not friendly bacteria, then,' Rhys said.

'I don't think there's any such thing as friendly bacteria. Some of them might be relatively indifferent, but I don't think they could reasonably be described as friendly.'

Like alien life forms that end up on Earth, she thought bitterly. Despite the best hopes of mankind, the universe seemed to her to be a pretty unpleasant place.

'Rhys Williams?' The nurse standing by the desk was looking around.

Rhys's hand shot up. 'Here.'

'This way, please.'

Gwen went with him to a small, curtained alcove where Rhys sat on a bed while a doctor examined him. She was younger than both Rhys and Gwen, and looked like she hadn't slept in a week.

'How did this happen, then?' she asked as Rhys pulled the tea towel away from his face. She looked over at Gwen. 'Or shouldn't I ask?'

'Rugby practice,' Rhys said firmly.

Gwen raised her eyebrows at the doctor, expecting her to take a look at Rhys's flabby physique and say something sarcastic, but she just looked him up and down and nodded. Surprised, Gwen glanced over at Rhys's stomach. It might have been her imagination, but it was looking flatter than she remembered. Maybe it was just the way the material of his T-shirt was plastered against the skin by the drying blood, but she could almost see some muscle definition. Was he going to a gym or something?

'I thought you rugby players wore gum shields,' the doctor said as she cleaned the wound with a pad of cotton wool. She kept dabbing the cotton wool in a kidney dish filled with something antiseptic. Thin strings of bloody liquid began to swirl around in the dish, forming shapes that came together and apart.

'They fall out.' Rhys winced as she patted the wound. The tooth-marks were livid against white skin now. 'By the time the training ends the ground is littered with gum shields. We have to send a boy out to collect them up at the end of the session. We pay him ten pence a set.'

'Right. I'm going to give you an anti-tetanus shot,' the doctor said, as if she hadn't been listening. 'And then put a dressing on the wound. I'll also prescribe a course of antibiotics, just in case. It's a pretty clean wound, and it should heal within a couple of weeks.'

'What about stitches?' Rhys asked.

'Not necessary. Go see your doctor in a week, just to check that everything's OK. If there's any swelling, or if the area gets tender to the touch, go and see them sooner.'

When they got outside, it was dark. A handful of people were hanging around near where the ambulances stopped. Rhys and Gwen paused for a moment, letting the fresh air wipe the tang of the antiseptic from their nostrils.

'I'd suggest going and getting a meal somewhere,' Rhys said. He indicated his bloody T-shirt. 'But they'd probably throw me straight out again.'

'We could get a takeaway,' Gwen said.

Rhys shook his head. He looked away, awkwardly. 'I don't really want to go back to the flat. Not now. Not straight away.'

'There's got to be somewhere still open where I can get you a shirt.' Gwen thought for a moment. 'Department stores will be closed. Asda will still be open.'

'Asda.' Rhys winced. 'Hardly my style.'

'Hey, you want dinner or not?'

He shrugged. 'All right. But you're going to have to go in and buy the stuff. I'll loiter outside, scaring small children.'

'OK. Extra-large?'

'Actually…' He paused. 'I think just Large will do.'

'Rhys, this is the kind of thing you should be saying to me but never do, but, are you losing weight?'

He shrugged, embarrassed. 'A little.'

'How?'

'Cutting out carbohydrates. Cutting down on the drinking. More walking.'

'Rugby practice, obviously.'

'Did you like that? I thought it was quite inventive.' A pause. 'And Lucy recommended some tablets she'd been taking,' he said, offhandedly. 'They worked on her.'

'Yes, we should obviously let Lucy be our role model on things involving food.'

'Ouch. Point taken.' He shook his head. 'This still feels like a dream to me. It's all moving too fast. I can't take it in.'

'Part of that's the shock. It'll pass. Tell you what – let's get a hotel room for tonight. A treat for the both of us. We can go back to the flat tomorrow.

It's Sunday, so that still gives us a day to recover before you go back to work – assuming you're fit.'

'That's the best idea I've heard all day.'

It would also, Gwen thought, give the rest of the Torchwood team time to investigate. There might be some clues back at the flat they needed to look for, something that might say where Lucy had gone. And, of course, the last thing she wanted was for her and Rhys to go back to the flat, fall asleep, and then wake up with Lucy bending over them, madness in her eyes, poised to rip their throats out.

Threesomes like *that* really didn't interest Gwen.

'What's a nice boy like you doing in a place like this?'

Owen laughed. The flagstones were cold beneath his crossed legs, and his vertebrae were grinding against the armoured glass behind him, yet he felt strangely comfortable. 'I sometimes ask myself the same question. I thought I'd be well on my way to being a surgeon by now.'

Marianne was sitting with her back against the glass in her cell, mirror image to his position. Their heads were separated by just a few inches of space. He could almost feel the heat from her body through the glass. Almost.

'Was that the big life plan?' she asked.

'Yeah, I thought so. Seven years of training and I still had it in my sights. Spent a year as a junior houseman at Cardiff Royal Infirmary. Then I blinked, and when I looked again it was gone.'

'And you ended up here.'

'Yeah.' He looked around, at the crumbling bricks and the lichen. At the rusted metal and the trickling water. 'I ended up here.'

'So you were at the Infirmary, but you're not Welsh, are you?'

He laughed. 'You can tell?'

'The accent.'

He paused. Thinking. 'Yeah, I'm from the East End. Plaistow. Terraced houses and council estates and old pubs. You could hear the Hammers playing at home from the back bedroom. Big cheer whenever they scored. Big groan when the goal went against them. I used to lie there and listen, Saturday afternoons. Used to make up my own commentary, as well.'

'So why did you go to medical school?'

Good question, and one he tried not to think about too often. 'Most of my friends ended up as car mechanics or estate agents. I could see all that ahead of me, and I couldn't face it. I wanted to do something that *meant* something. And then…'

'Go on,' she said softly.

'And then my dad died. Just upped and died. We found him in the bedroom one morning, slumped against the wall. He was wearing his shirt and his boxers and he had one sock off and one still in his hand. He looked… he looked like someone had said something to him that he couldn't quite hear, and he was trying to work out what it was. One of the arteries in his chest had just given way. Aortic aneurysm, it's called. I've done all the lectures, and I've seen photos in textbooks, and I've conducted autopsies of people who've died that way, but for me an aortic aneurysm will always be my dad, sitting there, one bare foot, and frowning.'

His face was wet. Tears were slipping from his eyes and spreading out across his cheeks leaving coldness behind. He hadn't even realised he was crying. The grief was something separate from him that his body could get on with while he was talking.

'I'm sorry,' Marianne said.

'And that's why I became a doctor.'

'So you could save people like your father?'

'No,' he said, shaking his head. 'So I could stop the same thing happening to me.'

Neither of them spoke for a few moments. Then: 'All right,' she said. 'Tell me about Tapanuli fever.'

'About what?'

'Tapanuli fever. This thing I've got.'

For a moment the flagstones seemed to tilt under Owen's backside. He didn't have a clue what she was talking about. Then he remembered. Tapanuli fever. He'd told her she'd been infected with a tropical disease and she was in an isolation ward.

'Oh, yeah, Tapanuli fever. Used to be known as the Black Formosa Corruption, back in Victorian days. Endemic to a few small regions of… er… South America. Argentina. I'm guessing that someone in Cardiff's just got back from doin' missionary work out there or something.'

'I've never heard of it.'

Not surprising, considering he'd made it up. 'It's very rare. Like Ebola. Nobody'd heard of that until there was a sudden spate of deaths.'

'And is that what's going to happen to me?' She was trying to be offhand, but he could hear the catch in her voice. 'What's the mortality rate? Isn't that what you call it – "mortality rate"?'

Almost involuntarily, his right hand reached out as if to take hers and squeeze it reassuringly, but all it encountered was smooth, cold glass. After a moment there was a small *thud* as something hit the glass on the other side. Her hand, seeking his.

'I won't let you die,' he said.

'You didn't answer the question.'

'We just don't know. In the jungle—'

Did they have jungle in South America? Or was it pampas? What the hell *was* pampas, anyway?

'—In the jungle, half the people who catch it die. But we've got you under observation, and we can treat it with antibiotics and stuff. I *won't* let you die.'

'You've got me isolated. It must be very contagious.'

'We have to take precautions.'

'You haven't even given me any antibiotics. You've just left me here, waiting.'

'The tests. We're looking at the results of the tests. Then we can treat the disease.'

Perhaps, he wondered, he could give her an injection. Just distilled water, but he could tell her it was an antibiotic. It might help her cope.

'I wish I could see my family,' Marianne said wistfully. 'They could just stand the other side of the glass, couldn't they?'

Owen knew that he shouldn't be talking to her this way, but he couldn't help himself. Jack would have told him to just leave her alone – do whatever tests were necessary and not engage in conversation – but he couldn't do that. Unlike most of the people and the things that had ended up in the cells, she didn't know what was happening to her. She needed reassurance.

She needed a friend.

'They've been notified,' Owen told her, 'but they've got to stay away. We're paid to take risks, here. They're not.'

'Could I write them a letter?'

He squeezed his eyes shut. Beneath the thin layer of chirpiness she put on, there was a deep chasm of vulnerability and fear. And he wasn't sure whether he was making things worse or better. 'Too risky. We'd have to spray the letter with antibiotics and stuff, to kill any bacteria, and the words'd just smudge and run off. It wouldn't look pretty.'

'Neither will I, if this goes on for much longer. I can't wash, I can't take a bath, and I haven't got a change of clothes.'

'Clothes we can find,' Owen said quickly. 'And I can probably get a bowl of hot water and some soap as well. If it's any consolation, you still look great.'

'Thanks. I bet you say that to all the dying girls in your care.'

'Only the beautiful ones.'

'Actually, some hot water would be nice. I must smell awful.' She paused. 'Talking of which, there's a really crappy smell in this place, and it's not me. It smells like the elephant house at the zoo. You know – that smell you get from things that eat hay all the time and then let it fester.'

It was probably the Weevil at the other end of the block, Owen thought, but he couldn't tell her that. 'It's the drains. This area of the… hospital… hasn't been used for a while. There's probably all kinds of stuff down there. I'll get someone to take a look at them.'

'At the very least you could get an air freshener.'

'Consider it done.'

'Thanks, Owen.'

He felt a shiver run through him at the sound of his name, said in her soft Welsh lilt. There was something almost erotic in talking to her and yet not seeing her. If they'd been face to face in a bar then he would have been touching her arm by now, gazing into her eyes, smiling, looking away and then looking back. But now, like this, it was like talking on the phone, but with the added *frisson* that she was only a few inches away from him. Close enough that he could hear her breathe; feel the glass vibrate if she shifted position.

'Owen,' she said, 'can I ask you a question?'

'Nothing's stopped you yet.'

'Is there someone else down here with me? Someone else in isolation?'

'What makes you think that?' he asked cautiously.

'Never answer a question with another question,' she said, a laugh in her voice; 'it sounds evasive. I thought I heard someone moving around. I tried talking to them, but they didn't answer.'

Marianne was at one end of the block of cells; the Weevil was at the other. 'You probably heard a nurse moving around,' he said, putting as much sincerity into his voice as he could. And Owen was the past master at faking sincerity.

'You're lying to me. I think there is someone there. I think they've got the same thing as I have, this Tapanuli fever. And I reckon they're even further gone than I am. Is that what I can look forward to: losing the ability to talk, just shuffling around in this awful place until I die? Is that what it's come to?'

'I won't let that happen, Marianne.'

'How can you stop it?' Her voice sounded muffled.

'I don't know yet, but I will. I promise, I will.'

He turned to face her, twisting around on the flagstones, but Marianne still had her back to him. Her face was buried in her hands, and her shoulders were shaking with the effort of holding back the tears.

Grangetown was the opposite of an up-and-coming area. It was down-and-going, if that meant anything. Gwen had spent a lot of time there when she was in the police – raiding houses, breaking up family feuds, making door-to-door inquiries – and the place still made her feel like someone was watching her, all the time. All the vegetation – the trees, the bushes, the flowers in the gardens – looked dry and faded. Desperation and curdled anger seemed to seep from the drains and the gutters. The place had a kind of leaden gravitational pull that made it easy to get in and much harder to get out again.

Gwen was sure that when she'd first arrived, parking her car around the corner and walking into the road she wanted, hands in pockets and looking casual, the first person she saw reached for a mobile phone. Maybe she was imagining things, but she could almost feel the invisible web of warnings fanning out from that one person: watch out, there's a stranger in the street. Might be the police.

The flat that Lucy shared with her junkie boyfriend was about halfway along the street. Gwen paused by the gate and looked at the outside. The curtains were drawn. One window was cracked. The house had been converted into flats: the hall appeared to have been divided, and there were two doors, one that presumably led to the ground floor and the other giving access to the stairs up to the first floor. Paint was peeling off both doors, and weeds formed a border along the junction between the concrete of the front garden and the walls and the front step.

She rang the bell for the right-hand door. Judging by the fact that the house to the left had its door next to this one, the stairs were on the left of the hall, meaning that the right-hand door gave access to the ground floor, where Lucy lived. She was there looking for Lucy, and if she just opened the door it would make Gwen's job easier. Alternatively, if her boyfriend opened the door it would save Gwen the trouble of having to break in.

Breaking and entering. How had it come to this? If there was one thing they had drummed into her in the police force it was that in order to enforce the law they had to uphold it. By committing minor infringements – illegal entry, planting evidence, forcing a suspect to confess to something they hadn't done – all the police did was to abandon the moral high ground. It didn't matter that they were doing it in the name of the greater good; by doing it, they subverted the greater good. They became criminals arresting criminals, which turned the whole thing into a glorified gang war.

And yet here she was, just about to break into someone's house, with a gun tucked into the waistband of her trousers. Prepared to do anything – even kill, if it was necessary in order to preserve her own life – and all in the name of the greater good. All in the name of saving the human race from the dark things that hid in the darkness, waiting for their chance to get in.

She shivered. What was it about Grangetown that made her suddenly feel dirty and old?

She rang the bell again, but there was no answer. Slipping her hand in her pocket, she took out a Leatherman, a multi-purpose folding tool that one of her police colleagues had introduced her to. The thinking person's Swiss Army Knife, he had called it. Quickly she folded out a flat knife blade. Making it look as if she was putting a key into the Yale lock then, blocking her hand with her body, she slipped the blade into the gap between the door and the jamb and, while she levered the blade, she used her shoulder to apply pressure to the door. Most locks only engaged for a few millimetres or so, due to clumsy fitting, and some pressure in the right place could just ease the cam of the lock away from the housing.

And it worked. The door gave under her shoulder, and she quickly eased her fingers around the wood as it moved, trying to ensure that it didn't suddenly fly in, banging on the wall.

Gwen moved into the shadowed hall and closed the door behind her, partly so she didn't alert anyone in the house to her presence, partly so she didn't alert anyone in the street to something unusual, and partly so her eyes could adjust more quickly to the darkness.

The first thing that struck her was the smell. Dirty washing, dirty plates, and something else. Sour metal. That very particular smell of blood.

She eased the Glock 17 from her waistband and held it high, pointed at the ceiling, safety clicked to *off*. Ready for anything.

Gwen entered the front room first, easing herself around the half-open door, alert for movement. There was nothing. The room was empty; bare floorboards, a sofa that had seen better days, DVD cases and discs scattered around the floor, and a surprisingly large HDTV set with full audio-visual set-up. Including speakers by the TV itself and on either side of the sofa. Her police training told her that it had probably been nicked; her knowledge of Lucy told her that the girl probably bought expensive toys for her boyfriend with her wages, which he eventually got around to selling to fund his drug habit. Cruel, but she'd seen it so often before.

After checking behind the door, she moved back into the hall. The kitchen was straight ahead, and she could see its length from where she stood. Piles of plates, crockery, cutlery, pans, all waiting to be washed. Several tinfoil takeaway containers with sauces of various kinds dried into them. No people.

The cupboard doors stood open, and there were packets of rice and biscuits on their sides, sticking out into the kitchen. Someone had been ransacking the place, looking for something. Looking for food, perhaps.

The door to the back room was closed, and she pushed it open with her gun.

The smell of blood – dryness, rust and sourness – intensified.

The body of Lucy's boyfriend was slumped across the bed in the back room. He was naked. His throat had been ripped out: blood had fountained across the ceiling, the bedspread and the wall behind the head of the bed. Chunks of flesh had been torn from his shoulders, his chest and his arms. His head was turned away but, judging by the blood that stained his cheeks, his eyes had been pulled out of his head.

Or sucked out.

Sucked out and eaten.

Gwen moved into the room, still alert for any movement but aware that she was probably too late. It looked as if Lucy had already had her snack.

The duvet had twisted about his lower half, probably as he fought to get away from his attacker, but there was a pool of glutinous blood congealing in its folds. Gwen had no desire to check, but she was pretty sure that his genitalia had been ripped away and swallowed whole. She only hoped he'd been dead when it happened. Junkie or not, nobody deserved that kind of death. Especially at the hands of their girlfriends.

Bile rose in Gwen's throat, bitter and acid, at the thought that this might have been Rhys. She might have returned from Torchwood to find him like this. On their bed. Twisted up in their duvet. Half-eaten.

'He tasted strange.'

The voice came from behind her. Gwen cursed, even as she turned and brought the gun up.

Lucy was standing behind the door. She stepped forward, the door starting to close as her body pushed past it. It was difficult to tell where the blood stopped and her clothes began. Her mouth and chin was smeared with it. Under other circumstances, Gwen might have thought she was vomiting the stuff, but she knew different. The blood wasn't Lucy's.

'It must have been the drugs,' Lucy went on. 'The heroin. It made him taste strange. Bitter, and a bit tingly.' She paused, and seemed to take in Gwen, and the gun, for the first time. 'How's Rhys?' she asked brightly. 'I hope he's OK.'

THIRTEEN

Gwen stared at Lucy.

The girl's eyes were wide, pupils surrounded by whites on all sides. She was licking her lips convulsively.

'I was looking for you,' Gwen said cautiously.

'That's good,' Lucy said. 'I was hoping someone would come. I thought it might be Rhys, but I was hoping it was you.' She smiled. 'I've already tasted Rhys. He's kind of spicy. Must be the amount of Indian food he eats. But I haven't tried you yet. I wonder what you taste of.'

Gwen brought her gun up in both hands, arms bent at the elbow, knees slightly bent as well, ready to absorb the recoil if she had to fire the gun. Classic shooter's pose, as taught to her not by the Cardiff police force, who had never armed her in eight years of duty, but by Jack, who had within three days.

'Cordite,' she said. 'I taste of cordite. Want to try some?'

'I'll skip the starter,' Lucy said, 'and go straight for the throat.'

She moved forward, and before Gwen could even think about pulling the trigger Lucy's left hand was knocking the gun away while her right hand gripped Gwen's jaw and wrenched it viciously to one side. Gwen's fingers tightened convulsively; the gun fired into the ceiling with a deafening blast. Plaster and fragments of wood fell around them. Lucy's forefinger and thumb were pressing deep into her flesh, bruising the bone, while the rest of her fingers were embedded deep in Gwen's windpipe. Somewhere in there, the carotid artery was faltering and spluttering, and Gwen's vision grew darker, as if something had parked in front of the window, cutting out the light from the street.

With her last shreds of strength, she brought the gun down on Lucy's head once, twice, and felt the girl's grip falter. She brought both arms down to her waist, thrust them up between Lucy's hands and then used what leverage she had to push Lucy's arms outwards. The girl's fingers reluctantly released their grip and Gwen sucked air noisily into her lungs as she backed away.

'Don't fight,' Lucy whispered, crouching. Blood was trickling down her face from the wound on her scalp. 'Fighting makes the muscles go all tense and bloody, but they taste better when they're relaxed.' Her gaze flickered sideways, to the remains of her boyfriend on the bed. 'He was so blissed out, he didn't even realise I was eating him. His muscles were like nothing I've ever tasted before. And his eyes... so, so sweet.'

'Lucy, look at me. *Look* at me. Why are you doing this?'

'Hungry,' Lucy wheedled. 'So hungry, all the time. Stomach feels like there's something twisting around and around in there, and it's never satisfied. Never ever satisfied. I have to eat all the time now, just to keep going.'

'But not me.'

'You're the only fresh meat here,' Lucy said, and launched herself at Gwen. She crashed into Gwen's chest, carrying her backwards. Gwen's feet caught in a piece of loose carpet and she toppled, Lucy's weight carrying her down. The room twisted around her as she fell, then it fragmented into shards of light as the back of her head hit the floor beside the bed. Lucy's weight fell directly on her stomach, driving the hard-won air from her lungs again. The girl's knees slid to either side of Gwen's chest, pinioning her. Hands held her wrists to the floor. The gun skittered away from nerveless fingers.

Pain scoured every nerve in her body, burning as it went. Gwen's breath hissed in her swollen throat. She wriggled, but Lucy's legs and hands were holding her body firm. She couldn't move.

Lucy leaned forward. Her breath smelled rank. Shreds of bloody skin were caught between her teeth. 'How romantic,' she hissed. 'Your flesh and Rhys's, reunited inside me. The ultimate threesome.'

'Why Rhys?' Gwen panted. 'I thought you fancied him?'

'I do. But you don't understand the hunger. Nothing is important compared to the hunger. It has to be satisfied.'

'Even when it means your boyfriend has to die? Even when it means that *Rhys* has to die?'

Lucy winced, eyes blinking closed and then looking away. 'It's like breathing,' she whispered. 'Even if I try to stop, I can't. I find myself just throwing food into my mouth to keep from screaming. Rice and bread don't do it. I need fresh meat.'

'But not mine,' Gwen shouted, twisting her legs so that one of her feet caught beneath the edge of the bed. She bucked, almost knocking Lucy off her chest. Lucy let go of one of Gwen's hands, grasping at the bedspread to keep herself from falling back. Gwen flailed around with her hand, looking for her gun but finding only something smooth and covered with fabric. Desperately she brought it up and hit out at Lucy's face with it, realising only as it passed in front of her eyes that it was a woman's shoe, black, probably a Manolo Blahnik knock-off, with four-inch heels.

The heel struck Lucy on her left temple, leaving a bloody gash behind it. She shot backwards, screaming, arms windmilling wildly. The back of her head thudded against the edge of the door, which had been left half-open when Lucy had pushed it earlier. It sounded resonant but liquid. Lucy bounced forward again, eyes wider than before but pupils rolled up so far they were staring at the insides of her sockets. Her head left a smear of blood and hair behind on the door. She fell towards Gwen, but Gwen rolled out of the way. Lucy's face impacted on the carpeted floor, and she didn't move.

'You're shit at this predator lark,' Gwen said, lying back on the carpet as she tried to get her breath back. 'You haven't watched nearly enough David Attenborough.'

Marianne was changing into the clothes that Owen had gone out and bought for her. He'd retreated down to the far end of the cell area near the imprisoned Weevil while Marianne undressed and dressed again, the two of them like men waiting for their wives outside a boutique changing room. He even found himself glancing sideways at the Weevil and raising his eyebrows without realising what he was doing. The Weevil just stared at him from its deep-set, piggish eyes. He couldn't tell whether it was sympathising with him or planning to rip his arms out of their sockets.

'I never asked before,' Owen called, 'but what do you do?'

'Eat and sleep and talk to you.'

'I meant when you're out in the real world. What kind of job did you do?'

'I install computer networks for financial companies. It's all right – I'm dressed now. You can come back.'

Owen walked the few metres down to the brick arch in which the armoured glass of Marianne's cell was set. She was standing close to the glass, arms folded shyly in front of her. She was wearing a pair of tight brown slacks in a moleskin material, and a T-shirt top. 'Looks good,' he said.

'You have interesting taste. I would never have thought to pair this shirt with these trousers.'

'They look fine to me.'

Marianne laughed. Holding her arms out, she twirled for him. 'Actually, it kind of works. Thanks for making the effort. I feel so much better in fresh clothes.'

'And you look great,' Owen said, appreciatively.

'I feel OK as well. Look, I'm not even showing any symptoms!' Marianne held her arms out for Owen's inspection. The contrast between the brown, freckled skin on the outside of her forearm and the soft whiteness of the inside made him shiver with its unexpected sexuality. 'See,' she continued, 'no rashes, no spots, no scabs or peeling, and no blisters. And I'm feeling OK. Really, I am.'

'Problem is,' he said, gazing at her through the armoured glass of her cell, 'that we just don't know how long the symptoms of Tapanuli fever take to emerge. And you may not be symptomatic, but you might be a carrier. We have to wait and find out.'

'How long?'

He shrugged. 'A week. I dunno.'

'A week!' She was on the verge of despair. 'I don't know if I can survive another week in this place. I mean, the company's great, but…'

Owen wished he could tell her the truth. He thought she *deserved* the truth. Trouble was, he didn't know what the truth *was*. Toshiko was still processing the ultrasound scans of Marianne's body and, given that the blood tests had shown nothing particularly out of the ordinary, there was no way at the moment of knowing what was wrong with her. As a doctor, he was stumped. Why had she attacked people, tried to eat them, and then tracked the Weevils through the city centre with a view to turning them into a mobile fast-food franchise?

'You'll survive,' he said. 'I'll make sure of it.'

She glanced up at him from beneath long eyelashes. 'Thanks,' she said. 'Your colleagues don't like me much, I know. You're the only one who treats me like a person, rather than a lab rat.'

'I'm sure they'd like you if they got to know you,' Owen said defensively.

'The Japanese girl doesn't want to look at me. She just comes in every now and then, points some gadget at me, makes it go "bleep", then goes away again. The American guy just stares at me for a while, wearing that big coat of his, then he goes away as well. He seems to spend more time with whoever it is in the cell down the end than he does with me. I can hear them talking – well, I can hear *him* talking, but I can't hear what he says. There was another woman who I saw on the night I was brought here, but I haven't seen her again. And there's a young bloke. I think he wears a suit. Sometimes, when I'm trying to sleep, and I turn over and open my eyes suddenly, he's standing there, watching me, but he always moves away quickly, before I can focus on his face.'

'It's their job to be dispassionate,' Owen said, as reassuringly as he could. 'They're all working on this Tapanuli fever outbreak. They can't afford to get emotionally involved with their patients.'

'And you?' She looked down at the ground. 'Is it *your* job to get emotionally involved?'

'It's not my job,' he said. 'It's just an optional extra.'

'You're really kind. I wish – I wish I'd met you before all this.'

Owen grimaced. 'If you'd met me before all this,' he said, the words spilling out before he had time to think about what he was saying, 'then you wouldn't have liked me.'

'But I do like you.'

'There's a barrier between us.' He slapped his hand against the glass, making a sound that echoed through the brick arches. Somewhere down the end, the Weevil grunted, surprised. 'I can't get to you and you can't get to me. All we can do is talk.'

'Don't remind me,' she said, with feeling.

'You don't understand.' He closed his eyes, rested his forehead against the glass. 'Look, if we were in a bar then I'd be all over you like a rash.'

'Don't mention rashes.'

'You know what I mean. You've seen guys like me before. Whatever we say, whatever we do, it's designed to get you into bed. That's the way it works with me. The only reason I'm talking to you now is because I can't get to you.'

'You're missing the point. You *are* talking to me. You could have walked away. Like the others.'

'I know. But I didn't want you to be scared of what was happening to you. That's my medical training coming out.'

'What changed?'

Owen frowned. 'What do you mean?'

'You said the reason you didn't walk away was that you *didn't* want me to be scared, not that you *don't* want me to be scared. Past tense, not present. So what's the reason that keeps you here now?'

'I like you. I like talking to you.'

'And if we'd been in a bar, and I'd taken you home, then we wouldn't have talked and you'd never have got to find out that you like talking to me. What does that tell you?'

He sighed. 'It tells me that I need a break.'

Gwen lay there for a few moments, listening to Lucy's breath bubbling through her nose. The girl wasn't dead, and Gwen wasn't sure whether that was a result or a shame. Part of her wanted to reach out, retrieve her gun and place a couple of rounds through the back of the bitch's head, just for the sheer cheek of trying to chat up Gwen's boyfriend, but that was the adrenalin talking.

Eventually, when she had got her breath back enough to talk, she pulled her mobile out of her pocket. Her finger hesitated over the 9, but reluctantly it moved on to the speed-dial button that got through to Torchwood. In principle, Gwen should notify the police straight away. In practice, what the hell would she tell them? Only four people in Cardiff – probably only four people in the world – could help her now.

Ianto answered the phone.

'Tell Jack that I've got one of these women who attack anything that moves,' Gwen wheezed. 'I'm over in Grangetown. Eighty-eight, George Avenue. I need the SUV and restraints.'

'We'll be there as soon as we can,' Ianto said. There seemed to be alarms going off in the background.

'What's going on?' Gwen asked. 'It's not fire alarm test day is it?'

'Some problem in the cells,' Ianto said. 'Jack has gone to investigate. I'll tell him as soon as he gets back.'

Gwen rang off, and pulled herself to a sitting position at the end of the bed. Something intruded in her field of vision; she turned her head to be confronted with a foot belonging to the corpse of Lucy's boyfriend. Most of the toes were missing: reduced to stumps. She winced. That might have been her.

'Thank God for high heels,' she muttered.

She rooted around in her bag until she found two pairs of restraints: braided plastic loops with a ratcheted toggle that could reduce the size of the loops and couldn't be slid back again. She put one of the restraints on Lucy's hands, pulled together behind her back, and another pair on her feet. Let her eat her way out of that.

While she waited for the Torchwood team to sort out their emergency and get there, Gwen searched the flat. It seemed to be balanced between chaos and order, with Lucy's boyfriend presumably leaving mess around him and Lucy trying desperately to clear it up all the time. Part of Gwen's mind felt sorry for Lucy, trapped in a dead-end relationship in a dead-end area of Cardiff, but the rest of her remembered the way the light had gleamed off Lucy's incisors as they parted, ready to rip her throat apart.

The cabinets on either side of the bed were obviously his'n'hers. The boyfriend's one she only gave cursory attention to, but Lucy's one was more interesting. On top of the various pieces of paper and hairclips in the top drawer was a blister pack, similar to the kind of thing that paracetamol came in but containing only two transparent bubbles. One of the bubbles had a pill in it; the other was empty. Gwen turned the blister pack over. The foil on the other side said nothing about the nature of the drug it contained. Two words were printed on it: the empty bubble was labelled 'Start', while the bubble that still contained a pill was labelled 'Stop'. No ambiguity there, and no need for the kind of triple-folded instruction leaflet that most pharmaceuticals came with these days.

Gwen slipped the pack into her pocket, and kept searching. Underneath where the pills had been was an A5 hardback book covered in a pink material. It said 'My Diary' on the front in big, childish letters. Gwen took it out and held it for a moment. Somewhere in those pages were Lucy's feelings about Rhys. Fantasies, perhaps, of him doing all kinds of things to Lucy that he'd occasionally hinted at doing with Gwen but never followed through on. Gwen's fingers curled around the edge of the cover. She could read it, while Lucy was still unconscious. There might be clues in there as to what had happened to her. There might be useful information she could take back to Jack.

There might also be descriptions of things that had happened between Lucy and Rhys for real, things that he hadn't admitted to Gwen.

She threw it back into the drawer. There were some questions it was probably best not to ask, not when things seemed to have improved between them.

Beneath where the diary had been was a flyer advertising a diet clinic: presumably the one that had helped Lucy lose so much weight. Was that what the pills were for? One to start losing weight, the other to stop. Could life really be that simple? No counting of calories, no cutting back on carbohydrates, no tedious exercise? Just two simple pills?

Gwen took another look at the flyer for the diet clinic. It was headed 'The Scotus Clinic', and there was a photograph underneath the heading of a thin and youngish man with a short, well-coiffured mass of blondish hair. The blurb underneath was written in short, pithy sentences, asking questions that begged particular answers, like *Do you want to lose weight and be the size you deserve to be?* and *Tired of not getting dates and getting passed over for promotion because of your size?*

Looking at the flyer, Gwen began to wonder. Lucy went to a diet clinic, and ended up wanting to eat everything in sight. Had Marianne – the girl they had back at Torchwood – been to the diet clinic too? Was something going on there that needed to be looked at? Jack would probably disagree – if there was no alien context then he was quite prepared to walk away, no matter how many lives had been lost or might still be lost – but Gwen still thought like a policewoman. If the Scotus Clinic was preying on young girls, screwing up their metabolisms with dodgy drugs, then they needed to be called to account. And if Jack wouldn't get involved then she would do it herself.

The rest of the search turned up nothing of interest. By the end, Gwen was sick and tired of sharing a room with a corpse and a cannibal. Torchwood were taking their own sweet time turning up, so she went into the kitchen and made herself a cup of tea.

'Why don't you like getting close?' Marianne insisted. 'Is it because you might get hurt?'

Owen shook his head. He still couldn't look at her. 'It's because it's never permanent. Everything dies. Everything gets destroyed. Even love. So we just make the best of it – get our pleasure where we can.'

'And what brought you to that conclusion?'

'Seven years of hospital, and then this place…' He paused, remembering his medical training: the gradual knowledge that there was nothing to humanity but flesh, blood, bone and brain, and the soul-destroying realisation of how fragile they all were. How easily broken. And then discovering through Torchwood that even the little comfort he had taken from the warmth of flesh was an illusion, that humanity was a small bubble of sanity floating in an ocean of madness.

'Poor Owen.' For a moment he thought she was being sarcastic, but her tone of voice was genuine, concerned. 'And I thought I was trapped.'

'That's enough about me,' he said. 'I have my cross to bear. I'm more interested in you at the moment. You're not showing any obvious symptoms. You're still lucid, I can see that, but what about how you're *feeling*? Any aches and pains? Any unusual tiredness? Mood changes?'

'No more than usual,' she said morosely.

'I can prescribe some stuff that might help. Paracetamol if you're feeling feverish.'

Marianne shook her head. 'I hate taking tablets. I'll just ride it out, I guess.' She paused, and wrapped her arms around herself. 'Strange thing is that I'm hungry, all the time. My stomach seems to be churning, although that might just be the stress of being locked up here.'

Owen looked at the pizza boxes and foil containers from the nearby Chinese takeaway that were stacked in the corner of the cell.

'Seems to me,' he said carefully, 'that you're doing pretty well when it comes to food.'

Marianne followed his gaze to the boxes and containers, and frowned as if she'd never seen them before. 'I didn't eat all those, did I?' she asked. 'I couldn't have. Not if I've only been here a day.' She glanced at Owen imploringly. 'Owen, tell me the truth – how long have I really been here?'

He thought for a moment. 'Honestly – about thirty-six hours.'

'That's what I thought. But I must have eaten ten pizzas and a shed-load of Shanghai noodles in that time. And I keep forgetting how much I've eaten, and I keep wanting more.' She was breathless, almost screaming now. 'What's *happening* to me?' She turned and threw herself against the far wall, hands pulled close to her chest, forehead pressed against the brick.

'Calm down,' Owen said reassuringly. 'It might be something to do with the Tapanuli fever. Your metabolism might have speeded up, raising your temperature to try and kill the virus off. Speeded-up metabolism means hunger. I'll check your temperature again. If it's normal then I could try prescribing some beta-blockers to suppress your appetite.'

'I get the strangest dreams,' she said quietly. Her voice was muffled, as though her hands were pressed up against her mouth. 'I dreamed I was chasing something through the city centre, and if I caught it I was going to eat it. And I dreamed I attacked a man in a bar. I was biting his face, and I couldn't stop myself. And I think there was a pigeon as well. I tore its head off with my teeth and swallowed it. I pulled its wings off and ate those as well. God, Owen, I can't stand these dreams. The hunger just rages through me, and I'd do anything to satisfy it. Can you give me something to stop the dreams? Please?'

'I could try Dosulepin,' he said, thinking. 'It's a tri-cyclic antidepressant, but it also acts as a sedative. It might take a few days to kick in, but it's worth a go.'

'Anything,' she said. He could hardly make out the words: her voice was so muffled. It sounded like she had something in her mouth, although she'd eaten her last lot of pizza an hour ago. 'I can't stand it much longer. I hate it here.'

Owen pressed his hands against the armoured glass. 'Just hold on,' he said urgently. 'We're working to find a cure. Just keep holding on.'

'I don't think I can,' she said, voice almost incomprehensible. 'The hunger… oh God, Owen, I'm so hungry.'

'Do you want me to get more food?' he asked. 'Pizza suit you? Or do you want to go for an Indian this time?'

Marianne turned around from the far wall. Her hands were held up in front of her face, and for a moment Owen couldn't work out what was wrong with them. Her fingers were streaked red and white, and they were thinner than they should have been. And the joints were exaggerated, arthritic.

It was the gore and the shreds of flesh that were clotting on her chin that made him realise.

While he was talking to her, while *she* was talking to *him*, Marianne had nibbled her fingers down to the bone.

Without thinking, he banged his hand on the control set into the inside of the brick arch. The armoured glass pivoted back into the cell with a grinding sound. Somewhere behind him, alarms went off in the Hub.

'Marianne, it's OK. Stay calm. I can help, OK?'

Marianne stared at him, eyes bright and wide with sadness and with agony. Blood dripped from her chin and onto the white T-shirt he'd bought her only hours before.

'Owen, I'm sorry,' she whispered.

And launched herself, skeletal hands outstretched, at his throat.

By the time Gwen got back to the flat it was dark, and she was so tired she just wanted to fall into bed and sleep for a week.

Ianto had eventually picked her up in Grangetown. He was alone in the SUV. When Gwen let him into the flat and noticed he was alone, she asked him where everyone else was. 'I believe Owen was attacked by the young lady we have prisoner,' he answered. 'He triggered the alarm, and Jack and Tosh had to subdue her whilst he escaped.'

'Subdue her?' Gwen said, thinking back to her epic battle with Lucy, 'How!'

'Jack used a fire extinguisher.'

'OK.' She nodded. 'That makes sense. I guess they distracted her with the freezing carbon dioxide.'

'No, they beat her back with the flat end. Caused quite a mess.'

Gwen winced. 'Is Owen all right?'

'He has some bruising.' Ianto glanced at Gwen's neck. 'Looks like you've suffered much the same thing.'

'Different attacker, but same intention, I guess. Talking of which…'

Together they had manoeuvred Lucy's tightly bound and still unconscious body into the back of the SUV. Ianto offered her a lift back, but she still had the car parked round the corner. Reluctantly she watched him drive off and then took a deep breath before braving the Cardiff traffic.

She hadn't eaten since before she set out to Grangetown, but the fight with Lucy had made her feel nauseous. The last thing she wanted was food. Now, pushing open the front door, she would quite happily have curled up on the hall carpet and slept if there was even a half-closed door between her and her bed.

'Oh my God!' Rhys appeared from the living room. The dressing on his cheek made him look like a lopsided hamster. 'Gwen – what happened?'

'What happened where?' she said muzzily.

'Your neck!'

'Oh, that. I got in a fight. With Lucy.'

He reached out to take her in his arms. She fell forwards, letting him take her weight.

'Are you all right? Did you win?'

'There's no video,' she said, eyes closed, pressed into his chest and smelling the mixture of aftershave and antiperspirant that she knew so well she could tell Rhys apart from a dozen other men in a darkened room. 'And we weren't fighting in mud, so you can stop getting excited.'

'I'm not getting excited,' he said. 'I'm just worried about you.'

'That's nice. I'm OK. I'll be even better when I get to bed.'

'You need to put some antibiotic cream on those scratches. Funnily enough, I actually have some you can use. It's in the bathroom cabinet.'

'OK.'

'You're not moving.' His arms went around her. 'What happened with Lucy?'

'She's in custody. In a secure unit.'

'Will I have to make a statement?'

Gwen shook her head against his chest. 'I don't think so. There's obviously something wrong with her.' She brought her hands up and pushed herself away from Rhys. 'Get yourself to bed. I need something warm to cuddle into.'

Rhys headed for the bedroom, pulling his shirt off as he went, and Gwen went into the bathroom. She reached for the door to the bathroom cabinet and pulled it open. Paracetamol, cotton buds, athlete's foot cream, tampons… where the hell was the antiseptic cream?

OK, there it was, sitting on the bottom shelf.

Right in front of the blister pack that only had two plastic blisters on it, one of which was empty.

And Gwen knew with a sickening lurch in her stomach that if she turned it around, the foil on the back would have two words printed on it.

'Start' and 'Stop'.

FOURTEEN

The Torchwood meeting next morning didn't get off to a good start, as far as Toshiko was concerned. Owen was bruised and surly; Gwen was bruised and moody; and Jack was irritated at one or the other or both of them. And Ianto was Ianto, fussing around the coffee machine just outside the Boardroom, trying to adjust the temperature of the steam, until Jack eventually said, 'OK: staff treat. We all need cheering up. We're going out for breakfast.'

They went out through Ianto's tourist information centre, and Jack led them to a Turkish-owned café that was perched on stilts out over Cardiff Bay. The waves were slate grey and topped with spume, washing over the pebbles that made up what little beach there was. Odd fragments of wood and plastic floated on the water's surface, eddying back and forth as if they weren't sure where they were going. A lone swan emerged from beneath the wooden pier that separated the water from the land, aloof and unassailable. In the distance, Penarth Head was almost lost in mist, grey against grey.

'We've had a hell of a few days,' Jack said after the waiter had taken their order. 'I know it's all looking bleak. It happens. Whatever's going on here is complicated, and I don't think we have all the answers yet.'

'*Nakitsura ni hachi*,' Toshiko murmured. At Jack's questioning look, she added: 'It's a Japanese saying: "The bee always stings when you're crying". It means that things go from bad to worse before they get better. If they get better.'

'I couldn't agree more. And I think that part of the problem is that some of us have pieces of information that the others aren't privy to. If we're going to make anything of this mess, we need to share whatever we have. Who wants to go first?'

'We have three people showing symptoms,' Gwen said, her voice flat, her gaze aimed at the tablecloth. 'Lucy Sobel and Marianne Till are both in custody in the Hub. We have to assume there are more people out there with this problem, whatever it is.'

'Owen,' Jack said, 'what exactly are we dealing with here?'

'I don't know, *exactly*. Tosh's computers are still processing the scans from that hand-held thing she knocked together. All I know from close observation is that the symptoms are extreme hunger leading to psychosis and exaggerated strength. Both Marianne and Lucy seem to be trapped in a mental state where the hunger is compelling them to attack people and eat them. Then their minds are glossing over the details and persuading them that they've been hallucinating. I suspect that whatever they are suffering from makes them suggestible, as well as psychotic. Blood work is normal, and there's no outward manifestation of disease. I'm picking up no bacteria or viruses in the atmospheric checks, so I can't see it being contagious.'

'It's not Tapanuli fever, then?' Jack enquired.

Owen glowered at Jack. 'I invented Tapanuli fever. It doesn't exist. It's not real.'

'You sure? I only ask because I don't think I'm inoculated. I missed that day at school.'

'Look, I was trying to reassure her! I wanted to keep her calm!'

'Right,' Jack drawled. 'That worked out well, didn't it?'

The waiter arrived with their orders, and they stopped talking while the plates were set down: full English breakfast, with black pudding, scrambled egg, sausage, bacon and fried bread.

'Should we be talking about all this?' Ianto asked. 'I mean…' He indicated the waiter with a nod of his head.

'Not to worry,' Jack said. 'I've got a blanking field generator under the table. Brought it with me from Torchwood. Nobody can hear us outside a six-foot radius.'

Ianto's eyes widened. 'You're joking!'

'Absolutely,' Jack replied. 'Actually, the waiter only speaks ten words of English, and three of those are swearwords. He can swear like a trooper in Turkish as well. In fact, last time I checked he could swear in fifteen different languages. I think he used to be a sailor. Then again, I think *I* used to be a sailor. There are periods in my life that are a bit vague. That's one of them.' He turned to Gwen. 'Oh, and by the way, you didn't say who the third person is who's affected.'

'It's Rhys.' She didn't lift her gaze from the tablecloth.

Silence fell across the table. Nobody seemed willing to say anything. Eventually, Toshiko leaned across and put her hand on top of Gwen's. 'Then whatever this thing is,' she said, 'we will stop it. Owen will find a cure and Jack will make everything the way it was.'

'And as an encore,' Owen muttered, 'peace in the Middle East and a resolution to the legal battle between the Americans and the Czech Republic over who brewed Budweiser beer first.'

'Shouldn't you be with him?' Toshiko asked. 'I mean, if he goes the way of the other two…'

Gwen winced. 'What was I supposed to do – tie him to the bed? I wanted to stay with him, I wanted to protect him, but I couldn't tell him why. He only took the pill, a day or two ago, so he's probably not as far gone as the other two. And if there's going to be a cure, it's going to come from here. From us. Staying with him would just… just mean I was waiting for the inevitable. At least here I can pretend I'm helping. So – what's the progress of this disease, if it is a disease? I have a vested interest now.'

Owen shrugged. 'If they don't get enough food, then they start eating themselves.' He caught the bleak look on Gwen's face and winced. 'Sorry, but it's true. Anyway, I dunno how far they could get before pain or blood loss made them pass out. Maybe both hands and both forearms. That's just a guess. Then again, given that this thing, whatever it is, seems to affect the brain, maybe it changes the way they feel pain. If they used tourniquets to control the bleeding then there's no reason why they couldn't munch their way through both arms up to the shoulders and both legs up to the knees. If they were gymnastic enough, they might get halfway up the thigh. Lips would go as well, of course. They'd probably save the tongue for last, if only because tourniquets wouldn't work and they'd choke on their own blood.'

175

Toshiko slid her plate towards the centre of the table. Suddenly she wasn't feeling hungry.

Judging by Gwen's white face, she didn't feel well either. 'And if they *do* get enough food?'

'Then I just don't know.' Owen speared a piece of fried bread with his fork and bit the corner off. 'There's always the possibility that they just keep on going, but I think that's unlikely.'

'Why?' Jack asked, succinctly.

'Because they aren't putting weight on.' Owen used his fork to cut a piece of black pudding. 'They're plugging massive amounts of calories into their systems, and those calories are going somewhere apart from hips and thighs. In fact, not only aren't they putting weight on, they're actually losing it. I reckon Marianne's lost half a stone since we caught her, and she's been eating like pizza's going to be reclassified as a Class A drug. If she keeps on going, she's liable to suffer from malnutrition.' Owen popped a piece of black pudding into his mouth. 'She could actually starve to death,' he said, and chewed.

'I've got to ask,' Jack said, staring at the remnants of the black pudding on Owen's plate. 'Although I probably don't want to. What exactly *is* black pudding?'

'It's a kind of sausage made from a blend of onions, pork fat, oatmeal and pig's blood,' Ianto said.

'OK,' Jack said slowly. 'Black pudding is made from blood. I get that. Nothing wrong with that. But you can get white pudding as well.'

'Yeah,' Owen said cautiously.

'So what's that then? The same thing but made with white corpuscles rather than red corpuscles?'

'It's just black pudding without the blood,' Gwen said reassuringly.

'Although earlier versions often had sheep's brains as a binding agent,' Ianto added. 'Are you going to eat that black pudding?'

'I think I'll pass,' Jack told him.

Rhys was woken up by a pain in his gut. It felt like stones were grinding together in there, rough surfaces grating on each other, and the membranes of his stomach were caught in the middle, torn and bleeding.

He curled up, pulling the sheets over himself and trying to force himself back to sleep, but it was no good. The pain was too intense.

Pain? It was hunger. He was starving.

Gwen had left before dawn, leaving a cup of coffee beside the bed before heading for her precious Torchwood, and Rhys had surfaced for long enough to phone work and leave a message on the answerphone saying that he'd been in an accident, and was taking a few days off. It seemed wiser than telling them the truth. He just hoped that nobody made the connection with Lucy being off work at the same time and came to the conclusion that the two of them were having an affair or something.

Eventually, he threw the duvet off and padded out, naked, into the split living room and kitchen area, taking the now cold cup of coffee with him. He and Gwen lived on the first floor of a converted house, so nobody was going to be gazing in through the window, and they lived in Riverside, so even if anyone could gaze in through the window at him they'd be too polite to do so.

He put the cup in the microwave and blitzed it until it was warm enough to drink. Sipping it, he went to the fridge and pulled out a tub of margarine, peeled the lid off, then walked across the living room and plonked himself down on the sofa.

What the hell was happening?

Scooping out a gobbet of margarine with his fingers he popped it into his mouth and tried to work out where things had suddenly gone wrong. Why, for instance, Lucy had suddenly attacked him. It wasn't like he'd made a move on her and she'd pushed him away and accidentally injured him; in fact, if anything, she was making a move on him before she took a chunk out of his cheek.

He excavated another gobbet of margarine and slipped it into his mouth, licking his fingers to get rid of the last traces, running his tongue along the sharp edge of his fingernails, then reached up to touch the wound dressing, pressing down lightly on the cotton wool to see how much residual pain there was. Strangely, he didn't feel anything. Whatever cream they'd used on him the night before had worked a treat.

As he scraped more and more of the thick yellow fat from the tub, Rhys began to wonder what his cheek actually looked like. He'd not dared look at it the night before. The lasting agony of Lucy's teeth latching onto the flesh and then tearing it away had made it feel like he'd lost the entire cheek. He'd been afraid that if he looked at himself in the mirror he would have seen his teeth and the inside of his mouth through a ragged hole. Even at the hospital he'd been wondering if they were going to operate – perhaps take some flesh from his thigh to replace the cheek, leaving him looking like a living jigsaw puzzle. Thank God Gwen had been there to calm him down. The pain had been intense, pulsing in time with his heart, sending tendrils of agony through the entire side of his face until the painkillers had kicked in. But now... now there was nothing.

Perhaps the nerve had died. Perhaps the skin was turning black around the edges. He sniffed, trying to detect some sign of gangrene, but he didn't even know what he was trying to find, and all he could smell was the rich oiliness of the margarine. Which, he discovered, looking down at the empty tub, he appeared to have finished.

His stomach had stopped complaining now. Draining the last of his coffee, he got up and went into the bathroom. In the mirror his face looked pasty. It also looked thin. He reached up wonderingly with his hand to feel the area under his chin. It used to bulge slightly, a chubbiness that he'd never really shed since childhood, but now there was a concavity where his neck and jaw joined. And the jawline itself stood out proudly. He smiled. He hadn't looked that good for years. If ever.

Rhys edged his fingernails beneath the transparent tape beneath his eye socket that held the dressing onto his skin, and paused for a moment. Did he really want to do this? Did he really want to see what was underneath?

Before he could talk himself out of it, he ripped the tape away from the skin. It pulled smoothly away, distorting the flesh in a wave as it went. The dressing fell away, held only by the tape on the bottom, by his jaw.

Leaving behind it an expanse of smooth, pink flesh, marred only by a set of small, crescent-shaped scars where Lucy's teeth had sunk into the skin.

Scars that he could swear were getting smaller even as he watched.

The waiter came over to clear the plates away and then pour them coffee. Conversation stopped while he worked. Toshiko spent her time looking through the window of the restaurant at the bay outside. A small ferry was docking as she watched. Passengers were waiting on its deck to disembark.

'OK, people – what's the connection between Marianne, Lucy and Gwen's boyfriend?' Jack asked.

'The Scotus Clinic,' Gwen said.

'And what's that when it's at home?'

'It's a diet clinic based here in Cardiff. Lucy definitely went there, and Rhys went there too. He told me about it last night. He wanted to lose weight because he thought I was falling out of love with him, the idiot.'

'And how does it work?' Toshiko asked.

'They get two pills: one to start the weight loss and one to stop it. I think if we investigate we'll find out that Marianne went there too.'

'She did,' Owen said.

Jack gazed at him with interest. 'OK, Sherlock – how did you know that?'

'Cos she had a leaflet in her handbag.'

'And what were you doing looking through her handbag?'

Owen looked affronted. 'I was looking for clues, and stuff.'

'And what were you *really* doing looking through her handbag?'

He ducked his head. 'I wanted to see whether she has a boyfriend or not.'

'And has she?'

'Dunno. You can't find anything in a woman's handbag. It's not organised along logical lines. I only found the leaflet by accident.' He looked around. 'That's why women don't make good surgeons, you know? Blokes, they put down their scalpels and retractors and stuff all in the right order so they can just reach out again and pick it up without even looking. Women, they just throw it all down higgledy-piggledy on the tray, and then wonder why they pick up a clamp when they want the forceps.'

Gwen looked over at Toshiko. 'Do you want to tear him a new arsehole?' she asked, 'or shall I?'

'He doesn't really mean it,' said Toshiko, but she avoided Gwen's gaze.

'How *is* Marianne?' Jack asked. 'Her fingers looked pretty raw from what little I saw.'

'Yeah, and her face wasn't looking too hot after you finished rearranging it with the fire extinguisher.' There was an undertone of dark anger in Owen's voice, but Toshiko couldn't tell whether it was directed at Jack or at himself. Or perhaps at both.

'If I hadn't, she'd have been treating your face like people treat kebabs on a Friday night.'

'Yeah, well…' Owen paused, gazing out of the window at the distant headland. 'I had to amputate her fingers,' he said finally, casually, as if he was talking about the weather, or last night's TV. 'The damage was too great. She'd stripped all the skin and bone off. I can't keep her unconscious – there's not that much sedative in the whole of Cardiff – so I've had to chain her up in the cell. Actually chain her to the wall so she can't eat any more of herself, with what remains of her hands bandaged up. Last I saw she was trying to reach the bandages with her mouth, she was that hungry.' It seemed to Toshiko that his gaze was fixed on something much further away than Penarth Head. There was something hard about his face. 'I remember taking an oath once to "Do no harm". I'm not sure with Marianne what "doing no harm" means. Whatever happens, she suffers.'

This time it was Gwen who reached out a hand to touch Owen's, an almost unconscious gesture of sympathy and understanding. Toshiko had been just about to reach out herself. When she saw Gwen's hand move, she pulled hers back, reaching instead to pick up her napkin, fold it, put it down again.

'What about Lucy?' Gwen asked. 'You didn't put her in the same cell, did you?'

This time it was Ianto who answered. Toshiko had almost forgotten that he was with them at the table. 'No, we managed to get her into the cell next to Marianne before she woke up.'

'And her boyfriend?'

'I went back and cleaned the place up. There's no sign that anything happened. I actually brought his body back to the Hub so that Owen could do an autopsy, if he wanted.'

'The fun never ends,' Owen muttered. 'Corpses, stacking up, every day. Bodily fluids and rotting flesh. I'd smell better if I worked in a fish and chip shop. And the hours would be better.'

'That looked like a nasty gash on her head when I picked her up,' Ianto continued, having paused politely while Owen talked, 'but it was healing fast by the time we got her into the cell. I wouldn't be surprised if whatever is affecting these women is helping them heal faster.'

'They're not alien,' Owen scoffed. 'They're ordinary Welsh girls. Whatever's happened to them hasn't given them magical powers. It just makes them hungry and psychotic.'

'I don't know.' Gwen was worrying her lower lip with her teeth. 'Remember what happened with the Weevils. For a start, they've obviously developed a far greater strength than normal. Lucy was close to breaking my neck, and Marianne – if it was Marianne – was able to take down a fully grown Weevil. Something's changing them physically, as well as mentally.'

'And remember the reactions of the other Weevils,' Toshiko added. 'The ones by the wharf, and the one in the cells in Torchwood. They were wary. They were *frightened*. I don't think that was just the fact that this girl had killed one of them.'

'No, that usually just makes them mad,' Jack said, with feeling.

Toshiko looked around at her colleagues. 'I know biology is Owen's area rather than mine, but I am wondering if these girls are giving off some kind of chemical scent which Weevils find disturbing.'

'I've just remembered something.' Gwen thumped the table with her fist. 'There's been so much going on that it just went out of my head, but Rhys told me that someone tried to kidnap Lucy a few days ago. I'd assumed that it was connected to her boyfriend – some kind of unpaid drug debt or something – but now I'm wondering if it's connected to whatever they're infected with. But who could it be?'

'Someone at the Scotus Clinic, perhaps?' Jack drummed his fingers on the table. 'I've got to say, I don't know whether there's anything here for Torchwood or not. It still sounds more like a shared delusion, or some tropical disease to me, pheromones and super-strength or not. We're set up to look for signs of alien activity in the area and stop it. I just don't see the evidence here.'

Toshiko looked over at Gwen. Her boyfriend was infected. If anyone was going to push Jack into investigating this, it had to be her.

Owen and Ianto gazed at Gwen as well, waiting for her to react.

'It might be alien influence,' she said, as if it were only her and Jack at the table, 'or it might be something more mundane. Either way, we need to find out. I think we should investigate the Scotus Clinic, and then make a decision based on what we find there.'

'Does Rhys remember enough about the clinic that he can draw us a map? Always useful to know where you're going.'

'I'll ask,' she said.

By the time Jack and Gwen had made their preparations, looked at blueprints and plans, checked out their weapons, argued over who was going to drive the SUV and then made their way, still bickering, through the Cardiff traffic to the office block that housed the Scotus Clinic, it was lunchtime. The lobby was crowded with men and women in smart office-wear, either heading out for coffee and sandwiches or back to their offices. People in green coveralls were watering the various plants and vines that were placed strategically around. The air was filled with the incessant *ping* of lifts arriving.

Jack looked around. There was something about lobbies that never changed. He'd been in hotels and office blocks from the nineteenth century all the way through to the forty-ninth, on a panoply of planets between Earth and the Horsehead Nebula, and it was always the same. People rushing around trying to look important, grabbing food on the move. Nobody taking time to sit down and relax, sip a cocktail, close their eyes and daydream for a while. Everyone had somewhere better to be, and they never seemed to get there.

The lifts were separated from the rest of the lobby by a glass wall. Booths embedded in the glass allowed people in and out via rotating glass doors, but only if they placed some kind of identity card in a slot. Gwen was standing in front of the glass, trying to make out the company listing on a big board by the lifts.

'Tolladay Holdings,' she read. 'Sutherland & Rhodes International, McGilvray R&D, Rouse and Patrick Financial… ah! The Scotus Clinic. Floor Twelve. Looks like it occupies the entire floor.' She glanced at the booths, then at Jack. 'How the hell are we going to get in? Have you got some alien device that will override the security on these doors?'

'Even better,' Jack said. 'I've got money.'

He strode across to the rose marble desk that sat in the centre of the lobby. A man in security guard's uniform sat behind the desk. His name tag read 'Martin'. He watched Jack approach with professional distrust.

'Hi,' Jack said. 'Look, I could spin you some kind of story about a snap health and safety inspection, or something equally implausible, but we're both busy men and we haven't got time to dance around. Let's cut to the chase. How much money will it take for you to let us through to the lifts?'

The man's face folded up into a scowl. 'Is this some kind of joke?'

'That entirely depends on whether you find the concept of hard cash inherently funny.'

Martin shook his head. 'You ain't getting in there.'

'Five hundred of your quaint British pounds.'

'No way.'

'Six hundred.'

'It's more than my job's worth, mate.'

'Sitting in a lobby being ignored by everyone who walks past isn't a job, it's just a way of watching your life slip away. Did you grow up wanting to be a security guard in an office block? Did you lie awake at night dreaming about handing visitor's passes out to stressed people turning up late for meetings? Seven hundred.'

'Look – who the hell do you think you are?'

'Come on, I'm on a tight budget here. Seven hundred and fifty pounds, and that's my final offer. Take an evening class. Follow your dream.'

Martin looked around. Nobody else was paying any attention to them. Catching Jack's eye, he glanced meaningfully down at something just below the level of the desk, then back again. 'I ain't got time for this,' he said loudly, and turned away. Jack leaned over and felt around with his fingers. There was a box down there, on a shelf hidden by the desk's surface, and there were four or five things like credit cards in the box. He scooped two of the cards out, replacing them with a thick envelope he'd taken from a pocket in his coat. 'Nice doing business with you,' he said. 'Hope the rest of your life works out OK. Drop me a line, OK?'

Gwen watched him return with an expression of disbelief on her face. 'Firstly, that was bribery. Secondly, did that envelope really have seven hundred and fifty pounds in it? Thirdly, if it did then how did you know that's how much it would take?'

'Funny thing,' Jack said; 'it always ends up at seven hundred and fifty pounds with security guards, no matter where we start off. Must be a union thing.'

He tossed a card to Gwen. Choosing a moment when the lift area was momentarily unoccupied, they went through their booths together.

The lift doors opened on the twelfth floor to reveal a hall area with a deep carpet in neutral brown, hessian weave wallpaper and some unthreatening abstract paintings. A door to the left identified the Scotus Clinic in large sans serif letters.

Gwen pushed the door open.

The lobby of the clinic was empty, apart from several comfy chairs in a waiting area, three doors, the right-hand one labelled 'Doctor Scotus', and a vacant receptionist's desk. Jack knew straight away that the place was deserted. There was a feeling, or rather, a lack of feeling to places that weren't being used. They were missing something: an energy, a vibration, a background hum. It was like the difference between a sleeping person and a corpse; they looked the same, at first glance, but you could always tell them apart.

Sleeping corpses were a problem, of course, but Jack had worked out different methods of identifying them. And they didn't turn up that often.

'I think we were expected,' he said, looking around. 'This place has been abandoned. And pretty recently.'

Gwen moved across to the right-hand door. 'Rhys said he talked to Doctor Scotus himself. We ought to start in there.' She knocked twice on the door. 'Just in case,' she murmured.

'Politeness costs nothing,' Jack agreed. 'Unlike security passes, which are quite pricey. I need to start cutting back on the bribes. I've almost blown this month's budget.'

'No answer,' Gwen said. She pushed the door. It swung open, revealing a shadowy office. If there were windows in there then they were covered by curtains or blinds. She stepped inside, quickly being swallowed up by the darkness.

'Can I ask you something?' Jack said, still looking around the lobby.

'Mmmm?'

'Why is it there's a Scottish pound note, but there's no Welsh pound note?'

'Mmmm!'

Gwen came staggering back through the door into the lobby, hands clawing at her neck. Something was wrapped around her throat, something about as thick as Jack's thumb but with a wildly thrashing tail. Something coloured black, with vivid blue stripes encircling its body.

And it was throttling the life out of Gwen.

FIFTEEN

Toshiko rubbed her eyes for what felt like the thousandth time. They were gritty and hot, and rubbing them just made them feel worse, but she couldn't stop herself. It was like scratching an itch, or sneezing: a reflex action that couldn't be suppressed.

'The problem with this place,' she muttered, 'is that I never know whether it's day or night outside. The world could end, and I'd be completely unaware.' In fact, she added silently, with Jack out there, the chances that the world could end in the next few hours were probably a lot higher. Things tended to happen when he was on the loose.

Her computer screen was still, infuriatingly, showing patterns of numbers as the processor crunched away at integrating the continuous readings from the hand-held scanner into a single coherent picture. It had been working for several days now, and gave every indication that it might churn away until the end of the world. Whenever that turned out to be.

Bored, she leaned back in her chair and gazed around the Hub. She still remembered the crazy mixture of feelings she had experienced when Jack had brought her in for the first time: terror at the huge responsibility that she had been given; pride that she had been chosen; excitement at the prospect of examining technology that no human had ever seen before; and, bizarrely, distaste at the place she would be spending her working life. The Hub was buried beneath Cardiff's Millennium Centre area, built in and around the crumbling remains of an old water pumping station, and remnants of the old Victorian architecture were everywhere to be seen.

The walls were perpetually damp, and the very lowest level of the central area was several inches deep in water that, in summer, usually hosted a colony of mosquitoes. At least, she hoped they were mosquitoes. Jack had once told her the water was actually home to the last survivors of a civil war on a planet of very small insectoid aliens. She hadn't believed him, of course, but come the summer she did stop swatting them. Just in case. No point in provoking an interstellar incident by accident.

Ianto was stood up by the Boardroom, fiddling with the coffee machine again. Seeing her looking up at him, he called down: 'Tosh, can I get you a coffee? I'm trying Jamaican Blue Mountain today.'

'Thank you, but no,' she said.

He turned back to the coffee machine. Toshiko was about to change her mind when she realised that the flickering of the computer screen in the corner of her eye had stopped. The processor had finished its job.

The screen was filled with a coloured display of a human body. Marianne Till's body. It wasn't an accurate representation – Marianne had been moving around while scanning herself with Toshiko's device – but more of a computer-generated representation based on the information from the scanner. Following Toshiko's instructions, the computer had mapped the data onto a standard human grid, legs slightly apart and arms held out from the sides, palms out. The picture was coloured according to the density of the material that was present in the body: bone was white, fat yellow, muscle red, with other colours winding in and around them to represent the rest of the stuff that bodies tended to be made up of: tendons, voids, lymphatic fluid, brain matter and other things that Toshiko couldn't even name. She could turn the body through any orientation, remove layers progressively until there was nothing left or slice through at any angle to get a cross-section of Marianne's body. Setting aside for a moment the sheer amount of time it had taken, it was actually a pretty impressive system. She would have to show Owen. He might be able to find a use for it.

A flash of crimson somewhere near Marianne's abdomen caught Toshiko's eye. She zoomed the image in. The area running from the stomach through the intestines to the bowel was effectively a void within the body: a space that might be empty or might be filled with solid or liquid matter, but either way it should always have a different density from the surrounding tissue. The problem was that Marianne's digestive tract seemed to be blocked by something that had a density close to that of muscle. It was coming up as red on the image. For a few moments, Toshiko thought it was a glitch in the software, but it was too localised, too self-contained. A tumour, perhaps? She was no expert – that was Owen's department – but she was pretty sure that tumours manifested themselves as lumps, not as long, thin, sinuous objects that wound all the way through the upper and lower intestines, terminating at one end in the stomach and at the other in the bowel.

And tumours didn't have a mass of smaller tentacles, as thin as cotton, emerging from one end in a cloudy mass.

Toshiko leaned back in her chair, feeling her stomach suddenly rebel at the thing on the screen.

There was something alien in Marianne's stomach.

Something alive.

Gwen felt the creature cutting into her neck. She could hardly get a breath past the constriction in her throat. Staggering backwards out of Doctor Scotus's office, she tried to call to Jack for help, but she couldn't get the words out.

Her head felt swollen with blood. Her eyes were bulging. A few seconds more and she was sure they would pop out of their sockets, the pressure was so intense. With every beat of her heart, spikes of pain were being hammered into her temples.

The world started turning grey around the edges. She managed to get her thumb between one loop of the creature and her skin. She tugged at it, trying to loosen the creature's grip, but it just kept tightening and her thumb was trapped with its circulation cut off.

One end of the creature's body waved in front of her face, thin strands of white erupting from a blue-ringed body, flat on three sides. The white hairs seemed to be aiming themselves at her face, like an albino medusa, except that she felt like she was turning to jelly rather than rock.

The door jamb hit her as she staggered sideways, but the pain was minor compared with the noose of fire that was tightening around her neck. All she could see now was a grey tunnel with the office very small and very far away at the centre of it. Tiredness washed up her arms. She just wanted to give up and fall asleep.

Something was fumbling at her throat, and it took a few seconds before she realised that it was Jack. She tried to tell him that it was all too late, too far away and too much trouble, but he didn't seem to understand. Something went *bang*, a long way in the distance, and then *bang* again, and she was being spun around. The pressure on her throat relaxed, and pain flooded up through the nerves, the veins and the arteries until her neck was incandescent with agony. She fell to her knees, retching, face burning and sweat coursing down her cheeks and forehead. Acid burned her mouth as she vomited thin strings of mucus onto the carpet. Firm hands were on her shoulders. She was being turned around again, slowly this time. Jack's face swam into sight through her searing hot tears.

'Last time I held a girl's head while she threw up,' he said comfortingly, 'it was too many hyper-vodkas rather than an alien worm thing that did it. I think the after-effects actually lasted longer. Nice girl – I think she went on to become President of somewhere. Or something.'

'What the *hell* was that?' Gwen coughed.

'See for yourself.' Jack helped her up, one arm around her shoulders and the other supporting her beneath her arm. She leaned gratefully against him. The warmth and the musk of his body enveloped her, a smell compounded of spice, leather and sandalwood. Her face touched the side of his neck, and she had to smother the sudden desire to lick his skin, tasting him.

'What's a hyper-vodka?' she asked, trying to distract herself. 'Is it some kind of cocktail?'

'Oh it's some kind of cocktail all right.' Jack's hand released its grip on her arm, but he still held her around the shoulders. 'Feeling OK?'

'Nothing a neck transplant wouldn't fix.' Gwen's eyes suddenly focused, and the world came into existence around her. They were back in the foyer of the Scotus Clinic. Directly ahead of her was the receptionist's desk, and attached to it, thrashing back and forth, was the most bizarre creature Gwen had ever seen. For a moment she thought there were two or three of the creatures all entwined together, all struggling to escape, but she quickly realised that there was only one of them. It had three sections, black with irregular blue rings the colour of cigarette smoke. They were triangular in cross-section, and joined together in the centre like a Catherine Wheel. Each section terminated in a mass of writhing white fibres. Two of the sections were stuck somehow to the desk, and the creature was thrashing around with a sound like paper being crumpled.

'I'm thinking of calling it Ringo,' Jack said. 'On account of the rings. I know it's corny, but I kinda think it's appropriate. It just doesn't look like a Brian to me. Or a Kevin.'

'What did you do to it?'

'I stapled it to the desk.' Jack reached down and picked a chunky electric stapler from the floor, something designed for fastening hundreds of sheets of paper together. A lead ran from the stapler to a socket in the wall. 'Found this on a shelf. Thought it was a weapon of some kind. If I'd actually considered the matter carefully I would have wondered what a personal assistant was doing with a weapon but, hey, maybe Doctor Scotus kept trying to get her bent over the photocopier. Anyway, it worked well enough for me to staple the thing to the desk.'

'That's... not of this Earth, is it?'

He looked carefully at the stapler. 'It says Rexel. Maybe that's the planet where it was built.'

'I meant the creature.'

'Oh, *that* is definitely not only not of this Earth, it's not of this solar system or even this arm of the galaxy.'

'Then how did it get here?'

'Slipped through the Rift, I expect. Although probably not in that form.'

'What is it – some kind of guard dog?'

Jack shook his head. 'I don't think so. I reckon it was left behind by accident. It looks like Doctor Scotus and his team left in a hurry. When you're feeling up to it, we'll search the place.'

Gwen eyed the creature warily. 'Leaving Ringo here?'

Jack shrugged. 'It's not going anywhere.' He stepped forward, grabbed the one free segment of the creature and wrestled it down to the desk, then brought the power stapler round and held it just below the writhing mass of white fibres. *Bang*, and all three of the creature's sections were fastened down, leaving only the central hub free to flex and thump against the desk. 'Especially not now.'

Casting nervous glances over her shoulder at Ringo – the name had unfortunately stuck in her mind – Gwen followed Jack back into the office, flicking on the light switch as she did so. Part of her was waiting for something to leap at her throat with a sound like rustling paper, but nothing happened. Jack just kept walking, oblivious.

'What happens if there's another one?' Gwen asked. 'Maybe they come in twos. Or threes.'

'And maybe they don't. If there's another one then the finest weapon that the people of the planet Rexel can manufacture will take care of it for us. But I think if there was another then it would have attacked by now.'

Together they searched through the office, Gwen starting to the left of the door, Jack to the right, meeting at the far side where Doctor Scotus's desk took pride of place, both of them circling around the oddly shaped chairs that sat either side of it. Apart from framed certificates on the walls and a bookcase full of medical textbooks on nutrition, digestion and, strangely, parasitology, Gwen didn't come up with anything. Judging by the speed at which he was moving, Jack wasn't having much more luck. When they got to the desk, Gwen took a moment to admire its solidity, and the slab of marble that formed its surface. Four marks in a rectangle on the surface indicated that something had been removed recently – probably a laptop, judging by the shape.

The drawers were all empty of anything apart from basic supplies; staples, bits of paper, rubber bands. Gwen was probably being over-optimistic thinking that there might be something incriminating there, but life could sometimes be surprising like that.

Jack, meanwhile, was looking though the waste-paper basket that sat by the side of the desk. 'Surprising how often people forget about the rubbish,' he said, pulling a crumpled piece of paper from its depths. He unfolded it, and the sound made Gwen's skin crawl. It sounded too much like the creature that was outside in the lobby, stapled to the desk. She raised a hand to her neck, which still ached.

Jack saw her shiver. 'Sorry,' he said. 'But I think this is important. It

looks like a recent list of clients at the clinic. Lucy Sobel, Marianne Till…'
His gaze locked with hers. 'Rhys Williams.'

She nodded. 'And how many others.'

'They had twenty-eight clients in all. Quite a profit, this Doctor Scotus
was making.'

'A profit on twenty-eight clients? How much were they paying?' Gwen
grabbed the sheet of paper from Jack's hands and glanced down the list.
'Rhys, you *arsehole*! That's our holiday fund gone for a burton!'

'Recriminations later. Investigation now.'

'OK, sorry. But still…'

'Gwen, he's likely to be punished enough over the next week or so. Cut
him some slack. He only did it because he wanted to look good for you.
And, frankly, who wouldn't?'

She sighed. 'OK. Thanks.'

'I don't think there's anything more we can find here. There were two
other rooms leading off the lobby. Let's give them a quick going over.'

They headed out of the office, bypassing Ringo, which was still thumping
the centre of its body frantically against the surface of the receptionist's
desk. Jack chose the middle door, Gwen the one on the left.

Gwen's choice was a well-appointed examination room. The walls and
ceiling were a clinical white. A desk was pressed up against one wall, with
one of the backless chairs in front of it. A curtained area off to one side
could be used for undressing. A trolley with a black PVC surface pushed
against another wall was presumably for examinations. Apart from some
abstract paintings on the wall, there was nothing in the room.

Gwen went through the desk drawers one by one, just on the off-
chance, but they had been hurriedly emptied of everything apart from the
normal detritus of office life: a handful of paper clips, the caps from three
ball point pens, a whole load of loose staples, some bits of grey lint, three
sealed pads of Post-it notes…

And a small foil blister pack containing two pills that had been pushed
to the back of the middle drawer. Gwen picked it out tentatively. It was
exactly the same as the one she had found in the bathroom cabinet back
in the flat, with the exception that this one contained both the 'Start' and
the 'Stop' pills.

'Look what I've found,' she said, walking out of her room and into Jack's.

'Look what *I've* found,' Jack retorted.

His room was exactly the same as hers, except that there was a body on the examination trolley. It was a woman. She was spread-eagled, head lolling off one edge, legs and arms hanging off the others. There was nothing peaceful about it: she looked like an abandoned doll.

'Client?' Gwen asked.

'Receptionist,' Jack corrected. 'She's wearing a name tag.'

'I guess she was killed by Ringo out there.'

Jack shook his head. 'No marks on her neck, and look at her mouth.'

Gwen leaned closer. The receptionist's mouth was wide open, locked in an endless scream, and there was blood around her lips. Some of it had trickled down her cheeks, leaving crimson stripes behind.

'Oh good God. Don't tell me—'

'That Ringo climbed out through her throat, probably rupturing something along the way? Owen can confirm it in an autopsy, but that's my reading of the situation.'

'What the hell are we dealing with?' Gwen asked.

Jack turned towards the door leading out into the lobby.

From out of the shadows, something black launched itself at his face, its skin torn where it had wrenched itself free of the staples that had been holding it to the desk.

Jack's hand came round holding his Webley revolver. His finger moved a fraction of an inch, and the creature blew apart as the gun made a sound barely louder than the power stapler. Shreds of flesh and droplets of liquid splattered against the walls.

'Something that just doesn't know when to quit,' said Jack.

The device Toshiko was looking at now – the third of the similar alien devices she had found the time to examine – was the one found in the wreckage of an alien escape pod near Mynach Hengoed in the 1950s. That was before she was even born, she reflected. It was flatter than the rest, lenticular, with sharp projections all the way around the edge, some of which had been knocked off over the years as it was moved from crate to crate. It was an orange colour, and had a hole right through the centre. Holding it in her hand, Toshiko thought it was slightly heavier on one side than the other, but she had no more idea about its function than about the rest of the devices in the series.

The series. That was how she was thinking of them. They were all different shapes, sizes and colours, but they were obviously related to one another. Made by the same hands, she was sure. Well, perhaps not hands. Made by the same claws, or tentacles, or mandibles. It didn't matter. She was convinced there was a consistent style running through them.

And perhaps more than just a consistent style.

Voices were echoing through the Hub from the Autopsy Room – Owen's personal domain – distracting Toshiko's attention from the device she held. It sounded like Jack, Owen and Gwen were arguing. Jack and Gwen had come rushing back from the Scotus Clinic looking like something had happened, but they'd headed straight into the medical section without saying anything to her. She'd tried to tell them about the image of the creature inside the girl, but Jack had snapped something about it being 'old news' and kept on walking.

Ianto had followed on a few minutes afterwards, wheeling a body in on a gurney. He too went past Toshiko without acknowledging her existence. Part of her had wanted to follow on to see what all the fuss was about, but she felt awkward. They would tell her when they needed to. When she could help.

Toshiko wondered if there was something technical she could be doing now, but she couldn't think of anything and neither Jack nor any of the others had made any suggestions. Having processed Marianne's medical scans, Toshiko had found herself at something of a loose end, which is why she had returned to looking at the alien devices matching the one that had been found in the nightclub where the young men had died.

Toshiko sometimes wondered whether the others truly felt she was part of the team. They valued her technical knowledge – she knew that – but there were times she felt as if she wasn't part of the decision-making process. Excluded from the action. Marginalised.

Perhaps she just wasn't outgoing enough. She certainly didn't join in the banter as much as the others did. She sometimes felt awkward at the informality of the Torchwood team – she was used to working in a more formalised environment. It was her fault that she didn't integrate with the team. She wished she knew how to do something about it, but she didn't.

Sighing, Toshiko slid the device beneath the scanner head that she had rigged up. It contained sensors that would examine the device in various spectra – microwave, infra-red, ultra-violet and others – and integrate the results together into one picture. Having already done this twice before on two of the other devices, she felt that she had it down to a fine art. And the changes she had made to the software would speed the process up.

As her computer laboured to integrate the various pictures it was receiving, Toshiko tried to hear what the argument was about, but she couldn't make any of the words out. Gwen appeared to be pleading with Jack about something, while Jack was being firm and Owen was throwing in the occasional jibe. Tension was seeping out of the medical area, and Toshiko could feel her shoulders and neck becoming tighter in sympathy. She hated conflict, especially in the Hub where things should have been calm and contemplative.

'Is that one of the objects from tunnel sixteen, chamber twenty-six, shelf eight, box thirteen?'

She jumped at the sound of the voice behind her. Twisting on her seat, she realised that Ianto was standing in the shadows.

'I signed it out,' she said defensively.

'I didn't mean to question you.' He stepped forward. 'I'm just glad that someone is taking an interest in the Archive. All too often we find these things, give them a cursory examination, then put them in a box and forget about them. It's nice that someone cares enough to pull them out every now and then and see if we can't find out something new.'

Toshiko opened her mouth to say something, although she wasn't entirely sure what, but her computer chimed softly. The integration routines had finished their work. She turned to view the screen. Ianto moved up to stand at her shoulder.

'What, if you don't mind me asking, is that?' he asked.

Based on what she had seen in the other two devices, Toshiko was pretty sure she knew exactly what it was. An image. A portrait of an alien creature, looking straight out of the screen at her, formed of components within the device: alien analogues of wires and capacitors, transistors and resistors, integrated circuits and power sources.

This picture was subtly different from the other two. The head was flatter than would be normal for a human, with a vertical slit for a mouth and eyes set at either end of a rugby ball-shaped head, but the head looked plumper than in the images from the other two devices; drooping less at either end and not as wrinkled. The mouth – if that was what it was – seemed more pronounced. If anything, the whole picture looked *younger*.

'I think,' she said carefully, 'it's someone's life story.'

SIXTEEN

'This is like performing brain surgery on a fucking *Smartie*,' Owen muttered as he bent over his autopsy table. He rested a scalpel on top of the yellow pill in the table's centre and pressed down gently. The pill slipped away and skittered to one side, bouncing off the table's metal lip.

Reaching out to a table on one side, where he kept his surgical tools on a metal tray, he retrieved a pair of forceps. With these in his left hand he could hold the pill steady while he gently drew the scalpel across the top of the pill. It left a fine incision behind. Something oily welled up through the incision.

'Interesting,' he murmured. 'I thought this was a dissolvable sugar coating, like you get on some headache pills, but it's more like a harder version of gelatin. It's flexible. With a bit of luck, I might just…' His voice tailed off as he moved the forceps around, getting a better grip on the tablet. Manipulating the scalpel carefully, he extended the incision to the sides of the pill, then slipped the blade beneath the coating and prised it away from the interior. Oil spilled slowly out. In less than a minute, he had removed the coating entirely, stripping it away from the thing that had been hidden inside.

'I hate soft centres,' he said.

'What have you got?' Jack asked from the balcony.

'Well, it's not Turkish Delight, that's for sure.' Reaching out to the tray again, he picked up a pen-like device with a lens and a light at one end. He pointed it at the thing on the autopsy table and pressed a button on the side of the device. The plasma screen above his head faded within a few seconds into a high-definition close-up of the thing. The tip of Owen's scalpel was just visible at the edge of the screen, the size and shape of a garden trowel.

'Oh hell,' said Gwen. She put a hand to her mouth. 'You know what we're looking at, don't you?'

The thing was no more than a centimetre long, and curled into a comma. It was charcoal in colour, with irregular blue stripes, and looked like three very small worms, all joined together at one end. A tiny fuzzy cloud that might have been thousands of minute, translucent, fibres surrounded the free ends. The small teardrop of oily liquid that had surrounded and protected it was spreading out across the metal topography of the table.

Jack nodded. 'Yeah. Yeah, I do.'

'It's an egg,' Owen said. He used the scalpel to unfold the foetal creature. 'It's not a pill at all; it's an egg. A fucking *egg*. And this is the embryo inside.'

'But…' Gwen seemed to run out of words. 'But *why*?' she finished eventually. 'Why would anyone knowingly swallow an egg, especially if it turns into something like *that*?'

'They don't do it knowingly.' Jack clenched his hands on the rail of the balcony, hard enough that Owen heard the metal creak. 'And I think they do it so they can lose weight. Tell her, Owen.'

'I'm guessing that the life cycle of this thing, whatever it is, is similar to that of our own, our very own, tapeworm,' Owen said. He leaned closer, fascinated by the thing on the table in front of him. 'It's probably activated by the acidic contents of the stomach, hatches, then makes its way to the intestine and latches on. It sucks up nutrients, drawn from whatever the host has been eating. There's so sign of a mouth, so I'm guessing it absorbs the partially digested food through its skin.'

'Chyme,' Jack suddenly said.

Gwen looked at him. 'What?'

'Chyme – semi-liquid, partly digested food leaving the stomach and entering the duodenum. Another candidate for my list of words that need to be saved from extinction and used in conversation as often as possible.'

'All eyes on me, please,' Owen said firmly. 'Unless you want to be sent to the naughty corner. Now, unlike a tapeworm, I suspect this thing is voracious. That's why the hosts are hungry all the time, and why they lose weight so fast. They're almost starving, because the thing in their gut is taking all the food away from them before they get a chance to absorb it themselves. It's like a cuckoo: relying on the host to do the hard work then taking advantage of the results.'

'I hope for your sake it's dead,' Jack said.

'Not dead as such, but it's certainly inert. It will only come to life if I swallow it. Which I have no intention of doing. Not even on a bet.'

'What about the other pill?' Jack asked. 'The one labelled "Stop"?'

Owen glanced over at the instrument tray, where three blister packs sat: the one Gwen had found in her own medicine cupboard, the one she had found at Lucy's flat and the one Gwen and Jack had found at the Scotus Clinic. All three packs were now missing their 'Start' pills. Two of them still had the 'Stop' pills remaining. The third was empty. 'I tested one earlier,' he said. 'Basic plant sterol – more or less harmless to humans, but I'm guessing it's deadly to the worm-things. It probably allows the host to digest the remains, so there's nothing left to give the game away.'

'Perfect.' There was something dark in Jack's voice. 'One pill to start the weight loss and another to stop it. Absolutely perfect. Symmetrical, in fact.'

Owen reached out and took a pair of tweezers from the tray. 'Perfect apart from all the side effects,' he said, picking the creature gently up from the autopsy table and holding it close to his face, turning it around so he could examine it from all aspects. 'That raging hunger isn't everything – there's psychotic behaviour as well. We don't know what causes that yet. And from what you said, the mature form of this thing leaped out of the receptionist's throat, rupturing a major blood vessel in the process before it attacked you. That's not the kind of behaviour that I've ever seen a tapeworm exhibit. It almost indicates awareness, perhaps even consciousness.'

'Is it intelligent?' Gwen asked. 'Could we communicate with it?'

'I don't think the brain's big enough to hold much intelligence. I think it's going on instinct, and some basic processing of sensory inputs. What surprises me is the way you say it attacked you. Tapeworms are just inert assemblages of self-replicating segments. This thing – whatever it is – has the ability to sense where things are, decide they are threats and move to do something about that threat. Wherever their natural habitat is, they probably stalk their prey in some way before either laying eggs inside it or colonising it in the adult form.'

The colour had drained away from Gwen's face. Her throat was working as if she was trying to stop herself throwing up.

'We'll call it George,' Jack said suddenly.

'Call what George?'

'The parasite that's inside your boyfriend. Makes it easier if we label them differently. Stops us getting confused. The one that attacked us in the Scotus Clinic was Ringo, the one inside Rhys is George, the one inside Marianne Till is Paul and that leaves the one inside Lucy Sobel as John.'

'You forgot this one,' Owen said, waggling the tiny alien creature back and forth in the air.

'This one can be Stuart. As in Sutcliffe.'

'Who was Stuart Sutcliffe?' Gwen's hand, still raised to her mouth, muffled her words, and Owen had to think for a moment before he could figure them out.

'He was the one who left the Beatles in Hamburg, before they made it big. Nice guy. Invented the mop-top haircut, believe it or not. Dab hand at the old collage technique. Girlfriend's name was Astrid, I think. Or Ingrid. One of the two.'

'Jack.' Gwen's voice was tremulous. 'We have to get rid of them. All of them. We've got the "Stop" pills. We can get Rhys and Marianne and Lucy to take the pills before anything worse happens to them.'

Jack looked down at Owen. *Tell her,* Jack's eyes were saying.

'We don't know anything about the life cycle of these creatures,' Owen said slowly. It was the same tone of voice he used to use when he was telling people that they had some inoperable cancer, or they were going to be paralysed for life. Slow, firm and reassuring. 'And we don't know how many other people are infected. I need one of the "Stop" pills so I can analyse it to see whether it can be synthesized, and we need to keep at least one of these creatures alive so we can study it and determine what it wants, what it needs, how it grows, how *fast* it grows and what its weaknesses are.'

Gwen turned towards Jack. 'We only need one of them. Owen just said so – you heard him. We can give two of them the pills.'

'And who gets to choose?' Jack asked. He looked from Owen to Gwen and back again. 'Which one of us gets to play God? Or would you rather we drew straws?'

'Rhys is my *boyfriend!*' she said, looking from one to the other. 'Doesn't that count for anything?'

'And Marianne's a nice girl with a family,' Owen snapped. Something in him felt close to breaking point. He'd failed Marianne so far: he wasn't going to fail her any more.

'And no boyfriend,' Jack reminded him.

'That's not the point,' Owen shouted, rounding on him.

'But what about Lucy?' Jack asked them both. 'I'm sure she's got a family as well. Doesn't she deserve the best chance we can give her?'

'She's a murderer,' Owen reminded them both. Turning to Gwen, he said, 'Do you want her to get away with killing her boyfriend? Isn't it right that we keep the creature in her alive and save Marianne and Rhys?'

'Punishment isn't the same as justice,' Gwen said slowly, shaking her head. 'Jack's right – we don't have the right to choose.'

Owen's fists clenched in frustration. 'I do. I'm going to give Marianne the "Stop" pill,' he said. 'She's suffered enough.' Before Jack or Gwen could stop him he grabbed one of the blister packs off the instrument tray and dashed for the door.

He could hear the sound of their pounding footsteps echoing off the Victorian brickwork as he sprinted through the tunnels of Torchwood. Gwen was shouting his name; Jack was silent but Owen could sense his steely determination.

His own breath rasped in his ears and burned in his chest. He could feel his blood pulsing through the arteries in his throat and in his temples. He couldn't tell how close they were; any second he expected a hand to close on his shoulder, pulling him back, but it never did.

Skidding round a corner, he reached the cells. The Weevil in the closest one was pressed up against the glass, sniffing at the air and exposing its teeth, but he paid no attention to it. He kept going, past the cell where Lucy was incarcerated and on to the end cell, where Marianne waited for him.

'I've got it!' he called. 'The cure. Just one tablet and you'll be fine! I promise!'

Marianne didn't answer. She was slumped in her cell, her bandaged hands with their damaged fingers still chained to the wall so she couldn't chew on them again.

Instead, she had found a different way to feed on herself. She had twisted her body around so that she could reach her upper right arm with her teeth. She must have dislocated her shoulder to manage it. Owen knew that she had dislocated her shoulder because she had chewed all the way through her arm, regardless of the pain, until there wasn't enough flesh left to keep it attached. With no joint there to hold the arm in, the weight of her body had pulled her shoulder and her arm apart, tearing through what few muscles and tendons remained. Her body had flopped forward onto the stone flooring, while her arm dangled separately from the restraint above.

The stone floor of the cell was a lake of glutinous blood.

Marianne's head had dropped forward on her chest, and her hair, her gorgeous blonde hair, hung over her eyes.

Owen slumped to his knees. The blister pack dropped from his fingers. He felt as if a yawning chasm had opened up within him, an abyss into which his heart was dropping.

'Owen,' came Jack's voice from beside him. Strong fingers took his head and turned it until he was looking straight into Jack's eyes. Jack was kneeling beside him, and Gwen was kneeling beside them both. 'Owen, I will ask many hard things of you. This is not the hardest, not even close, but it will seem that way. It will seem like the hardest thing in the world. Owen, I need you to cut Marianne's body open as quickly as you can and get that thing out of her. It might be still alive, and we need to find out all we can about it. I won't ask you if you can do that for me, because you *will* do it for me. Do you understand? You *will* do it.'

Owen nodded bleakly. Of course he would do it. What else was left? He used to be a doctor. He used to cure people. Now… now he couldn't even cure himself, let alone anyone else.

While Gwen went back for a trolley, Jack opened up the door to the cell. He had his Webley ready, just in case the creature – what had Jack christened it? Paul? – made some attempt to escape the cage of dead flesh that was holding it.

Owen just watched, still kneeling on the ground, as the two of them released Marianne's left arm from the restraints, placed her body on the trolley, then released her right arm from the restraints and placed that beside her. His heart had dropped away into that unfathomable abyss within him. He couldn't feel anything. There was nothing left to feel.

With Marianne on the metal surface of the autopsy table, and with Gwen and Jack watching silently from the gallery, Owen carefully cut the clothes off her body. Part of him remembered how desperately he had wanted to see her naked, but the sight of her body did nothing for him now. Marianne wasn't there any more. What was her was the way she had held herself, the way she had tilted her head, the way her eyes had seemed to come alive when she got talking about her favourite things – that had been Marianne. And that had gone.

Mechanically, Owen made a deep lateral incision from shoulder to ruined shoulder, dipping down to touch Marianne's xiphoid process as he crossed the sternum, then a second incision from the xiphoid process down to the groin, cutting through muscle and yellow body fat. Blood welled thickly from the incisions. Using his hands, he pulled the incisions apart, revealing the internal organs. Normally he would cut through the ribs and cartilage next, exposing the heart, lungs and trachea, but he wasn't conducting an autopsy – he was looking for one very particular thing.

Looking up at the gallery, where a grim-faced Toshiko and Ianto had now joined Jack and Gwen, he nodded at Toshiko. She pressed a button on a remote control she was holding, and the image of Marianne's torso, taken by Toshiko's ultrasound scanner, flashed up on the high-definition screen that hung above the table. The colour-coding showed where the creature was – or where it had been. Palpating Marianne's duodenum, Owen quickly located the right stretch of intestine. He could feel something in there more solid than pre-digested food. It seemed to shift slightly under his questing fingers. Reaching out to the instrument tray, he retrieved a couple of clamps and used them to secure either end of the organ, above and below the creature. A few strokes with a scalpel and he had isolated that entire section – about a metre's worth of wet, pink flesh. He lifted it clear and placed it in a metal bowl, then placed the bowl on the table beside Marianne's abused body.

Ianto, unbidden, had retrieved a large glass jar from storage. It had a lid that could be fastened securely on top, and nozzles top and bottom so that liquid or gas could be introduced or extracted. It was about the size of Marianne's head. Owen had sometimes used it for chemical experiments, but it suited his purpose now. From his chemical store, he obtained some hydrochloric acid and poured it into the jar, along with some distilled water and various other chemicals. By this time, guessing what he was doing, Gwen had scoured the Hub for whatever scraps of food she could find – old pizza crusts, sandwiches, bags of sweets, stuff from the refrigerator, anything that could be used to replicate the internal environment of a digestive system. Owen tipped them into the jar. Within moments the mixture had turned cloudy and curdled, and the sharp smell of the acid had been replaced by something nastier and more faecal.

Owen retrieved the section of Marianne's intestine from the metal bowl and held it up above the jar. This was going to be the tricky bit. Somewhere in the background, he could sense Jack bringing his revolver out of his coat, holding it ready in case the creature tried to escape, as it had from the receptionist at the Scotus Clinic.

Owen held the scalpel in steady hands, preparing to make the final cut. He held the length of intestine by one end, just above the clamp, and sliced vertically downwards. The cut gaped open, pressed by something heavy within. For a moment, Owen was worried that the creature wouldn't relinquish its grip, but it must have sensed a change in the health of its host. Whatever means it used to maintain hold on the inside of the gut, whatever hooks or suckers it was using, had been released. As Owen watched, a slimy black and blue mass slid out of Marianne's intestine and fell into the jar, splashing the liquid up the sides where it stuck in globs, which then slid down again to rejoin the mass.

Ripples spread across the surface of the liquid, but Owen thought he could see the creature moving, digging itself deeper into the biological muck.

'Ladies and Gentlemen, meet Paul,' he said, the first words he had spoken since he had found Marianne's body. 'Paul is formerly the occupant of Miss Marianne Till. Paul will be staying with us for a while. Please make him feel welcome.' He gazed up at Toshiko. 'Tosh, you're the most technical one here, so I'm going to tell you what to do next. The hydrochloric acid and the scraps of food will resemble the contents of a gut, which will make Paul here feel at home. I don't fancy keeping it like this, however – too messy and it's going to stink to high heaven. What I want you to do is drain the jar in about four hours, and while you're draining it, flush it through with nutrient solution. You'll find bags of it labelled up in the fridge. Set up a drip so the nutrient solution gets introduced into the jar at the same rate as it's removed. Set it up so that a bag lasts about two hours. That may be overdoing it, but I don't think these things can be overfed, somehow. All clear?'

Toshiko nodded.

Gwen tried to catch his eye, but he wouldn't look at her. 'Owen,' she said: 'what happens now? You're talking like you're not going to be around.'

'I'm not, for a while,' he said. 'I'm going to go and find a dark corner somewhere, and I'm going to get as drunk as I can, as fast as I can. And then I'm going to have sex with as many people as I can in as short a space of time as I can. I don't know how many records I'm going to break, but alert the media anyway. Someone named Owen will come back later on, when he's ready, but it won't be me. I'll be gone.'

He placed his mobile phone on the instrument tray and walked out without looking back.

Owen left the Hub via the lift that led up to the water tower in front of the Millennium Centre. He stood there, on the slab of stone that had been touched by something special in the past and from where nobody could see him, no matter how close they were, and he watched people walk by, individually, in couples and in groups.

The world went on. Life went on. Just because Marianne had died, it didn't mean that anything else had changed.

After a while he stepped forward, off the slab and onto the wooden slats that paved the entire area in front of the Centre. Still, nobody noticed him. They walked around him, barely avoiding touching his arms, but nobody would look him in the eye. It was as if he had ceased to exist.

He headed for a bar on Bute Street where he could get absolutely wrecked in the sure knowledge that they would keep on serving him drinks. He started on beer with a whisky chaser, on the basis that it was fast and effective. While he was drinking, he tried to let all conscious thought drain away. Sensation washed over him and receded. The only things that mattered were the warm, smoky taste of the whisky and the coldness of the beer, sluicing his throat.

When he realised that he had lost count of how much he had drunk, he moved on to another bar, and then another. All around him people were picking each other up or picking fights with each other, but nobody tried to talk to him. There was a deadness in his eyes, or in his soul, that discouraged them. Life just washed around him.

Eventually, of course, he went back. Where else was there to go?

The Hub, unusually, was empty. Owen kept walking, towards the Autopsy Room.

Ianto was standing outside. He was peering nervously around the edge of the doorway.

'Where is everyone?' Owen asked.

'Gwen has gone to be with her boyfriend,' Ianto replied. 'Jack has said that if she can persuade him to take the "Stop" pill then he's happy to let it go. Jack and Tosh are out looking for Doctor Scotus, and I've been spending my time either here or the cells.'

'Doing what?'

'Watching the creature Jack calls Paul develop and looking after Lucy Sobel. The things you should have been doing.'

Owen felt like hitting Ianto square in the face. 'What's up?' he asked instead. 'Why are you skulking out here?'

'Ah – we had a slight problem with Paul,' Ianto said, edgily. 'I think I may have had the nutrient solution pumping in too fast. It seems to have absorbed too much too fast.'

Owen pushed him out of the way and glanced into the room.

The Autopsy Room was much as he had left it, except that the glass jar that he had put Paul in was lying on its side, smashed into large fragments.

Paul was on the autopsy table. It wasn't a worm any more. It was about the size of a rat, but consisted of a long black body, sharpening to a vicious point at both ends, striped with electric blue. Two gauzy, gossamer fans which had emerged from the central body were thrumming the air.

'Fuck me,' Owen said. 'It's Paul McCartney, with wings!'

SEVENTEEN

The SUV drifted like a polished black ghost through the streets of Cardiff, reflecting the cars and buildings that it passed. Every now and then, Jack would take it past the half-silvered glass of an office block, and Toshiko would look out of the window to see a corridor of multiplied images extending to infinity, mirrors reflecting mirrors.

What with that, Jack's driving and the device she was holding, Toshiko was beginning to wish she hadn't come up with her Big Idea.

'How are you feeling?' Jack yelled back.

'Irritated,' she called over the engine hum. 'And tired. And exhilarated. And bored.'

'But not hungry?'

'No more than usual.'

She shifted the map from her lap and raised the alien device slightly to aim it more squarely out of the window. It was the one they had found in the nightclub. It seemed like weeks ago that she had turned over Craig Sutherland's body to see it lying there, but it was actually only four or five days. Things had moved so fast.

A pang of suppressed sexual longing ran through her, making her feel as if her heart was about to burst, then it was gone, leaving her shuddering and empty. She moaned.

'OK?'

'It's… difficult. So many emotions.'

'I know. We have to keep going, Tosh.'

'Yes. We do.'

Toshiko had set the device up as best she could to amplify distant traces of emotion and reflect them back to her. The problem was, driving round the city left her at the mercy of a thousand different feelings. Emotions were what differentiated humans from animals, that's what they said, but Toshiko was finding herself swamped by an animalistic mass of basic drives and fears. For a person who valued logic and order above all things, it was terrifying. Or was she just picking up on someone else's terror, somewhere close by?

The car drove past another anonymous office block, and she felt a wave of crashing tedium sweep over her. Why was she even doing this? It was as boring as chewing sand.

She was just about to throw the device out of the window and curl into a ball on her seat when Jack took a corner, and the boredom was replaced with edginess. She glanced at the back of Jack's head, sure that he had turned to check her out while she wasn't looking. He hated the fact that she was technologically cleverer than he was. He only kept his position as leader by destroying those who could replace him. He'd done it to Suzie, and he was going to do it to her if she didn't kill him first.

Her hand curled around the butt of the automatic pistol that she kept beside her. One quick shot to the back of the neck and she could take control of Torchwood.

She raised the pistol and took aim at Jack.

Gwen looked across at Rhys. They were standing on the edge of Cardiff Bay, on a small beach of grey and black pebbles, looking out across the water. Gulls bobbed nearby, hoping for a crust of bread or a fragment from a burger bun. She knew she should be at Torchwood, helping to track Doctor Scotus down, but she needed to make sure that Rhys was safe.

What was the point in saving the world if you weren't allowed to save the ones you loved?

There was almost no sign that Rhys's cheek had been almost torn off, just days before. The skin was pinker, less weathered than the rest of his face, but it wasn't like he was the kind of guy who spent his life halfway up the Amazon or halfway across the Gobi, and consequently had a face weathered to buggery. A couple of days of sun and wind and you wouldn't be able to tell the difference between one side and the other.

'Look, I'm having trouble grasping this,' he said. 'That tablet – you're saying it was *contaminated?*'

'I checked with the Department of Health,' she said smoothly. 'They're worried that the tablets might be adulterated with something. It's a bit like that scare a few years back about the Chinese herbal remedies, when they discovered that in high doses they could cause liver failure, but because they are classified as a herbal supplement rather than a drug people are still allowed to sell them. Same story here.'

'Why is it,' Rhys asked, 'that we have a Department *of* Health but a Department *for* Transport, a *Ministry* of Defence and a Home *Office*. There's no consistency there at all.'

'Rhys – focus!'

'Yeah, sorry.' He thought for a moment, and his face crumpled into a worried grimace. 'The thing is, they worked! I've lost a good stone and a half since I took the first tablet.'

'And you look great,' she said, reassuringly. And it was true. Rhys hadn't looked as slim for as long as she had known him. His stomach was flat, his arms and thighs were taut and his arse… that was just fantastic. Part of Gwen wished she could get that effect as quickly, but she wouldn't pay the price that Lucy or Marianne had. No, it was back to running through darkened hospital corridors and alleyways for her.

'And you reckon this is why Lucy had such a bad reaction?'

'Psychotic episode brought on by whatever complex biochemical stuff was in the pill. Apparently they've had complaints from all over South Wales.'

'Hasn't hit the news,' he said, puzzled.

'BBC Wales have been doing an undercover investigation. Apparently they're going to blow the lid off it in a new documentary in a month or so.'

'Oh.' He seemed strangely impressed at the mention of BBC Wales, as though it lent the story some extra credibility. 'OK, I understand about the pills, and I understand about Lucy. What I *don't* understand is, if the pills are potentially so dangerous, why do you want me to take the second one?'

* * *

Owen stared at the squat, black shape and goggled.

The tentacular arms seemed to have melded together, forming a long, thin body, and then the whole thing had grown two pairs of diaphanous wings, each one a third of the way along the body, that looked like they were beating at several hundred beats per second. The thing was both radially and bilaterally symmetrical, with the body knobbly in the middle but coming to a sharp point front and back. From what he could see, there were clusters of deep-set eyes, like jewels, at both ends. With those wings it was likely to be fast, and if it could go in both directions then it was likely to be highly manoeuvrable.

It was like a flying knife.

Ianto looked over his shoulder. 'What happened to it?' he asked.

'I think we're dealing with a multi-stage life cycle,' Owen replied. 'There's the egg, of course, and there's the creature that sits in the gut, absorbing nutrients. And then there's this. Probably the egg-laying stage.'

'What does it do – cut its way out of the host and fly off?'

'Don't be melodramatic. That's more like *Alien* than it is real life.' He thought fast, trying to connect what he knew of biology with what he'd observed of this thing in its various stages. 'I'm working on the assumption that something this evolved isn't a parasite at all. It's not in its best interests to kill the host, cos it wouldn't last long without a source of food. And I don't think the worm form is built for hiking long distances in search of one. No, it wants to keep the host alive so it keeps getting fed, but what if the host dies? Then it's faced with a mass of flesh which it can metabolise quickly, triggering a new stage of development.' His voice was getting faster as he worked through the implications of what he was saying and saw the conclusion that he was coming to. 'So when the host dies, it grows wings and turns itself into a flying dart.'

'But why?' Ianto pressed.

'So it can aim itself at some animal moving along the ground, fly at it really fast and embed itself in the animal's body, either killing it or causing severe wounds. It lays its eggs and it dies. Then scavengers come along and eat the remains of the dead animal, unwittingly snaffling up a whole load of eggs at the same time. And the cycle starts again.'

'That *is* like *Alien*,' Ianto pointed out, 'with some modifications so it makes more sense.'

'Shut up,' Owen said, absently. He tried to imagine what life was like on this creature's world. Nasty, brutish and short, he thought, which for some reason also reminded him of a girl he'd shagged a few months back.

'OK,' Ianto said. 'Now that you've cleverly worked out that it's a flying, egg-laying dealer of death, I have another question.'

'What's that?'

'Which one of us is going to go in there and get it?'

The corrosive paranoia dripped away from her, and Toshiko was suddenly confronted with the fact that she had badly underestimated this device. The emotions she was receiving were too strong. She wasn't able to cope. She threw the automatic away from her, onto the seat that Owen usually occupied, horrified at the terrible mistake she had almost made.

Toshiko's position as technical expert to Torchwood was based on a couple of lucky guesses she'd made early on, but ever since then she had failed at whatever task she had been set. Jack only kept her on out of pity. The best thing she could do was to pack her bags and return to London. A despairing wail escaped her lips. There was no escape!

'Tosh, stay focused.'

'I'm trying. I'm really trying,' she wept.

The device's field of view passed across a man dressed in a tattered and stained overcoat and ragged trousers. His shoes were tied to his feet with string, and he was pushing a shopping trolley ahead of him. It appeared to be filled with old magazines. Toshiko cringed, expecting madness to wrap itself around her mind, infiltrating black tendrils into every aspect of her thoughts, but instead all the colours in the sky and the road and the cars seemed to intensify, as if a rainbow had descended from the sky and coated everything with light. She wanted to lean out of the window and let the wind ruffle her hair while she called out to passers-by, telling them how wonderful the world could be if only you opened your heart to it.

The car drove on leaving the vagrant behind, trailing his cloud of joy, and Toshiko felt like crying at what she had lost. For a moment there she'd had the secret of existence in her hand, and it had been snatched away.

Hunger squirmed inside her, and her mouth suddenly filled with saliva.

She could smell meat on the breeze, and it was almost driving her mad. She was just about to tell Jack that she thought she had something when she noticed that the device was pointing across a dual carriageway at a Mexican restaurant. She must have been picking up on the hunger of the diners inside. She adjusted her aim away from the restaurant to take in another section of the city.

It was as if she had driven off the edge of a cliff and was falling into a chasm of starvation. Her stomach knotted tight and her hands began to shake. She couldn't think straight: every sight, every sound, every smell reminded her that she desperately needed to eat.

She nudged the device sideways, perspiration beading her forehead, and the feeling was gone, melting away to leave nothing behind. If what she had felt before, passing the restaurant, was hunger, then this had been famine, multiplied many times over.

Quickly she worked out the bearing that the feeling had come from and drew a line across the map, starting at the rough position of the car and extending across the city. She turned to Jack and said: 'I think I have something. It's coming from the east.'

'Strong?'

'Almost overpowering.'

'OK.' He swung the SUV into a tight turn. 'Sorry to do this to you, Tosh, but we need to triangulate that signal. Keep scanning until you get it again. Let's hope it's what we're looking for.'

Oh bollocks, Gwen thought. 'The second pill isn't made from the same plant extracts,' she said carefully. 'It's more of a standard drug, like paracetamol, but it flushes the body of… of impurities. It sensitises the liver to the stuff that was in the first pill and helps your body eliminate it. The Department of Health have given it a clean bill of health. As it were.'

'Right. OK.' He shrugged. 'I'll take the second pill when I get home, then, if that's what you want.'

Gwen fished in her pocket and brought out the blister pack that she'd removed from their bathroom cabinet. 'Here – take it now.'

'God, you're keen.'

'I worry about you.'

216

He smiled. 'Really? Cos I like it when you worry.'

'Take the pill, Rhys.'

He slipped it into his mouth and swallowed it straight away. Gwen didn't know how he could do that without a glass of water. Was it a bloke thing? Did they practise with aspirin, just so they could impress girls with their manly pill-swallowing abilities?

'Done,' he said. 'So what's going to happen to Lucy?'

'She's under medical supervision. The pill affected her quite badly.'

'Yeah.' He shook his head. 'Now she's lost some weight, she should really dump that boyfriend. He's nothing but trouble. I keep telling her that.'

'I think she's digested the message,' Gwen said, looking away to suppress her shudder at what she'd found in Lucy's flat. She still had to talk to Jack about what they could do with Lucy, who was still back in Torchwood, imprisoned.

'So…' Rhys said, reaching out to stroke her cheek, 'you got to get off back to Torchwood, or have we got time for a quick shag?'

She looked around at the pebbles and the seaweed. 'What – *here*?'

'Not here, stupid. Back *home*.'

She considered. On the one hand, Jack and Toshiko were out tracking Doctor Scotus while Owen was missing, presumed drunk, and they probably needed her help. On the other hand, she really should stay with Rhys until she knew the pill had taken effect, otherwise they might have another of those creatures on their hands.

'You've talked me into it, you smooth-tongued bastard,' she said, but Rhys had stopped listening. He was clutching his stomach in alarm.

'Oh hell,' he said. 'I need a bog, and I need it fast!'

As Owen edged into the Autopsy Room, the creature stirred, flexing its body and raising both ends up from the table. Owen could hear a sound coming from it, a rustling sound, like someone wading through dry grass.

'Nice Paul,' he said. 'I really liked "Magneto and Titanium Man". Classic track, in my opinion.'

He eased himself into the room. The creature moved to track him with its tiny eyes. Owen assumed it was tracking his body heat, seeing him in the infra-red.

Owen moved to the right, leaving enough space for Ianto to slip into the room and move to the left. They separated, each one moving in a different direction around the gallery that encircled the walls. The creature wasn't sure which one of them to go for, moving its 'head' uncertainly from one to the other and back again.

'"Band on the Run" was great as well,' Owen went on, trying to distract the creature with sound as well as movement. He didn't know whether it could hear him or not – maybe it could track vibrations as well as heat. Worth a go, at any rate. 'Although I never understood that line about the rain exploding with a mighty crash as they fell into the sun. What's that all about then?'

He and Ianto were about ninety degrees apart now, and the creature was still uncertain which of them to concentrate on. Perfect. From behind his back Owen pulled out the alien device that Toshiko had found in the Archive, the one that looked like a pumped-up clover leaf with a stalk hanging down, the one she said projected small electrical shocks along an ionised path, like a low-power ray gun. 'Right,' he said, 'get ready to—'

With a sickening lurch in the pit of his stomach, Owen suddenly realised that he and Ianto had kept on moving past the ninety-degree point and were now almost in a straight line with the autopsy table in the middle. That would have been fine if the creature had had just the one head and had to still keep looking at both of them, but Paul effectively had two heads, one at each end. And with both Owen and Ianto now safely under observation, it attacked, flinging itself off the table and propelling itself through the air at fantastic speed using its insectile wings.

At Ianto.

'Get down!' Owen yelled. Ianto dropped out of sight behind the railing on the gallery. The creature hit the brick wall, embedding itself an inch into the mortar, then flexing its body back and forth and using its wings to pull itself out. It hovered in mid-air for a moment, looking around for sources of heat. And it found Owen. One moment it was there, the next it was a blur, heading for his chest.

Owen brought the alien device up and pulled what Toshiko had confidently told him was the trigger. It shuddered in his grip, and the air between him and the living missile was filled with light. The creature bucked, losing its aerodynamic form and suddenly becoming something more like a boomerang. It spun crazily through the air before bouncing off the wall next to Owen's head and falling to the gallery, stunned. Or dead. Owen didn't much care which.

'Wouldn't it have been easier to just gas it?' Ianto asked.

Owen gestured towards the doorway. 'No door,' he said, breathless. 'Whoever designed this place didn't count on anything in the Autopsy Room wanting to get out again, which just goes to show how little they knew about Torchwood.'

Jack and Toshiko came breezing into the Hub at the same time as Gwen. Well, actually, as far as Gwen could see, Jack was breezing and Toshiko was more like a slight waft of air.

'Tosh – are you OK?' she asked.

Toshiko offered up a wan smile. 'I've been better,' she said.

Jack took the spiral metal stairs up to the Boardroom three at a time. 'Everyone get together,' he said. 'We're going to go for the big finale.'

Gwen and Toshiko exchanged glances before following him up the stairs and past the large portholes – former pipes that had been sealed off – that looked out into the murky waters of the bay. Small fish were playing around in the crevices in the brickwork.

Owen and Ianto arrived from the medical area, having presumably heard the commotion. Owen was carrying something under a blanket.

'Coffee?' Ianto asked as they all congregated in the Boardroom and sat down around the conference table.

'You're going to need it,' Jack said. 'We've got a packed programme ahead of us.' As Ianto fiddled with the machine outside the door, Jack took up a position in front of the wide window that looked down into the Hub, legs apart and hands on hips. 'Right, let's clear up some loose ends. Gwen – what's the story with Rhys and George Harrison?'

'Rhys has taken the second pill, and he's flushed the disintegrating remnants of George down the toilet in the noisiest and most unpleasant way possible. But he's clear. Thanks.'

'No problem. Ianto, where are we with young Lucy and John Lennon?'

Ianto glanced in from the platform outside. 'Miss Sobel is still confined in the cells. Having learned our lesson from the unfortunate Miss Till, we've made sure her arms and legs are firmly pinioned and she has a metal gag in her mouth – a scold's bridle, I think it's called. And we're pumping a vaporised form of anaesthetic into the cell to keep her sedated.'

'Yeah, and who's idea was that?' Owen snapped. 'I thought I was the doctor around here?'

'You went AWOL,' Jack said calmly, 'so we had to improvise.' He turned back to Ianto. 'I think we're safe to feed her the second pill now. Put it in her food or something. Owen can clear the cell out when she's finished clearing John Lennon out of her system.'

'Thanks a bunch,' Owen muttered.

'Hey, don't complain. You left us in a mess, so I'm leaving you with a mess. What goes around, comes around.' Jack glanced around the faces at the table. 'OK. George and Ringo are dead, John is on the way out and Stuart never got a look in. So where's Paul?'

Owen pulled the blanket from the object that he'd brought up with him. It was an old-fashioned bird-cage made of metal rods, flat on the bottom and curved on the top, but the thing inside wasn't a canary. In fact, Gwen wasn't sure what it was. It's body was long and thin and winged, but it looked cowed.

'This,' Owen announced, 'is Paul. He's gone solo and reinvented himself.'

'Seriously,' Jack said. 'What *is* that thing?'

'Seriously, it's the next stage in the life cycle of the worms.'

'It's a flying egg-layer with extreme prejudice,' Ianto added helpfully, bringing in a tray full of coffees.

'The worm lurks in the gut, absorbing nutrients, until the host dies,' Owen explained. 'The worm then turns into this thing, which flies around until it can bury itself in something living – probably some kind of grazing animal, but I'm sure anything would do. We'll call that the secondary host. This thing lays eggs, and dies. The eggs are then eaten by whatever eats the secondary host, and the cycle starts all over again.'

'And I'm sure that on its home planet it works out perfectly,' Jack said, 'but here on Earth it's trying to impose itself on a different set of hosts, and

I'm not going to let that happen. And I also want to know where Doctor Scotus fits into all this, which brings us on to what Toshiko and I did this afternoon. Using that alien tech which amplifies distant emotions, we triangulated on a place on the outskirts of Cardiff where there's a large concentration of very hungry people. Either there's a Weight Watchers convention going on, or Doctor Scotus's clinic is up and running somewhere else.'

'Why would he get all the people who have taken the pill already to congregate together?' Gwen asked. 'It doesn't make sense.'

'Remember the attempt to kidnap Lucy Sobel?' Jack asked. 'I think Doctor Scotus has realised his little pills are having side effects, and he's trying to get the evidence off the streets. I think when we get there we'll find that he's managed to scoop up most, if not all, of the kids who bought into his little weight-loss scheme, and he's probably wondering right now what he's going to do with them. So get ready, boys and girls, because we're not going to let this go on any longer. I can accept a lot in life, but preying on the helpless and the gullible is out of line. I want you armed and ready to go in ten minutes.' He glanced over at the cage on the table, and the creature that sulked within it. 'And bring Paul. I think I may have a use for him.'

EIGHTEEN

The sun was setting over towards the centre of the city, silhouetting the expensive high-rise hotels against a background of scarlet, purple and blue. From her position squashed in the back of the SUV, Gwen could see past a concrete jetty to where water roiled, thick and slow.

'Where the hell are we?' Owen asked as the SUV coasted to a halt under Ianto's careful hands. He got out of the car and looked around, hands on hips. 'Don't think I've ever been around here before.'

'You know the bit of Cardiff Docks that was redeveloped into an expensive marina where they hold dragon boat races and stuff?' Jack asked as he too climbed out of the car.

'Yeah.'

'This isn't it.'

Gwen slid out of the passenger side. 'Somewhere over near Bute East Dock?' she ventured, recognising the angle at which she was seeing some of the taller tower blocks. She reached back into the car and retrieved the bird-cage in which Owen and Ianto had imprisoned the flying thing. An improvised cover had been placed over it, shielding the creature from casual attention.

'Spot on,' said Jack. He looked around, hair ruffling in the breeze coming in off the bay. 'Ianto – I want you here, with the engine running. We may need to get out in a hurry. Everybody else, are you tooled up?'

Last out of the SUV, Gwen checked her Glock 17. It was big and clumsy and heavy, and every time she fired it she thought she was going to fracture her wrist, but she knew she was going to need it. That was Torchwood for you. 'Check,' she said.

'Check,' Owen confirmed.

'Check,' softly from Toshiko.

'And that's a big Texas check from me too,' Jack finished. 'Just because I'm the boss it doesn't mean I can get out of these things.' He indicated a low building with a much larger extension on one end over near where the water rolled back and forth like a caged animal. 'This whole area was part of the dock operations a hundred years or so ago. That building over there was a meat-packing factory, turning imported frozen carcasses from Argentina into stuff you can put on shelves and keep for ever. The place closed down back in the 1970s, and there were so many holding companies and front companies involved that nobody can track down who owns it now, so it's standing right in the way of redevelopment. Toshiko and I identified it as a hunger hotspot earlier on. Apt, I suppose. I'm guessing this is where Doctor Scotus is hiding out.'

'What's the plan?' Gwen asked, coming alongside Jack.

'We go in, we get the innocent parties out, kill any worm or flying thing we can find, destroy all the diet pills, leave, have dinner and sleep the sleep of the just. Did I leave anything out?'

'That's a strategy,' Gwen said. 'What about the tactics?'

Jack stared at her. 'We go in,' he repeated, 'we get the innocent parties out, kill any worm or flying thing we can find, destroy all the diet pills, leave, have dinner and sleep the sleep of the just.'

'OK, just checking.' Gwen raised her eyebrows. 'I always like to know what's expected of me.'

'Problem is,' Jack said, 'we don't know what's going on in there. Always difficult to come up with tactics when you don't know what you're facing. If you try, you might end up facing a tank with a peashooter or trying to kill a mosquito with an elephant gun. Best tactic is not to have a tactic. Play it by ear.'

'And what happens when it all goes wrong?'

'That's the great thing about not having tactics,' Jack grinned. 'Whatever happens, you can claim that's what you intended.'

He led the way across to the building. 'According to the plans that

Toshiko called up,' he said over his shoulder, 'there's a side door along here. We'll go in that way.'

'Tactics?' Gwen muttered.

'Nearest door,' Jack replied.

The door was padlocked, but a few seconds with the Leatherman and it was open.

'Where did you learn to do that?' Owen asked, impressed.

'You pick these things up when you're in the police.'

The door opened inwards onto a corridor that ran left and right along the side of the building. Jack looked both ways, then pointed down to the right. 'Owen, Tosh – you take that way. Gwen and I will head left. Scout the place out, don't alert anyone to your presence, meet back here in ten minutes, try not to touch anything or set off any alarms.'

'Tactics!' Gwen said beneath her breath as she picked the shrouded bird-cage up from where she had left it.

'Common sense,' Jack said.

As Owen and Toshiko went off to the right, Jack set off along the corridor to the left. The floor was dusty along the edges, but clear in the centre, Gwen could make out wheel tracks in the dust. 'There's been some traffic along here,' she said, nodding towards it. 'And recently.'

'I'd feel more comfortable,' Jack admitted, 'if we actually knew what this Scotus guy is up to. That way we could just burst in and stop him. Trouble is, we need to find out what he's doing *first*, and *then* stop him, which complicates things.'

They passed a series of square metal doors with thick glass windows set at eye level and little control boxes beside them, which Gwen assumed controlled some kind of refrigeration. She glanced in through one of two of the windows, but it was dark inside and she couldn't see anything apart from a flutter that may have been a reflection of something behind her, a moth or a fly or something. Placing her hand on one of the doors, she thought she could detect a slight tremor, but she wasn't sure.

She looked off to her right. Toshiko and Owen had vanished around a bend. They were on their own.

Jack had reached the end of the corridor, where a fire extinguisher was attached to the wall, heavily coated in fluffy dust.

A door was set into the wall. 'Shall we see what's inside?' Jack asked.

'Tactics?' she smiled.

'Foolhardiness,' he grinned, and threw the door open.

Owen and Toshiko walked cautiously along their half of the corridor. The floor was tiled in black Formica, and the walls were patchily painted. Rectangular neon lights hung from chains on the ceiling. A pair of double doors terminated the corridor: they had plastic sheets attached along their bottom edges and, judging by the curved marks they had left, would scrape along the ground when the doors were opened. Toshiko assumed that their job was to keep moisture out, which indicated that whatever was on the other side was open to the elements, at least some of the time,

Toshiko's foot caught on a raised floor tile, and she staggered to the wall, placing her hand against it to steady herself. A deep vibration transmitted itself from the wall to her arm. She took her hand away, but realised that she could still just about make the vibration out, transmitted through the floor and the air.

'Can you hear something?' she asked Owen.

He cocked his head to listen. 'Heartbeat?' he asked uncertainly.

'Generator,' she corrected.

Owen placed his hands in the centres of the doors and pushed them open. The noise suddenly intensified, and the two of them stepped forward, through the doorway and into a large roofed space. It probably took up a good half of the entire building, Toshiko estimated. Two-thirds of the way along, the floor dropped down five feet or so. The remaining area, running up to a series of massive doors at the far end, was paved with tarmac. The inescapable conclusion was that this was some kind of shipping area, where lorries would drive up at the end and back up to the raised area, where boxes of tinned goods would be loaded in. But that wasn't what it was being used for now.

The place was set up as an impromptu medical ward. It looked to Toshiko like something from the 1950s: between the doors and the line where the ground dropped down were four rows of tubular metal bedsteads with crisp white sheets. Their occupants, lying comatose and connected to drips and monitoring equipment, contrasted bizarrely with the darkness, the concrete floor and the skylights above through which rose-coloured light filtered in, making everything beneath look surreal and fantastic. Cables ran off to the edges of the room to where the generators probably sat.

There was nobody around. No nurses, no doctors, nothing.

Owen moved to the first bed and picked up the clipboard from the end. Toshiko walked across to join him.

'Jodie Williams,' he read. 'Age twenty-five. Blood pressure and heart rate seem OK.' He replaced the clipboard and went around to the side of the bed to check the monitor and the drip. 'She's being sedated. That's more confirmation that the worm's been removed from her body: we know that sedatives and anaesthetics don't work well on people who are infected.' He brushed the girl's hair from her face. 'Pretty,' he said, and began to pull the sheet down to expose her naked body.

'Owen!' Toshiko said, shocked.

He looked up at her. 'It's OK,' he said, 'I'm a doctor. I'm allowed to do this kind of thing. I have a licence, and everything.'

Pulling the sheet down to her hips, he indicated a sterile dressing on her stomach. 'She's had something removed,' he said, 'and I think we all know what it is.' He quickly ran professional fingers up her body. Her ribs were pronounced and her stomach, at least, what could be seen of it beneath the dressing, was concave. 'She's almost malnourished. OK, we can assume she's had one of these things inside her and it's been taken out. Where is it?'

He walked across to the next bed and pulled the sheet down. Another sterile dressing, another concave stomach. It was the same with the next girl he tried, and the next. The fourth one was a boy, a teenager.

'It's a production line,' Toshiko breathed.

'Not a production line,' Owen replied, standing in the centre of the two rows of beds. He looked around. 'There must be forty or fifty of them here, and they've all had their worms removed. It's more like a battery farm.'

'These must be the patients from the Scotus Clinic,' Toshiko said. 'Doctor Scotus must have had them all kidnapped when he realised that the worms were causing problems.'

'But he wouldn't have had the time or the expertise to kidnap them himself,' Owen mused. 'So who did it for him?'

'That would be us,' a voice said in a marked Welsh accent.

Toshiko whirled around. A man was standing just inside the doorway leading back into the building. He stepped forward. He was thick-set, with a close-shaven scalp on which Toshiko could see numerous white scars.

'And who are you?' Owen said, stepping forward, fists clenched.

'Never mind that,' the man said. 'What makes you think you can just wander in here like you owned the place?'

'And what makes you think you'll get out alive,' came a voice from the far side of the space. Toshiko looked over her shoulder. Another man was pulling himself up from the dropped section of floor; muscular arms pistoning his body upwards. He straightened up.

'Don't try to run,' said the man in the doorway. He reached behind his back and brought out a gleaming brass knuckle-duster from a pocket, slipping it onto his right hand and raising it up so that the light from the skylights shone from the sharp points above each knuckle. 'You'll only make things worse for yourself.'

'Not that it gets much worse,' said his companion. He was holding a length of bicycle chain. It looked to Toshiko like he'd soldered nails along its length until it resembled heavy-duty barbed wire, only much more flexible and much more deadly. 'We were told to stop anyone from interfering with this lot, but we weren't told to do it quickly.'

Jack breezed through the door and into the room beyond.

It was where the canning had taken place. The room was filled with machinery, through which Jack could just make out a ribbon-like path, a walled conveyor belt that wound around and about the various devices that would have sterilised the cans, pumping them full of whatever kind of meat slurry the factory was producing that week, sealing them, labelling them and sending them on their way.

In the centre of the room was a cleared space and in the centre of the space a folding wooden desk had been set up with a canvas director's chair behind it. Doctor Scotus was sitting in the chair, reading a report.

'I love what you've done with the place,' Jack said cheerily. 'The whole retro-industrial thing is really big these days. Quite a change from that nice expensive office you used to have, with that big granite desk and those ergonomic chairs. Still, you go with what you've got, right? Like *Changing Rooms*.'

'And who the hell are you?' Scotus replied, standing up. His long blond hair drifted around his head as he moved.

'Health and Safety,' Jack said, feeling rather than seeing Gwen move into the room behind him, gun held high. 'We've been getting reports that you're giving women tablets that implant alien creatures in their stomachs which drive them into hunger-fuelled frenzies which lead to murder and self-mutilation. The question is, have you filled out a proper risk assessment for this activity? Because if you haven't, we're going to have to take action.'

Scotus stared at Jack. His face reflected various emotions, one after the other; anger, confusion, realisation, understanding, concern and, finally, surprise. 'Alien?' he said thoughtfully. 'Yes, I suppose they would have to be, wouldn't they?'

'You didn't know?' Gwen asked, moving up beside Jack. She was still carrying the shrouded bird-cage, he was glad to see. He had plans for that.

'It's not the first explanation that comes to mind,' Scotus said. 'I assumed they were some newly evolved species, or something that we'd just never seen before.'

Jack moved to one side, concerned that if anything went wrong then he and Gwen were both in the line of fire. He wanted them separate, so that at least one of them would survive an attack long enough to fight back. It was a lesson he'd learned the hard way, more years ago than he cared to remember. 'How did you come across them?' he asked.

'Tell me who you are first,' Scotus said quietly, firmly. He had considerable charisma, Jack noticed.

'Let's just say we're interested in anything that's alien. Especially if it starts affecting people.'

Scotus nodded. 'Very well. I wasn't always a nutritionist,' he said. 'I used to be a vet. I owned a place just outside Cardiff, specialising in farm animals.' He grimaced. 'Have you seen the way that farming is going recently? It's enough to turn your stomach. If scientists could breed square chickens, so that you could stack more of them together in one place, then farmers would beat a path to their door. It's all about maximising the amount of profit per cubic foot, because the supermarkets will absolutely nail the farmers to the wall with the contracts they force them to sign.'

'Fascinating though this is,' Jack said, 'I'm still waiting for the aliens to turn up.'

'I was called out to a cow that had died,' Scotus said. 'It had apparently been acting strangely for days; eating much more than usual, attacking the other cows and taking bites out of them, getting thinner and thinner. I thought it was BSE, but if you report that then there's a panic which results in every cow within fifty miles being slaughtered, and I didn't want to be responsible for that. I conducted an autopsy, and I found this thing in its stomach. It was barely alive.'

'Drifted through the Rift,' Jack murmured to Gwen. She didn't reply.

'It looked like some kind of tapeworm,' Scotus continued, 'so I put it in a nutrient solution while I worked out what to do.'

'Don't tell me – it changed into a thing like a flying dagger and tried to impale you.'

'I was out, on a call. I came back to find my dog dead and the creature gone.' Scotus reached a hand up to his forehead, brushing the fine blond hairs away and placing his palm over his eyes. 'I autopsied the dog, and found a cluster of these… egg-like things. I kept them for study – cutting some of them open, implanting others in rats and cats and other dogs until I had worked out their complete life cycle.'

'Without bothering to inform the authorities?'

'And what good would that have done? They wouldn't have understood what an opportunity I had!'

'Opportunity?' Jack asked. 'To do what – kill people?'

Scotus winced. 'That was… unfortunate,' he said. 'It was never meant to go that way. I thought I'd invented a way of making people slim and making me rich at the same time. Obesity is such a problem these days. People would pay a lot of money for a guaranteed way of losing weight, and I developed a toxin that would just dissolve the creatures when their hosts had reached their ideal body mass without affecting the hosts. It was perfect – my patients would never realise what was inside them! I didn't realise that the creatures could actually influence people's actions if they weren't getting enough nutrition!'

'The road to Hell is paved with good intentions,' Jack said. 'But you're going to turn around and walk back along that road.'

'I don't think so,' Scotus said.

Jack raised his pistol, but a muffled sound behind him made him turn.

Gwen's head was twisted painfully around to one side, pointing up at the ceiling. Her eyes were wide and it looked like she might have been screaming, if the hand that was holding her head hadn't been cutting off her breathing.

The hand belonged to a man in a leather jacket, who was holding Gwen's automatic in his other hand.

'Drop the gun,' he said, 'or I'll snap your girlfriend's neck.'

Somewhere in the distance, a gun fired.

Owen raised his gun and aimed it at the head of the thug with the nail-encrusted chain, which looked like something barnacled and crustacean. 'One more step and I'll conduct a radical transsphenoidal hemisectomy using a copper-jacketed bullet rather than a scalpel,' he said, trying to put a firmness into his voice that he didn't really feel.

'You talk too much,' the thug said. He lashed out expertly with the chain, flicking it.

The end of the chain sliced across Owen's knuckles, sending fiery pain shooting up his arm. He dropped the gun. It hit the floor, butt-first, and fired, sending a plume of flame up towards the ceiling and deafening Owen with the blast.

'I do everything too much,' Owen muttered, sucking blood from his fingers.

The recoil caused the gun to skitter across the concrete floor towards the thug. He looked at it disdainfully, and kicked it away, over the edge of the concrete floor and onto the tarmac beneath. 'Tricky safety design on the P220,' he said. 'The company abandoned the traditional catch for a decocking lever that lowers the hammer to a safety notch.' He glanced up at Owen, and there was a terrible humour in his eyes. 'But that's by-the-by,' he said. 'Now it's fairer. We're both unarmed.'

'You've got that chain thing,' Owen pointed out.

The thug looked at the spiked chain.

'Oops, my mistake,' he said, and smiled.

He stepped towards Owen, bringing the chain back behind him and coiling it, ready to strike.

Owen risked a glance to one side, where Toshiko was confronting the other thug. He'd hoped she would have him on the floor with her gun in the back of his neck by now, but she seemed to be weighing up her options, deciding how to take him on. As Owen watched, Toshiko's thug stepped forward suddenly and sliced his knuckle-dusters horizontally through the air at eye level. She brought her hands up to protect her face. The knuckle-dusters caught her palm, their brass spikes tearing the flesh and spraying blood in all directions. Toshiko staggered backwards, the gun falling from her hand and hitting the concrete floor but not, Owen noticed, firing. Perhaps he should switch to a Walther.

Something moving in the corner of his eye made him glance up. The nailed chain was flicking towards his eyes. He instinctively put his left arm up to defend himself. The chain wrapped itself around his forearm, the nails tearing through the leather of his jacket and into his flesh. The pain caused his breath to catch in his throat and his heart to go into arrhythmia with the shock. Instinctively he wanted to pull his arm closer to his body, protecting himself, but years of fighting in bars had taught him two valuable lessons.

Lesson one: you can ignore pain, if you really try.

Lesson two: do what the other guy is least expecting, even if it hurts.

Owen took two steps towards the thug. The chain sagged between them, its tension removed by Owen's actions. The thug pulled at the chain, but instead of dragging Owen towards him, pulling him off his feet, he merely succeeded in taking some of the tension back up again. Owen took a step to one side, blood pulsing hot and wet inside his sleeve. Raising his right leg, he brought his foot down hard on the side of the thug's knee.

Owen felt, rather than heard, a wet snapping sound. The thug's leg crumpled in a direction it wasn't supposed to go. He screamed, shrill and loud.

'And that's what seven years of medical school did for me,' Owen gasped, tugging the chain from the thug's suddenly nerveless hand and unwrapping it carefully from his arm. 'I know every vulnerable point on the human body, and several inside it as well.' Stepping forward, he brought his heel down squarely on the thug's temple. The screaming stopped.

The inside of his sleeve was hot and wet and throbbing, but he didn't think the damage was anything more than superficial. He turned to where Toshiko was fighting her own corner. She was backing away fast, blood dripping from her injured hand. Owen looked around for her gun. If he could retrieve that, he could even the odds somewhat.

Before he could do anything, Toshiko reached down with her uninjured hand and pulled her leather belt out from her jeans. Still backing away, she doubled it over and moved her grasp from the metal buckle to the pointed and pierced end.

'What's this – the fashion police?' her thug taunted.

Toshiko flicked the belt at him the same way Owen's thug had flicked the nailed chain at him. The square belt buckle caught him on the bridge of his nose. Blood gushed as he stumbled backwards. His heel caught on Toshiko's Walther and he missed a step. Toshiko flicked her belt again. The buckle hit him right between the eyes. He crumpled to the floor.

Owen looked at Toshiko with astonishment. 'That was awesome,' he said.

'That was Fendi,' Toshiko replied smugly. She looked at his arm, and winced. 'We need to get that seen to,' she said.

Owen indicated her ripped hand. 'And that,' he said.

Toshiko looked at it as if she hadn't noticed it before. 'Should we get to a hospital?' she asked hesitantly, 'or call Ianto?'

Owen indicated the beds lined up behind them, each with its comatose occupant. 'They've all got sterile dressings on,' he pointed out. 'There has to be a cupboard full of medical supplies around here somewhere. And when we've got ourselves sorted out, we'll go and see what's up with Jack and Gwen. They're probably having a really boring time, compared to us.'

NINETEEN

Jack let the Webley fall from his hand onto the tiled floor.

'OK, big boy,' he said to the goon who was holding Gwen's neck, 'you can let go now.'

The goon twisted Gwen's head around a little further. Jack could see her tendons standing out. Her cheeks and forehead were suffused with blood and her eyes were almost popping out of their sockets. One more turn and her neck would break.

'If anything happens to my friend,' he said calmly, 'I will take my pistol and shove it so far up your ass that you'll gag on it. And then I'll reach down your throat and pull the trigger.'

The goon kept smiling at Jack, and shook his head in mock-chastisement, but he relaxed his grip a fraction. Gwen sucked in great whooping gulps of air, her face gradually returning to its normal colour. She was still holding the bird-cage in her hand, and she shakily set it on the floor without disturbing the shroud.

'Not sure where this guy fits into the scheme of things,' Jack said, turning to Doctor Scotus. 'Are you branching out into fitness? Hiring personal trainers?' He eyed the goon up and down. The man obviously lifted weights every day. No need for diet pills there. 'Cos I could do with a workout, if you know what I mean.'

'I've… made a deal with some of the Cardiff criminal fraternity,' Scotus said. 'They protect me, and carry out some small tasks, and in return I give them a cut of the profits.'

'Small tasks like kidnapping your customers off the street because you can't afford to have them running around going psychotic?' Jack gazed at the goon, who was getting edgy at the attention he was getting. 'I wouldn't start counting on those profits if I were you,' he said. 'The bottom's dropped out of the diet-pill market, what with all the problems with murder and cannibalism and stuff.'

'Issues, just issues,' Scotus said, rubbing his hand across his eyes. 'The creatures are growing too fast, requiring too much nutrition. I've developed a hormone that will delay their growth, slow it down. It will require my patients to take another tablet every day, of course, but I will tell them that it's just a part of the treatment. One tablet to start the treatment, a tablet every day to keep it going, and a tablet to stop. It's simple, and effective.'

'How long did it take to develop this hormone?' Jack asked. 'And how many people died along the way? Was your receptionist one of them?'

Scotus grimaced. 'Poor girl,' he said. 'She missed taking a tablet. Just forgot. The creature inside her reacted... badly. It escaped, and hid somewhere in the air-conditioning system, or under the floor. I had to move out of the office suite in a hurry, before it attacked anyone else.' He shook his head. 'It should be a fairly simple process to adjust the dosage to ensure that my customers can miss one or two tablets in a row without the creature becoming agitated.'

'But you need the eggs,' Gwen rasped, rubbing her throat. 'You need *lots* of eggs if you're going to develop an efficient business model.' She spotted Jack's sceptical glance, and shrugged. 'Rhys bought a book called *Fifteen Ways to be an Effective Manager*,' she said. 'I had a flick through, one night, when I was bored.' Turning back to Scotus, she said, 'So where do all these eggs come from? As I understand it, a host needs to be implanted by one of those flying things, and I doubt you got more than a few dozen eggs from that dog of yours. You're going to need *thousands*, even *tens* of thousands, if this thing takes off. What's the secret? Where are the eggs going to come from?'

Scotus looked away, discomfited. 'There are... possibilities,' he said. 'I have identified a new source of supply.'

'No.' Jack felt a rage building within him, burning through his heart and brain. 'This stops, here, now.'

Scotus shook his head. 'You don't understand,' he said. 'The potential impact of my diet pills is *immense*. They could literally change the world. They are the only diet pills *guaranteed* to make you lose weight. Not "help". Not "assist". Not "only in conjunction with a calorie-controlled diet". No, if people stick to the regime, then the pills actually *make* them lose weight. Overnight, there's no more obesity epidemic in the western world. The National Health Service can turn its resources away from treating heart disease and diabetes, and all the other things that obesity causes, and start working on the things that matter, like curing cancer and Alzheimer's disease. The government can redirect its resources to fighting global warming. Just one simple thing, like making people slim, and the effects are incredible. Is it so much to ask that a few people sacrifice their lives in the early stages of testing?'

'Yes,' Jack said. He could feel the rage darkening his voice. 'It is.'

Scotus was almost pleading now. 'But there are always risks in drug tests. Do you think that antibiotics came for free? Do you think that drugs for controlling blood pressure didn't cause any problems during testing? Even when new drugs go into a few years of double-blind tests to check their efficacy, the people given the placebos have to suffer a continuation of their symptoms when the other people on the trial are being given a cure. Is that fair? All medical research is built on pain and death. We accept it, when we think about it at all, because the potential benefits are so great!'

'There is a difference,' Jack said, 'between research that may have an unfortunate side effect and research that's guaranteed to kill your test subjects.'

'It's no good,' Gwen said. She was staring at Scotus. 'You won't convince him. He will keep on going, producing his pills, whatever arguments you make.'

'She recognises the truth in what I'm saying,' Scotus proclaimed. 'She recognises the passion behind my words.'

'No,' Gwen said. 'I recognise the fact that you've been infected yourself. There's one of these creatures inside you, and it's controlling your thoughts.'

Halfway along the corridor, past the door they had come in by, Toshiko stopped by the first of the massive riveted metal slabs.

'What's this?' she asked Owen.

He rushed past her. 'Cold store,' he said. 'It's where they would have kept the frozen carcasses they offloaded from the ships, before canning them and taking them away to the shops. Transport area's back *that* way,' he gestured over his shoulder, 'so the canning area is probably up ahead.'

'The power is on,' Toshiko said simply.

Owen stopped. 'It can't be. This place has been deserted since the 1970s.'

'There's a generator,' Toshiko pointed out.

'But that was set up to keep the medical monitoring equipment running, and provide lighting.' Owen was getting irritated; Toshiko could tell from his tone of voice. He didn't like people disagreeing with him. 'There's no point cooling the cold store down to some ludicrous temperature. That's just a waste of energy.'

'It would be,' Toshiko said, 'if there wasn't anything in here.' She pressed her face against the thick glass. 'But I think there is.'

She turned her attention to the control box by the side of the door. It had a thermostat on it, plus a couple of buttons that turned the cooling on or off. The thermostat was set at just above freezing. There was also a button that opened the door, although there was a massive handle on the door itself which would do the same in case of power failure. She guessed there was a similar handle on the inside just in case anyone became trapped.

Owen moved alongside her. She edged to one side, careful not to brush against his arm. She had poured antiseptic over it, back in the large area where they had fought and vanquished their opponents, and then placed dressings over the area where the nails had ripped his skin and bound the whole thing up with bandages. He had then done the same with the back of her hand. Owen had left their opponents tied to two empty beds at the end of one of the rows. He had wanted to use the nail-studded chain to tie them down with, but Toshiko had vetoed the idea.

'Let's take a look inside,' she said. She pressed the button on the box that she thought would operate the mechanism. Somewhere inside the door, something went *clunk*. A hydraulic system wheezed into life, pulling the door slowly open. Toshiko and Owen both stepped backwards as the door swung ponderously towards them and a cloud of freezing vapour puffed into their faces.

As the vapour cleared, Toshiko stepped forward. She had retrieved her Walther from the floor of the medical area, and now she held it in front of her in both hands, ready to fire.

'Oh hell,' Owen said. His breath turned to white vapour as it left his mouth, condensed into water droplets by the cold that rolled towards them from the opening door. 'Are those what I think they are?'

'They look like…' Toshiko started, and then trailed off as her thoughts caught up with her words. 'Oh fuck,' she said primly.

The cold store was about the size of the Boardroom back in the Hub, but twice as tall. It was empty of carcasses, shelves or anything else apart from meathooks hanging from the ceiling and what looked at first glance like a series of sticks that had been thrown onto the floor and frozen to the walls and ceiling. At second glance, they weren't sticks. Sticks didn't have wings that had frozen into solid boards, but which were still beating slowly.

'That's where the things from those patients' stomachs went,' Owen breathed. 'Scotus must have removed them surgically, and then put them in some kind of nutrient solution until they turned into these flying egg-laying things. God alone knows why he wanted to. I mean, if he's that much of a psycho, he could just have killed the patients and let the worms feed off the nutrients in the dead bodies. They would have turned into the flying things naturally. I wonder why he went to all the trouble of taking them all out by hand?'

'Maybe he wanted the patients for something else,' Toshiko said. She turned to look at Owen. He looked back at her. Neither of them wanted to guess what Scotus wanted the patients alive for, but they just couldn't help themselves.

'If we assume he wants to make lots more eggs,' Owen started. 'I mean, a regular production line of eggs, then the best thing he could do would be—'

'To turn the eggs he already had into worms,' Toshiko continued, 'then turn the worms into flying egg-layers and let them find secondary hosts, then each flying egg-layer would lay hundreds of new eggs.'

Owen's face was bleak. 'And as long as Scotus keeps some back, he can have a continuous production line! Oh, that's just too sick to bear thinking about.'

A handful of the flying creatures were moving sluggishly towards the door, attracted perhaps by Toshiko and Owen's body heat. They were using their wings to push themselves along the icy floor.

Toshiko pressed the button that closed the door. Cumbersome, unwieldy, it started to move.

And caught the first of the creatures as it pushed itself over the lip of the doorway, crushing it. The creature's shell cracked, leaking yellow ichor, and the door started to open again.

'Safety cut-out!' Toshiko cried. 'It thinks someone's trapped their foot!' She hit the button again, but the door kept swinging outwards. More of the creatures teetered on the lip of the door, then fell out. As the warm outside air hit them, their wings lost their rigidity, becoming flexible and diaphanous again. Toshiko could hear the wings buzzing as they beat faster and faster. Their little red eyes, so like jewels, seemed to glow in the light from the corridor as they tracked Owen and Toshiko's movements.

One of them started to rise shakily into the air.

Jack gazed levelly at Doctor Scotus.

'How can you tell he's a host?' he asked Gwen.

'Look at his hair,' she replied.

'Yeah, OK, I grant that he's got that whole "mad scientist with wild crazy hair" aesthetic going, but I see that a lot. It's not proof.'

'His hair is waving in the breeze, isn't it?'

Jack looked at Scotus, who was staring at Gwen in disbelief. 'Yeah, so?'

'So there isn't any breeze.'

Jack looked back at Scotus. Thin blond strands haloed the man's head, but Gwen was right. Now that he was concentrating, he could see that the strands weren't only waving in the absence of any breeze; they weren't even moving in the same direction as each other.

'What the hell...?' he muttered.

'Remember the worm thing that attacked us in Scotus's office?' Gwen moved to one side; the goon who had been standing behind her, guarding her, moved too, but so did some of the tendrils on Scotus's head, shifting to track her motion. 'That thing had a whole bunch of thin white tendrils at both ends of its body, didn't it?'

'I had other things to worry about at the time, like stopping it from throttling you, but let's say I do remember that.'

'Imagine those tendrils much longer. Six feet, maybe. Imagine them finding their way up his throat, out into the air. Imagine them finding their way in between the cells of his body, infiltrating themselves past arteries and veins, through muscles and into his brain, and then out through his scalp. Imagine—'

'Thanks. I get the picture.' A thought struck Jack. 'Hang on – that worm thing had tendrils at both ends.'

They both glanced down to Scotus's groin. Was it Jack's imagination, or was there something stirring down there as well?

Jack looked up at Scotus's face. 'What happened?' he asked simply.

'I tried one of the pills,' he said. 'I had to. Who would buy diet pills from a fat nutritionist? I got the same cravings as the others, the same desire to eat anything, no matter what it was. I suppressed it, with powdered protein supplements at first, then using drugs. Eventually, I discovered that by taking sedatives I could cause the creature's appetite to reduce. Its weight is stable now, but the tendrils you mention – the way it perceives the world – continued to grow. They permeate me. They have infiltrated me.'

'Then why not take the second pill?' Gwen asked. 'Why not flush the thing from your system?'

'Because the tendrils are too entwined with my brain and my nervous system,' Scotus said simply. 'Killing the creature would most likely kill me. That's one reason. The other is simpler. It won't let me.'

'It won't let you?' Jack stepped forward.

The goon behind Gwen tracked Jack with her gun, but let him go. The man was too engrossed in what was going on. It was obvious from the expression on his face that he thought he'd fallen into a pit of madmen. 'You mean, it's controlling you?'

'Nothing that obvious. It's not intelligent; not as we measure intelligence, anyway. But it does have instincts, which it communicates to me. The instinct to survive is *very* strong.'

'I think I've heard enough,' Jack said. 'Have you heard enough?'

'More than enough.'

Jack reached into a pocket of his greatcoat. His hand closed around the alien device that they had found at that Cardiff nightclub what seemed like years ago now. Toshiko had already set it up so that it would pick up local emotional reactions and amplify them further away. All he had to do was to press a couple of buttons to activate it. His fingers found them quickly.

He nodded to Gwen. She bent and quickly pulled the shroud off the bird-cage before the goon could stop her.

The winged alien creature in the cage shifted, confused by the sudden flood of infra-red signals.

'Jesus!' the goon said, and stepped backwards, raising the gun and aiming it at the cage.

One of the other alien devices that Toshiko had determined was part of a matching set was wired to the cage, shoved in through the little flap through which the creature had originally been shoved. It transmitted electrical charges along a plasma path generated by a low-power laser beam. It was aimed directly at the creature, which didn't have any room to squeeze out of the way.

Before the goon could stop her, Gwen pressed the button that activated it.

A lambent orange glow filled the cage, and the creature suddenly bucked as a charge of electricity went through its body for the second time that day.

The pain it felt was picked up by the original alien device and amplified all around. Scotus doubled over in agony, throwing up on his desk; Gwen collapsed, eyes rolling up in her head; and the goon just keeled over. Gwen's gun fell from his fingers.

Jack fought against it. Pain and he were old friends. He could keep going through agony that would fry the nerves of any other human.

While the effect lasted, Jack walked slowly through the pain like a man walking underwater, collecting all the weapons and dumping the goon's body next to that of Doctor Scotus, fastening both of them to the canning machinery with some flexible metal restraints that he'd brought with him from the Hub. Then he turned both alien devices off.

Gwen recovered first. He'd expected that. She had more force of will than almost anyone he'd ever known.

Owen pulled Toshiko to her feet.

'What was *that*?' she asked.

'That was Jack's plan working,' Owen said grimly.

'It was as if someone was drilling out all my teeth at the same time.'

'Let's hope it bought Jack the time he wanted.' Owen looked around at the winged creatures that had spilled out of the cold store. The pain felt by their brother had obviously hit them hard, but they were beginning to recover. 'Quick, let's get out of here.'

He half-dragged Toshiko through the door and into the room beyond, pulling the door shut behind him. He didn't have much time to take in the sight of all the canning machinery, and the two men fastened to it. Jack was standing in the centre of the room, propping Gwen up. He smiled at Owen and Toshiko as they arrived.

'Are we having fun yet?' he asked.

'There's something you should know—' Owen started.

'There's many things I should know, including how to mix the perfect hyper-vodka and how to recover from its effects. What's this one?'

'There's about thirty of those winged things loose outside, and a hospital ward with about the same number of sedated patients,' Owen said rapidly. 'The winged things are going to head right for them, plunge themselves right in and lay their eggs. The eggs we can deal with – I recommend a flamethrower and then some acid on the ashes – but that leaves us with thirty-odd dead people, and I'm not comfortable with that.'

Jack raised his eyebrows. 'I can't leave you alone for a moment, can I?'

'I reckon we have about three minutes before it's too late.'

Jack's gaze flicked left and right as he considered his options. 'Bullet's will take out those flying things, won't they?'

'Yeah, but there's a swarm of them. You'd never get them all before they get you. Remember, they're attracted by body heat.'

'Yeah, I remember.' A grin burst across Jack's face. 'Did I see a fire extinguisher out in the corridor?'

Owen shrugged.

'Yes, you did,' Toshiko answered.

'Carbon dioxide or foam?'

Toshiko thought for a moment. 'Judging by the colour coding, carbon dioxide.'

'Perfect. Can someone get it for me without getting hit by one of those things?'

Gwen, Owen and Toshiko exchanged dubious glances. Eventually, Toshiko opened the door, Gwen grabbed the fire extinguisher from the wall and Owen held his automatic at the ready in case any of the creatures flew at them.

He needn't have worried. They were all crawling or flying unsteadily along the corridor, gaining strength by the moment, towards the medical unit. Towards their new hosts.

Jack had taken his coat and shirt off, and was standing bare-chested, arms extended. 'Come on,' he said. 'Do it.'

'But—'

'Do it.'

Owen raised the fire extinguisher. He looked uncertainly at Gwen and then at Toshiko. They just stared back.

He pulled the safety pin out and pressed the handle firmly down.

Carbon dioxide gushed from the fire extinguisher's nozzle, enveloping Jack in a pall of white fog. The gas, expanding as it emerged from its pressurised state, sucked heat from the air. Jack's hands were just visible, emerging from the cloud, white with frost, the fingertips glistening. He was turning slowly, letting the vapour hit him from all sides.

Owen released the handle and let the fire extinguisher drop.

Jack stood there like a marble statue, every muscle on his stomach and his arms standing proud and firm.

He opened his eyes and winked at Owen. Then he scooped up the guns – his and Gwen's – from the table. Gwen held out a spare magazine she had taken from her pocket. Jack took it, then walked stiffly out of the room and down the corridor.

There was silence for a few moments, then Owen heard the sound of gunfire – six rapid shots from Jack's Webley, then a series of deeper roars from Gwen's Glock. Owen imagined the creatures whirring around the cavernous room with the hospital beds in the centre, and Jack, standing there, picking them off like a man firing at clay pigeons. The firing started up again, higher and flatter than the Glock. He must have reloaded his Webley. Another pause, and then the firing started again, deeper this time: the Glock again.

Owen had lost count of the number of shots he'd heard, when suddenly everything went silent. Had Jack killed all the creatures, or had one of them plunged itself into his chest, filling him full of eggs? Still, no sound. No footsteps. Nothing.

Fingers appeared around the edge of the doorway. White, cold fingers.

Jack walked slowly back into the room.

'That was fun,' he said. 'Forget about diet pills: I think we've just discovered the logical successor to paintballing.'

TWENTY

The sky was bright and clear, a wash of purest azure from horizon to horizon. Penarth Head stood out crisply against the sky, almost as if the whole scene were a collage and the headland had been cut out of a picture in a magazine and stuck onto blue card. Even the water of the bay seemed purer than usual, sparkling in the sunshine.

Standing at the quay that led down to the ferry, Jack and Gwen were comfortably silent. They had shared life and death together, and although they had plenty they wanted to say to one another, for the moment they were content.

'What happened to the patients in Scotus's medical facility?' Gwen asked eventually.

'Owen brought them out of sedation, one by one, and spun them some story that they'd been drugged in a bar. He's very fond of that story. I think it has some kind of resonance for him.'

'How did he explain the dressings and the scars?'

'Told them they were missing a kidney, which was probably on its way to the Middle East to be transplanted into a billionaire oil tycoon. Hey, if it means they're more careful about what they eat and drink in future then it's a plus as far as I'm concerned.'

'And they bought it?'

Jack smiled. 'Owen can be very convincing, when he wants to be. I think he's taken four of them out for dinner so far, and he's working on the rest.'

Far out across the bay a small boat was bobbing around. Normally, Gwen wouldn't have been able to see even half that distance, but the air was so clear she felt she could see all the way across to Weston-super-Mare if she tried.

'What about Doctor Scotus?' she asked.

'Owen and I talked about that. In the end, it wasn't our job to punish him. We suggested he try one of the "Stop" pills, under medical supervision, to see whether it would get rid of the thing that was inside him, infiltrating its way through his flesh. He couldn't take it himself, of course – the thing wouldn't let itself be harmed – so Owen dissolved it in solution and injected it.'

'OK. And..?'

'And Scotus was right. The creature had wound itself too tightly around him. He didn't survive the process.'

'Oh.' A moment's pause. 'And Lucy?'

'Returned to full physical health.'

Gwen thought for a moment. 'She killed her boyfriend, you know. She *ate* her boyfriend. There's got to be some kind of payback for that.'

'I said full *physical* health. She's under psychiatric supervision. I doubt she'll ever come to terms with what she did.'

'Hmm.' She didn't sound convinced. 'I know Toshiko will survive,' she said eventually, 'but what about Owen? He took that thing with Marianne pretty hard.'

'He always does. He'll get over it.' Jack looked sideways at Gwen. 'And what about you? We haven't seen you around for a while?'

'You haven't texted me.'

Jack grinned. 'I mislaid the number. Everything OK at home?'

Gwen nodded. 'Everything's fine. Well, as fine as it'll ever be. After I got the police to raid that factory and arrest the gang members, we went away for a few days. Rhys wanted to go to Portmeirion, but I held out for Shrewsbury.'

'Very nice.' He paused, weighing up whether to continue. 'You know,' he said eventually, 'those diet pills weren't the answer. They just address the symptom, not the cause. Changing your body isn't the point. You have to change the behaviour that's changing your body.'

'Very wise,' she said. 'You should go on TV. Maybe write a book. *Change Your Tack With Captain Jack.* You'd sell a million.'

'Too much like setting up a religion, and I'm not going *that* route again.' He noticed Gwen shiver. 'Cold?'

'Getting that way. Shall we go back?'

'Let's.' On a whim, Jack slipped his greatcoat off and placed it around Gwen's shoulders.

'What's that for?' she asked, surprised.

'Because you earned it,' he said.

All of the alien tech was safely in storage back in the Hub, sitting in boxes in the Archive, but Toshiko couldn't stop thinking about them. Not about the devices per se, but about the information they contained. The images. The story.

Sitting cross-legged on the futon in her flat, candles burning on shelves and tables, Toshiko laid out the nine photographs in a line on the tatami mat in front of her, moving them around until they were in the order she wanted.

The image on the left showed the alien – the *designer*, as she thought of it – at what she guessed was its youngest age. The skin, from what she could make out, was unlined, the eyes bright and firm. As she looked from left to right, the alien got older. Its skin became more wrinkled, more pachydermous, and the hammerhead-like extrusions which housed its eyes began to droop. In the last but one image, it looked sad and old.

Hidden within the devices it had made, had been the story of its life; of how it had grown, developed and aged. Perhaps it had happened a few decades ago, perhaps a few million years, but the story was as real as if it had happened yesterday.

The last image of all was different. It had come from one of the pieces of tech found at the scene of an alien spaceship crash near Mynach Hengoed. It had also, coincidentally, been the last one Toshiko had examined.

It was a long shot, showing the designer from head to toe, if those concepts had any meaning. Toshiko found it difficult to tell, but she thought it had three massive legs and two arms that emerged from either side of a thick neck. She didn't know where in the sequence the picture came, except that the designer looked neither young nor old. Middle-aged, perhaps.

What made the image unique was the other alien with the designer: a smaller version, with deer-thin legs and eye-extensions that pointed upwards, like a 'Y'.

A son? A daughter? Something for which there was no word in any Earth language, perhaps, but Toshiko got the impression that it was an offspring of some kind. And that the designer was very proud.

In the end, she thought, the slow decay of the body didn't matter. We all continue on, renewing ourselves, through our offspring.

They are what matter.

They are what survive.

Acknowledgements

Thanks to: Stuart Cooper, for contacting me in the first place, and for helping me refine the plot; Gary Russell and Mathew Clayton, for making the book a pleasure to write; Peter Anghelides and Dan Abnett, for the support network; and Steve Tribe, for a superb, friendly and detailed copy-edit.

TORCHWOOD

ANOTHER LIFE
Peter Anghelides

ISBN 978 0 563 48653 4
UK £6.99 US$11.99/$14.99 CDN

Thick black clouds are blotting out the skies over Cardiff. As twenty-four inches of rain fall in twenty-four hours, the city centre's drainage system collapses. The capital's homeless are being murdered, their mutilated bodies left lying in the soaked streets around the Blaidd Drwg nuclear facility.

Tracked down by Torchwood, the killer calmly drops eight storeys to his death. But the killings don't stop. Their investigations lead Jack Harkness, Gwen Cooper and Toshiko Sato to a monster in a bathroom, a mystery at an army base and a hunt for stolen nuclear fuel rods. Meanwhile, Owen Harper goes missing from the Hub, when a game in *Second Reality* leads him to an old girlfriend…

Something is coming, forcing its way through the Rift, straight into Cardiff Bay.

Featuring Captain Jack Harkness as played by John Barrowman, with Gwen Cooper, Owen Harper, Toshiko Sato and Ianto Jones as played by Eve Myles, Burn Gorman, Naoki Mori and Gareth David-Lloyd, in the hit series created by Russell T Davies for BBC Television.

TORCHWOOD

BORDER PRINCES
Dan Abnett

ISBN 978 0 563 48654 1
UK £6.99 US$11.99/$14.99 CDN

The End of the World began on a Thursday night in October, just after eight in the evening...

The Amok is driving people out of their minds, turning them into zombies and causing riots in the streets. A solitary diner leaves a Cardiff restaurant, his mission to protect the Principal leading him to a secret base beneath a water tower. Everyone has a headache, there's something in Davey Morgan's shed, and the church of St Mary-in-the-Dust, demolished in 1840, has reappeared – though it's not due until 2011. Torchwood seem to be out of their depth. What will all this mean for the romance between Torchwood's newest members?

Captain Jack Harkness has something more to worry about: an alarm, an early warning, given to mankind and held – inert – by Torchwood for 108 years. And now it's flashing. Something is coming. Or something is already here.

Featuring Captain Jack Harkness as played by John Barrowman, with Gwen Cooper, Owen Harper, Toshiko Sato and Ianto Jones as played by Eve Myles, Burn Gorman, Naoki Mori and Gareth David-Lloyd, in the hit series created by Russell T Davies for BBC Television.